Rice

Rice

Su Tong

Translated by Howard Goldblatt

WILLIAM MORROW AND COMPANY, INC.

NEW YORK

LIBRARY OF CONGRESS CATALOGING-IN-PUBLICATION DATA
Su, T'ung, 1963–
[Mi. English]
Rice / Su Tong ; translated by Howard Goldblatt.
p.   cm.
ISBN 0-688-13245-6
I. Goldblatt, Howard, 1939–   . II. Title.
PL2904.T86M513   1995
895.1'352—dc20   94-38307 CIP

Printed in the United States of America
First Edition
1 2 3 4 5 6 7 8 9 10
BOOK DESIGN BY FRITZ METSCH

Rice

I

SUNDOWN. A FREIGHT TRAIN FROM THE NORTH COMES to a rocking halt at the old depot. A young man, jolted awake, feels the train shudder to a screeching stop; lumps of coal shift noisily under him as he squints into the blinding depot lights; people are running up and down the platform, which is blurred by steam and the settling darkness; there are shadows all around, some stilled, others restive.

Time to jump. Five Dragons grabs his bedroll, dusts it off, and carefully tosses it to the roadbed, then leans over and jumps, effortlessly as a bundle of straw, landing feet first and uncertain on alien territory, not knowing where he is. Cold winds from nearby fields carry the smell of lampblack. He shivers as he picks up his bedroll and takes one last look at the tracks, stretching far into the murky distance, where a signal light changes from red to green. A rumbling noise pounds off the depot ceiling above and the tracks below; another train is approaching, this one from the south. He ponders trains and railroad tracks; even after two days and nights of being tossed around atop a lumpy coal car, he feels oddly detached from the whole experience.

After threading his way through a maze of cargo and passengers, Five Dragons heads for town. He has gone three days without food, until his intestines seem to be oozing blood. Taking a small handful of hard kernels out of his bedroll, he tosses them into his mouth one at a time. They crunch between his teeth.

It is rice. Coarse, raw rice from his home in Maple-Poplar Village. The last few kernels disappear into his mouth as he enters town from the north.

Runnels of water in the cobblestone street from a recent rain glisten like quicksilver. Streetlamps snap on, immediately carving out silhouettes of an occasional home or tree; the air in the squalid northern district, home to the city's poor, stinks of excrement and decay. Apart from the hum of spinning wheels in nearby textile mills, the deserted streets are silent as death. Five Dragons stops at an intersection, near a middle-aged man sleeping under a streetlamp, his head pillowed on a gunnysack. To Five Dragons, who is dead on his feet, it seems as good a place to rest as any, so he sits down at the base of a wall. The other man sleeps on, his face absorbing the pale blue cast of the streetlamp.

Hey you, wake up! Five Dragons says. You'll get a cold that way.

The sleeping man doesn't stir. Dead tired, Five Dragons assumes. Travelers from home are like stray dogs; they sleep when they're tired, wherever they are, and their expressions—lethargic and groggy at times, ferocious at others—are more doglike than human. Five Dragons turns and looks at the gaudy painted advertisements on the wall behind him: soap, cigarettes, and a variety of herbal tonics in the hands of pouty, pretty young women with lips the color of blood. Tucked in among the sexy women are the names and addresses of VD clinics. Five Dragons grins. This is the city: chaotic and filled with weird things that draw people like flies, to lay their mag-goty eggs and move on. Everyone damns the city, but sooner or later they come anyhow. In the dying light Five Dragons sees the legendary city smoke rising into the air, confirming his image of what a city is: one gigantic smoke-stack, just as Maple-Poplar villagers had told him.

As he gets up to leave, Five Dragons glances over at the man lying under the streetlamp. He hasn't moved, but now his tangled hair is covered by hoarfrost. Five Dragons walks up and shakes him. Wake up, time to get moving. Cold and hard as a stone. Five Dragons holds his finger under the man's nose. Nothing. A dead man! he screams as he turns and runs. How could he know the man was dead? Up one unfamiliar street and down the other he runs, but the bluish face of the dead man follows him like a hornet. He is too shaken to look back, too scared; dark, shadowy shops, factories, and piles of rubble streak past until the cobblestone street ends at a wide and mighty river. Lanterns fore and aft cast their light on the dark hulks tied up at piers; some men around a pile of cargo are smoking cigarettes and talking loudly; the smell of alcohol hangs in the air. Stopping to catch his breath, Five Dragons sizes up the waterfront, with its late-night oc-cupants. Still shaken, he must calm down before deciding where to go next.

They saw him run up to the wharf like a scared rabbit, a bedroll over his back, his face ashen, neck and nose coated with coal dust. They had been sitting in a circle eating peanuts and stewed pig's head and getting drunk, but now they were on their feet watching the scared rabbit.

Where's the fire? Abao grabbed Five Dragons by the collar. What did you steal?

Dead man. Five Dragons was still gasping for air. A dead man!

A dead man's chasing you? Abao laughed loudly. Did you hear that? he asked the others. He even steals from dead men.

I didn't steal anything, I'm no thief. Completely surrounded by the gang, he looked down at the liquor bottles and greasy chunks of pig's head on the cargo and unconsciously moved toward them. Moonlight and lamplight shone upon the blotchy faces of the men, who watched him without saying a word. A gurgle rose in his throat. With a shaking hand he reached out for the food. I'm so hungry. Anxiously he searched the men's eyes. Were those smiles on their faces? I'm really hungry, I haven't eaten in three days. His voice quaked as he picked up a piece of stewed meat. He screamed in pain; his hand, the meat still clutched in it, was pinned to the ground by someone's foot.

Call me Daddy. Abao ground his foot. Then you can have it. **Just call me Daddy.**

Please, Elder Brother, show some pity. Five Dragons looked up at Abao's face and cleanly shaved head. I'm so hungry. Can't you show some pity?

All you have to do is call me Daddy, Abao said. What is it—you don't get it or you won't do it? Come on, say the word, and I'll give you the food.

Five Dragons stared helplessly at Abao. **Daddy,** he said at last.

Abao laughed wildly. Keeping his foot planted squarely on Five Dragons's hand, he pointed to the others. Don't forget them. They won't go along unless you call them Daddy, too.

The men were so drunk they could hardly stand; one

leaned against the cargo and swore without letup. Their bloodshot glares made Five Dragons's skin crawl. Mournfully he lowered his head, his eyes drawn to Abao's black sandal and the two pale toes, hard as rocks, grinding down on the back of his hand.

Daddy. In the night air his voice sounded hollow and weak. Somehow their merriment was contagious. But then he lowered his head and saw his own shadow, crouching like a lowly dog. Who's my daddy? Daddy was not a term he had used before. As an orphan in Maple-Poplar Village, he had more uncles, aunts, and cousins—distant and close—than he could count, but no father and no mother. Villagers said they had died in a great famine twenty years earlier. He was asleep on a haystack, sucking a silver necklace, when they were taken off to be buried. Five Dragons, the villagers remarked, you looked like a stray dog back then. All fatherless children look like dogs. Finally Abao lifted his foot, and Five Dragons crammed the piece of meat into his mouth. His taste buds were so numb that the meat had no flavor, but what did he care, now that he was putting real food into his body? His spirits were on the rise when Abao walked up with a cup of rice wine and patted him on the side of his jaw. Drink this. Understand? One good swallow should do it.

No, not me, Five Dragons said between bites. Abao squeezed his jaw painfully. I don't drink, Five Dragons complained. All I need is the meat.

Meat without wine? Come, now, act like a man. Abao held the cup up to Five Dragons's lips. Drink. If you don't, I'll snatch the food right out of your mouth.

Instinctively Five Dragons jerked his head backward, drawing a loud curse from Abao; other men rushed up to hold Five Dragons; one squeezed his jaw to force open his mouth, another poured five cups of wine into the dark pit, one right after the other. Five Dragons fought and kicked and coughed as the liquor burned its way down his throat. He thought he was going to die. Dimly he heard their crazed laughter. What's going on? As the alcohol began to take effect, his spent body seemed to float like straw—again. Stars in the sky, masts poking out of the river, and the men's bloodshot eyes all glittered somewhere off in the distance.

After flinging Five Dragons to the ground, the men watched him roll over agonizingly and lie on his side. Moonlight framed his waxen face and the meaty froth in the corners of his mouth. Incoherent sounds emerged from his quivering lips.

What's he saying? one of the men asked.

He's saying **hungry**. Abao kicked Five Dragons's leg. Hunger has turned him into a raving lunatic.

A ship's whistle drew the men's attention to the river's edge. Their massive shadows passed over and around his body, then vanished behind piles of cargo. Five Dragons, dead drunk, had no idea who the men were. Later on, whenever he met up with the Wharf Rats, a gang of murderous thugs, he would shudder to think how he had stumbled into their lair on his first night in town.

At daybreak Five Dragons dreamed of Maple-Poplar Village: floodwaters converging from all directions swamped five hundred acres of paddy land and scores of hamlets, destroying every mud hut and tree in their path. Golden rice tassels covered the surface of water carrying dead pigs and dogs, broken limbs and branches, and the faint smell of rotting flesh. Men and women trudged out of the water, their sobs and wails thudding into him like raindrops, like hailstones. He was part of the exodus, but only he wore a benign, carefree expression. He carried a branch to knock down the withered fruit of wild jujube trees along the way.

The wharf came to life. Five Dragons woke to morning noises all around; men rushed past him, loads of cargo on their backs; sailors and stevedores shouted back and forth. As he struggled to sit up, he tried to recall what had happened the night before. But his mind was a blank. The taste of alcohol and greasy meat clung to the inside of his mouth. It was like a bad dream.

Five Dragons walked around the wharf, and no one noticed. The men from the night before were long gone; a line of freight wagons stood beside a steel-hulled ship whose cargo of snowy white rice was being unloaded by stevedores. Five Dragons watched in silence, entranced by the scent of new rice.

Where did *that* come from? Five Dragons asked one of the men. That's good rice.

Don't know and don't care. The man ignored Five Dragons as he emptied his wicker basket into a wagon bed and clapped his hands together. There's famine everywhere these days, so any rice is hard to come by.

Sure is, Five Dragons agreed as he scooped up a handful. We lost five hundred acres of paddy land. All that rice, just as good as this, swallowed up.

It's the same everywhere. Floods here, droughts there.

The floods came just before harvest time. A year of blood and sweat, buried in water. A self-mocking smile accompanied Five Dragons's comment.

The four wagonloads of rice headed out in single file; Five Dragons, mesmerized, followed them down filthy streets, through crowds of people, past fruit stands, rickshaws, and an array of shops. The hunger pangs returned, so out of habit he popped kernels of raw rice into his mouth. Rice, it didn't matter whether he crunched it, chewed it, or slurped it, so long as it filled his belly.

At the intersection of Brick Mason Avenue he spotted an ancient brick pagoda amid a clutter of run-down buildings. Rising fifty feet in the air, it, too, had a light blue cast. Birds circled, wind chimes resounded crisply; he gazed up at the pagoda. What's that? he asked. No one answered, for by then the wagons had drawn up in front of the Great Swan Rice Emporium. Clear the way, the wagoners shouted at people lined up at the door. We've got rice!

Sitting on the shop counter eating sunflower seeds, Cloud Weave cast sidelong glances outside. She was dressed in an emerald-green cheongsam and high-heeled leather pumps, which she clicked against the counter—it was the tempo of agitation. Her sister, Cloud Silk, was helping a clerk weigh out rice for customers in front of the nearby storeroom, her pigtail sweeping lightly across her shoulders. Cloud Weave and Cloud Silk had gained notoriety as Brick Mason Avenue's rice-emporium girls.

Porters streamed in the gate with sacks of rice over their shoulders, passed through the chaotic shop to the rear compound by way of a narrow path, where Proprietor Feng made tallies and squeezed each sack as it passed by. Dust from the freshly milled rice hovered in the air. A row of aging brick buildings with black tile roofs occupied the rear compound. Rice was stored at the eastern and western ends; three rooms with a southern exposure were where Proprietor Feng and his daughters lived. Above the outer gate hung a black signboard with four gold inlaid characters, although most people could only read the word for rice: **MI**. Rice-laden porters all knew that the establishment occupying this particular corner of Brick Mason Avenue had been passed down from generation to generation for two centuries, and none cared what the remaining three characters said.

Water dripped from colorful laundry on a clothesline above the flow of pedestrian traffic. Obviously belonging to the rice-emporium girls, it smelled faintly of laundry soap as it dried in the sun and hinted at the feminine bodies it was meant to cover. Nineteen-year-old Cloud Weave and seventeen-year-old Cloud Silk were at an age when they were, if anything, lovelier than the fancy clothes they wore.

Cloud Weave spotted Five Dragons sitting on a wagon and scraping loose rice into a pile with both hands, then spreading it out again, mechanically, over and over. After the rice was unloaded, Proprietor Feng paid off the porters, who climbed onto the wagons and departed, leaving Five Dragons standing alone at the entrance, his shabby bedroll at his feet. He gazed curiously into the shop, a strange expression on his pale yet handsome face; his lips were chapped and cracked. Cloud Weave jumped down off the counter, walked to the door, and tossed out a handful of sunflower husks. She leaned against the doorframe and eyed him with interest and curiosity.

What are you hanging around for? Didn't you get paid?

Five Dragons backed up a step and gaped at Cloud Weave. No.

You're a porter, aren't you? She looked down at the bedroll. Or are you just looking for a handout? That's it, isn't it? I'm a good judge of people.

No. Five Dragons shook his head, looking past her into the shop, where clerks and customers were taking care of business. Is rice sold here? he asked.

Sure. What are you looking at? She giggled, one hand held to her mouth. Who are you looking at, me or my sister?

Neither. I'm looking at the rice. You have a lot.

You're looking at rice? What for? Disappointed, Cloud Weave noticed that in the sunlight the stranger's skin was dull as a stone. Your face looks like a dead man's. How come? Don't stand around here if you're diseased. I don't want to catch smallpox or cholera or anything like that. I'd be ruined.

I'm starving, not sick, Five Dragons said indifferently. Can I have a bowl of leftover rice? I haven't eaten in three days.

I'll get you some. I'd just feed it to the cat, anyway. She stretched in the doorway. You won't find anyone with a bigger heart than mine, did you know that?

By the time she returned from the kitchen with a bowl of leftover rice, Five Dragons had come into the shop and was arguing with a couple of the clerks. Cloud Silk pulled her sister outside by the sleeve. He's got lice! She was nearly shouting. Their kind always has. Five Dragons's gaunt face reddened with embarrassment as he was thrown out of the shop. He turned and cursed angrily. Cloud Weave didn't catch the words, but she saw Cloud Silk pick up a broom and attack him. How dare you talk to us like that, you filthy beggar!

A moment later, as Five Dragons sat dejectedly on the steps, his shoulders heaving, Cloud Weave said, You poor man. She hesitated briefly, then handed him the bowl of rice. Why get so upset? she asked with a smile. Here, eat

this before you leave. Don't you know it's taboo for beg-
gars to enter a rice shop? Five Dragons raised his head
and looked at the bowl of rice for a long, silent moment.
He knocked it out of her hand. Fuck you and your whole
family! I'll show you if I'm a beggar or not. Cloud Weave
stood in the doorway gaping at the spilled rice. She
laughed after regaining her composure. I see you've got
character, she said approvingly. A man ought to have
character. But I don't care whether you eat it or not. People inside the shop were watching them. Cloud Weave!
Her sister rapped on the counter. Get in here, and quit
acting like that. Cloud Weave walked inside. What's
wrong? she asked. I only took pity on him because he was
so hungry. How was I to know he'd fly off the handle
like that? A dog will sink its teeth into a saint these days.
People just won't let you do what's right anymore.

Customers watched this scene play itself out in silent
puzzlement. With full sacks over their shoulders or under
their arms, they waited their turn at the scales, where they
redirected their attention to the price and quality of rice.
With reports of famine increasing, people carried their rice
home feeling at once anxious and melancholy. In times of
war and turmoil, rice shops were paradise on earth in
south China. The Great Swan Rice Emporium on Brick
Mason Avenue prospered as never before.

So many customers flooded the shop that Cloud Weave
had to assist as cashier, a task for which she had neither
the patience nor the interest. Every so often she turned to
look outside. Brick Mason Avenue was, as always, gloomy
and drab. The stranger, who was still hanging around,
was the only sight that truly captured her interest. Like a
chicken fleeing from the butcher, he headed up one side
of the street and down the other, over and over, an object

of pity and scorn. Cloud Weave watched him, confused by feelings of tenderness: His young, tired face and eyes, filled with a cold glare, affected her deeply.

In the afternoon a curtained rickshaw pulled up to the door. Cloud Weave emerged from the shop and climbed proudly into it. Her face was powdered and rouged, her brows plucked and trimmed into thin black arcs, her lips painted red. She left a heavy cosmetic fragrance in her wake.

Where to? the puller asked. Where does the elder mistress want to go today?

The usual, Cloud Weave said, patting her own leg. And hurry. You won't get paid if I'm late.

Heads emerged from windows on Brick Mason Avenue, their owners assuming that Cloud Weave was off to another of Sixth Master's parties. They surmised that she was his mistress, since they often saw her leave, but not return. She might have come home very late, but then again, she might have stayed the night.

Upon her arrival at the Lu mansion she learned that today's party was being held in honor of two businessmen from Beijing. Most of the guests were strangers to her. Sixth Master entered from the garden in the company of several men and women and sat at the head table. Cloud Weave moved toward them. Excuse me, excuse me please, she repeated as she passed through the crowd, until a servant blocked her way. The master says he won't need female companionship at the head table tonight. It took a moment for what he said to sink in. Then: Who wants to sit there, anyway? I wouldn't sit next to him if he asked me.

At dinner that night Cloud Weave drank so much that

at one point she rested her head on the table and clamored to be taken home. The other women at her table whispered back and forth, trying to determine who she was. Finally someone said, Her father runs the rice emporium. Cloud Weave banged a small vinegar plate with her chopsticks. What's wrong with that, you gossips? What would you be eating, if not for our emporium? Shit? The shitty north wind? Shocked by the vulgar outburst, her fellow guests frowned. Cloud Weave stood up and glared at them. If I'd known this was going to be such a terrible party, I wouldn't have come.

She walked to the door, where Abao and some of the Wharf Rats were playing cards. Take me home, Abao, she demanded, grabbing his collar. Aren't you spending the night? he asked. She hit him with her fist. I'll rip that dog snout right off your face, she threatened. Spend the night with whom? Your Ladyship wants you to call her a rickshaw, and be quick about it. I'm bored, so I'm going home to get a good night's sleep.

At that late hour Brick Mason Avenue was dark and deserted. Cloud Weave stepped down from the rickshaw and turned to Abao. Go back and tell Sixth Master that he and I are through. Abao laughed. Not me. Maybe you're not afraid of Sixth Master, but I am. Cloud Weave said contemptuously, Who does he think he is, snubbing me all evening? I've never been so humiliated.

Someone was sleeping in the doorway, curled up in a bedroll, with only a matted head of hair sticking out. Cloud Weave kicked the bedroll. The sleeping man rolled over. She saw his eyes open briefly before he went back to sleep. It was the man from earlier that day. He's back. She wondered why he was sleeping in their doorway.

Who's back? Abao asked from the rickshaw. Want me to get rid of him?

No. Cloud Weave stepped over him. Let him sleep there, she said. I feel sorry for homeless people. I hate to see a wretched man like that.

The sky was just turning light when Proprietor Feng got out of bed, coughed, and walked outside to empty the chamber pot at the base of the wall. Then he crossed the yard, went down the narrow path, and entered the shop to take down the door slats and hang out the blackened shop banner. This had become a ritual over the years. On those occasions when he looked up at the word **MI** he was struck by how weatherbeaten the board was getting, with more tiny holes in the silk borders all the time. But since he had no control over the elements, he gave such omens of decline as little thought as possible. Maybe it was time to make a new sign.

Proprietor Feng had noticed the man sleeping in the doorway three days in a row.

By this time Five Dragons was sitting up staring at mist-enshrouded Brick Mason Avenue. When he heard stirrings in the shop behind him, he turned in time to see the scarlet slats come down, one at a time, revealing the chilling blue of Proprietor Feng's cotton robe against the darkness of the shop's interior. The subtle fragrance of raw rice released into the air energized him. It was the only smell that brought warmth and affection into his life, especially so far from home.

Why do you sleep in my doorway every night? Proprietor Feng asked him.

Five Dragons looked up and shook his head.

There's an awning over there. Proprietor Feng pointed to the grocery store across the street. It will keep you dry at night, so why not sleep there?

I like it here, where I can smell the rice. Five Dragons climbed to his feet and rolled up his bedding. I just sleep here. I haven't stolen any of your rice.

I never said you had. Proprietor Feng frowned. Where are you from?

Maple-Poplar Village. Far away, a couple of hundred miles. People from the city have never heard of it.

I have. It's like one big granary. I hauled rice from there as a boy. Why aren't you there working the fields? How come you all swarm to the city?

Floods. The rice is under water. If I'd stayed, I'd have starved to death.

Do you really think you're going to do any better here? Who lives and who dies in times like this is in the hands of fate, and there's nothing anybody can do about it. Life's as hard in the city as it is in the countryside.

With a sigh, Proprietor Feng turned and began cleaning the shop, sweeping up loose grains of rice and dumping them into a dustpan. Thinking about the fate of home and country always depressed him. But this time his thoughts were interrupted by a voice. Do you need a helper? Proprietor Feng, who was slightly deaf, straightened up. He saw Five Dragons's head poking in the door, his matted hair decorated with bits of straw.

What did you say? You want to be my helper?

Five Dragons gripped the doorframe nervously and stared at the floor. Keep me around, Proprietor, he said in a strange, raspy, heavily accented voice. I'm strong, I can do anything you need. I can even read a little.

I already have two clerks, Proprietor Feng said, sizing up the man. That's all I need. I can't afford to pay more wages. We barely earn enough to get by as it is.

I don't need wages. I'll work for food.

Yes, I can see that. Food always comes first when you're fleeing from a famine. Proprietor Feng laid down his dustpan and walked up to Five Dragons, squinting to get a better look. He kept his thoughts to himself, but a subtle change came over him. He patted Five Dragons on the shoulder. You're good and husky, that's for sure. But where would you sleep?

Anywhere. Five Dragons's face lit up. He pointed to the floor. Right here. I could sleep standing up if I had to.

Yes, I can see that, too. Proprietor Feng laughed. Come in, he said. As the saying goes: Saving someone's life makes you a seventh-stage buddha.

One of Five Dragons's legs went slack, as if he were about to kneel. But the other remained stiffly on the step. He looked at his knees, wondering what was going on down there. His jaw swelled from all the excitement, an ache spread to his heart.

What's the matter? Proprietor Feng saw Five Dragons stiffen. I said come in. Don't back out now. This was your idea, not mine.

Oh. Like a man waking from a dream, Five Dragons stepped inside. There, I'm in.

Cloud Silk entered the shop just then, combing out her long braid. She eyed Five Dragons suspiciously and asked her father, Why are you letting him in the shop at this hour of the morning? What about all the bad luck? Here, I'll get rid of that beggar.

I've taken him on as a helper, Proprietor Feng told his daughter. He gets food but no wages.

A helper? Cloud Silk's eyes nearly popped out of her head. Are you crazy? We don't need any help, why take on a beggar? So you can stuff him like some kind of pig?

Don't make such a fuss. Proprietor Feng eyed his daughter. You don't know anything about the business. I know what I'm doing. Besides, I feel sorry for him.

You two pretend you're so good. There are lots of people out there worth feeling sorry for. Why not bring them all home? She stomped her foot. You're infuriating! Just wait till people start laughing at us for hiring a beggar. What am I supposed to say?

I'm no beggar. Five Dragons, red-faced, defended himself. Why do you have to degrade people like that? I told you I'm not a beggar, that I left home looking for work, like all the men in Maple-Poplar Village.

I don't care what you are! Who's talking to you, anyway? Don't come near me, you're disgusting!

Five Dragons's world changed dramatically when he crossed the threshold of the Great Swan Rice Emporium. He heard the blood flow through his limbs once more, after a long period of quiescence—he really did hear it surge through veins and arteries long used to a sluggish flow. That misty morning would forever remain in his memory.

Customers streamed into the shop all that morning. After giving Five Dragons two sesame buns, Proprietor Feng sent him to the storeroom to haul rice into the shop. But Five Dragons felt the soles of his feet flutter when he tossed the first sack over his shoulder. Weak from a lack of food, he assumed. A couple more meals, and his strength would return like new grass. With bits of sesame seeds in the corners of his mouth, he carried sack after sack into the shop with a growing sense of elation, ignored by all but Cloud Silk, who occasionally glanced at him with loathing. They ran him ragged until about ten o'clock, when he was permitted to rest and catch his breath. As he sat in an old redwood chair, trying not to look as uncomfortable as he felt, his attention was divided between people entering and leaving the shop and the silent bins of rice; sunlight reflecting off the water in the city moat raised white ripples on the street; city noises covered Brick Mason Avenue, and once in a while there was riflefire beyond the city gate; a woman standing in the doorway of the grocery store wept, the victim of a purse snatcher. It was like a dream. Have I really escaped the poverty and destruction of Maple-Poplar Village? Have I really made it to the city?

Cloud Weave woke up a little before noon. Five Dragons watched her walk sleepy-eyed to the table, take a bowl of rice from the clerk named Wang, and sit down. She yawned as she ate. Her face was white, her cheeks rosy, her eyes dark: last night's makeup. She wore a pink satin nightgown, from which a fair-skinned and nicely tapered thigh emerged. Five Dragons, who sat at an adjoining table with the two clerks, concentrated on his food to keep from looking at her. Masters at one table, servants at another, he noted. As he was helping himself to a fourth bowl of rice, he turned to see Cloud Silk staring at his hands. See, Father, he's going back for more. You thought you hired a helper, but you got yourself a hungry pig. Five Dragons's hand stopped in midair. Is it all right? he asked. If not, I'll stop. The laughter from both tables stung.

Are you still hungry? Proprietor Feng asked. If not, then stop. We have to pay for our rice just like everyone else.

Then I'll stop, Five Dragons said, still red-faced. I've had three bowls already.

Cloud Weave doubled up with laughter. Eat, she said, holding her sides. Don't listen to those misers. Eat all you want. No one should have to leave the table hungry.

Do you realize how much he can put away? Cloud Silk asked her sister. He's got the appetite of an ox. He'd clean out the pot if you let him.

Five Dragons's face darkened. I'm finished, I don't want any more. He slammed his bowl down on the table and walked outside. But the joy of having finished off three bowlfuls of rice took the edge off his anger. He picked his teeth and looked around the yard. The sky turned dark, swallowing up the afternoon sunlight. Chilled, moist air in a slate-gray sky promised rain. The emporium girls' underwear and stockings still hung from the clothesline, and the door to the rice storeroom was open, sending the unique aroma of new rice drifting toward him. Five Dragons couldn't help but wonder if he had finally found the haven that would bring an end to his wanderings. Mounds of snow-white rice; beautiful and desirable women; trains on one side, steamships on the other; close to the center of town, yet within sight of industry; surrounded by people and wealth. The dream of every man from Maple-Poplar Village was within his grasp. A private utopia was taking shape in his head.

2

NO GIRL ON BRICK MASON AVENUE ATTRACTED MORE attention than Cloud Weave. Her days of innocence ended without a trace, as if washed away by a night rain. She was like a lovely wildflower, plucked by Sixth Master, who had taken his pleasure from her for years, as everyone on Brick Mason Avenue knew only too well.

They had met when she was only fifteen, the story went, when the rice-emporium mistress was still alive, and Proprietor Feng spent all his time in opium dens. Madam Feng, formerly Zhu, ran the business. Day in and day out she sat behind the counter cursing her husband, then sending Cloud Weave to go bring him home. Like a good daughter, she always did as she was told. One rainy day, she would recall, she sloshed down Brick Mason Avenue and turned into Coolie Hat Lane, trying to stay dry under an umbrella as resentment toward her father grew. This particular opium den, located in a bathhouse, could only be reached by walking around the indoor pool, where Cloud Weave saw several men walking naked amid the steam. Not daring to go any farther, she yelled: Come out here, Father. Her shout drew looks from the men inside. I'm not calling you, she complained as she looked away. I'm looking for my father. The opium den's inside, a bathhouse worker told her, he can't hear you. Go in there and call him. You're young enough, nobody cares. So she gritted her teeth, covered her eyes with her hands, and ran past the men's pool into a series of dark, narrow corridors, at the end of which two yellow lanterns framed the entrance to the den. Tears of humiliation ran down her cheeks.

Dense smoke inside the den carried the distinctive smell of opium. Umbrella in hand, Cloud Weave moved from bench to bench to find her father among the blurry faces. Finally she spotted him in conversation with a middle-aged man. Proprietor Feng had an obsequious, even reverent expression on his face. The other man, looking like a well-dressed member of the landed gentry, was sitting on a sofa, newspaper in hand and a big cigar in his mouth. A long chain was looped around his wrist, the other end attached to an enormous German shepherd. Cloud Weave, too upset to be scared, rushed up and dragged her father off the opium bench. Aren't you having a wonderful time, she complained, sobbing. Do you know what it's taken me to find you? Accidentally stepping on the chain, she drew snarls from the dog and leaped back in fright. She watched the man quiet the dog, then look up and leer at her.

Don't shout like that in here, Cloud Weave, Proprietor Feng said as he laid down his pipe. This is Sixth Master, he added in a soft voice. Kneel down and wish him health.

Why should I? Cloud Weave said, glancing at Sixth Master. Is he the emperor or something?

Watch your mouth, Proprietor Feng warned her. Not even the emperor is as rich and powerful as Sixth Master.

Cloud Weave looked more closely at the stranger. He wasn't angry, that was clear, and she was surprised to discover a softness hidden in his long, narrow, keen eyes. Her cheeks reddened. Shifting her body gently and twirling her braid, she said, If I kneel down and wish Sixth Master health, what will Sixth Master do for me?

The man shook his wrist to rattle the chain, and let out a clipped, hoarse laugh. Carefully eyeing her profile, he said, Aren't you a clever little girl? Tell Sixth Master what you want, and you shall have it. What will it be?

Cloud Weave looked confidently at her father and said without hesitation: I want a mink coat. Or is that too rich for Sixth Master's blood? She bent down to kneel, but he stopped her. He had a strong grip.

No need for that, he said. A mink coat, is that all? You shall have it.

She could not forget Sixth Master's hand. Large and damp, it slid over her shoulder and down to her waist, stopped for a moment, then pinched gently like two rows of teeth. A tender pain to take home with her.

The next day Abao showed up at the rice emporium with a large department-store box. Proprietor Feng knew that Abao was Sixth Master's man. He told one of the clerks to serve him. You can't carry rice in that, he said. Abao walked up and handed him the box. Don't be a fool. This is a present for the daughter of the house from Sixth Master. He has decided to become Cloud Weave's patron. Proprietor Feng blanched, his hands shook under the box. Abao laughed. Afraid to take it? It's nobody's head. It's a mink coat. But even if it was a head, you'd have to take it, since it's from Sixth Master. Proprietor Feng smiled weakly. It was all in fun. I never meant for Sixth Master to take her seriously. Now what? Abao drew up to the counter. Now what? he grinned. You're a businessman, count it as a business deal.

Proprietor Feng summoned Cloud Weave, cursing her as soon as she emerged from her room. See what you've done? How am I supposed to accept him as your patron? Cloud Weave snatched the box out of her father's hands and opened it. With a squeal of delight she removed the mink coat and draped it over her shoulders. Don't you dare put that on, her father demanded as he grabbed her. I forbid it! She scowled. It's my gift, why shouldn't I wear it? Proprietor Feng softened his voice. Cloud Weave, you're too young to understand, but this could be the biggest mistake of your life. Take my word for it. But she would not let go of her fur coat. She stomped her foot. I'm going to wear this, and that's all there is to it! I've been frantic just thinking about it.

Proprietor Feng called his wife out to reason with their daughter, but Cloud Weave refused to listen. Instead she ran into her room with the coat and bolted the door behind her. After a while, she emerged wearing Sixth Master's gift, and stood defiantly in the doorway facing her parents. Proprietor Feng glowered at his daughter for a long moment. Do what you want, you little demon. Your time to weep will come sooner or later.

The late-autumn days were cool and crisp, and Cloud Weave loved to flaunt her fur coat on Brick Mason Avenue. Of course, things turned out just as Proprietor Feng had predicted, and it didn't take long. One day an invitation to Sixth Master's birthday party was delivered to Cloud Weave at the emporium. Her parents stood dejected in the doorway watching her ride off in a rickshaw. Cloud Weave is just a girl, Proprietor Feng said. Barely fifteen. How can that old bastard sleep at night? Madam Zhu was reduced to leaning against the doorframe and weeping. Proprietor Feng sighed. She was born to come to grief, he said. Let her go. We'll just pretend we never had her.

From that day onward, Cloud Weave was a puzzle to all. Every day she waited breathlessly for Sixth Master's summons. His world fascinated her. Intoxicated by his hedonistic life-style, she changed dramatically that autumn, face and figure, and the neighborhood girls began to avoid her. Suddenly she was a young woman, regal in her silver-gray mink coat. One day she and Sixth Master were playing mah-jongg. He told her to mix the tiles. Give me good ones, he said, then sat her on his knee and put his arm around her. She purred like a kitten, a discontented little feline that had bounded out of the stifling, confining rice emporium onto Sixth Master's knee. None of the other girls from Brick Mason Avenue would have done that. But she had, and she was proud of it.

One day she said to the girl across the street, You know who Sixth Master is, don't you? Well, if you ever spit at me again, I'll have Sixth Master put you out. Know what that means? It means he'll kill you. Now let's see you spit at me.

By then Cloud Weave was beyond her parents' control, so one day Proprietor Feng bolted the gate and locked her out. Later that night they heard shouts of Are you going to open the gate for me or not? I was just having a little fun. I'm not working in some whorehouse, so why won't you let me in? They could only sigh and ignore their daughter's shouts. Eventually they heard her climb onto the woodpile and pull out pieces of dry kindling. Calling her mother and father by name, she shouted, If you don't let me in I'll set fire to this run-down rice shop and let it spread to the other run-down shops on this run-down street!

Cloud Weave soon had the worst reputation of any girl on Brick Mason Avenue. Her comings and goings were gossiped about by neighbor women; their talk reached the ears of children, who then mimicked what they heard behind Cloud Weave's back: Worn-out old shoe! Cheap trash! Most people assumed that the rice-emporium owners let their daughter come and go as she pleased not only because they had given up on her, but also because they feared Sixth Master. Normally, Brick Mason Avenue shop owners knew everything about one another, but now the shady relationship between Cloud Weave and Sixth Master threw a blanket of secrecy over the emporium. Some people even spread rumors that Great Swan had become a stronghold for bandits.

That winter Madam Zhu, proprietress of the emporium, died. During the days leading up to her death she sat behind the counter all day, holding a handkerchief to her mouth and coughing. Over the winter solstice, when the rice wine was being drunk, she tried to cough, but no sound emerged. Using one of the door slats as a stretcher, Proprietor Feng rushed her to the mission clinic. As she was being carried off, people noticed how pale she had grown and how her eyes were filled with tears. She never returned. The doctors said she died of consumption, but neighbors, recalling all that Cloud Weave had done, insisted that she died of a broken heart. Eventually even Cloud Silk came to share that view. She was thirteen when it happened. Having despised her elder sister for as long as she could remember, now when they argued, she pointed at Cloud Weave and swore, Who the hell do you think you are? All you know is how to shame yourself with horrible old men, you stinking piece of trash! Cloud Weave would reach out and slap her younger sister. But even as she wept and held her face, Cloud Silk kept up the barrage: You killed our mother, you piece of trash! One of these days I'll get even!

Five Dragons didn't learn all this history until he had been there quite awhile. Since he had nothing to do after the shop closed at night, he fell into the habit of crossing the street to visit with the blacksmiths, who never tired of gossiping about the rice emporium. And whenever Cloud Weave's name came up, their eyes shone. Five Dragons warmed his hands at the forge, lost in thought. So? he said. Isn't that what all women are like? Aha! one of the blacksmiths replied spiritedly. So now you're her protector. Has she let you feel her tits? Five Dragons, his face taut, turned his hands to warm the backs. Why ask me? I'm not going to marry her. Who cares about her tits? I wouldn't touch them if she begged me.

Autumn faded with the falling locust leaves. Chill winds blew through the cracks in buildings and across intersections, like muffled sobs. Five Dragons paced in his bare feet, feeling uncomfortably cold. Winter was back. For him it was the worst season. He did not own a comforter, he had no lined shoes, and cold weather made the hunger pangs worse. His thoughts drifted back to home in Maple-Poplar Village. The floodwaters would have receded by then, leaving behind ruined crops, fallen buildings, and homeless dogs barking frantically; the ground would be covered with rotted rice plants and dead twigs and the leaves of cotton plants. He wondered how many people had returned to the village. But what did that matter? Maple-Poplar Village would still be a scene of desolation and death, and he wasn't going back, no matter what.

From where he stood, midway between the blacksmith shop and the rice emporium, Five Dragons looked up and down the length of Brick Mason Avenue. The setting sun cast his gaunt shadow on the cobblestone surface, where it stuck like the silhouette of a tree. Children were rolling iron hoops down the street; the high-pitched screeches of a two-stringed *huqin* and the hollow notes of a bamboo flute, followed by the childish, lackluster strains of a female voice, came from a local opera troupe at a distant intersection. Odd aromas from the pharmaceutical plant and smoky chimney smells from factories to the west arrived on the same winds. A man roasting chestnuts across the street wrestled his cauldron out of the way of a rickshaw traveling down the street. Who could that be? the man wondered aloud.

It was the elder daughter of the rice emporium, Cloud Weave, slumped and ashen against the backrest, no longer the lively young woman they were used to seeing. A man in black sat beside her. Recognizing him as Abao, Five Dragons was reminded of what had happened on the wharf that night, and his scalp went cold. Quickly hiding behind a lamppost, he watched anxiously as the rickshaw passed him and stopped in front of the rice emporium.

Abao helped Cloud Weave down. Obviously she had been crying; her eyes were red and puffy. With his hand resting on her hip, Abao guided her through the gate. Something stirred deep inside Five Dragons. Kill Abao, kill the bastard. Back home in Maple-Poplar Village, he would certainly have translated his anger into action: clubbed him with a stone, hacked him with his scythe, or strangled him with his bare hands. But in unfamiliar territory—Brick Mason Avenue was a long way from Maple-Poplar Village—he knew that the city itself and the circumstance of living under someone else's roof had turned him cautious, even cowardly. It was a thought, just a thought. He would never follow through on it.

From the doorway Cloud Silk called to Five Dragons; he rushed over. She had a scornful look on her face. Go see to Cloud Weave, she said impatiently. She's carrying on about being sick, and I don't feel like dealing with her. Some man brought her home, didn't he? Five Dragons asked. Shut up, and do as I say. Don't let Abao hang around her room, understand?

Why me? Five Dragons grumbled as he headed out back, where he encountered Abao emerging from Cloud Weave's room. Abao glared suspiciously at Five Dragons, who tried to get out of his way. Abao grabbed him by the wrist and dragged him toward the shop. Cloud Silk met them halfway. What are you doing, Abao? she demanded. He's our new helper. He's what? You hired someone like him? It was my father's idea. But he's a good worker. Abao released Five Dragons's arm. I don't like the looks of him, so be careful. Cloud Silk was alarmed. Do you know him? Is he a thief? Abao grinned. If he isn't, he's as bad as one. I can see myself in him. He's probably every bit as cruel as I am. What do you mean by that? she asked. Abao pointed his thumbs at his own chest. Everybody's afraid of me. I'm warning you, keep an eye on this one.

Five Dragons turned and went inside, his head bowed. He nearly bit through his lip as he thought, I can't shake that mad dog. I'd give anything to murder him. Still flustered, he pushed open Cloud Weave's door and took another look behind him, where Abao was strutting toward the front gate. If you really want to do something for this family, Cloud Silk shouted at his retreating back, tell Sixth Master to keep his hands off Cloud Weave and stop treating her like a worn-out old shoe. You people make me sick.

Cloud Weave lay in bed sobbing and tearing her hair. It hurts, she moaned, it's killing me. Finding her agony strange, Five Dragons squatted down to remove her shoes. Where does it hurt, Mistress? She gave him a blank look. All over. It's killing me. She fought his attempts to remove her shoes. Get away from me! What do you think you're doing? Who said you could climb into my bed? I wouldn't dare, he said, managing to slip off one of her high heels. Second Mistress told me to look after you. If you're sick, get some rest. Cloud Weave stunned him with a kick in the face. He stumbled backward, holding his hand to his face and suppressing his anger. Is that all you men have on your mind? What makes you all think I'm so easy? Maybe that's what other men want, but not me. He filled a basin with hot water, rinsed out a washcloth, and wrung it dry. Someone has made you very mad, Elder Mistress. He handed her the washcloth. You'll feel better after you wash your face. Clearly, he had touched a nerve, for Cloud Weave pounded her pillow and burst into tears. Mad? Who wouldn't be mad? she sobbed. I'm so mad I could scream. What right did that old sex fiend have to hit me? He's got the heart of a wolf and the lungs of a dog. After all the years of pleasure I gave him, he goes and hits me. He actually hit me!

Now Five Dragons knew what was wrong. It was Sixth Master who had hit her. But so what? He saw nothing wrong with a man hitting a woman, here or anywhere else. They usually deserve it. What was she getting so upset about? She probably had it coming. He grinned and turned to leave.

Stop right there! A pillow thudded into his back. You've got one hell of a way of looking after me.

Five Dragons lowered the door curtain. You should sleep now, Mistress, and I shouldn't be hanging around.

What do you mean, shouldn't be hanging around? What about me? I ache all over, and all you can think about is leaving.

What do you want from me? he asked. Tell me what to do, and I'll do it. Shall I call you a doctor?

I don't want a doctor, I want a massage. With a coy smile, she added, And I want *you* to give it to me. Come on, what's there to be afraid of? Brightly painted fingernails moved nimbly across her buttons, and he saw the top of her cheongsam part to reveal a pink undershirt. His mouth fell open as the top of her arching, snowy-white breasts came into view. But what really surprised him were the purple welts. He gulped nervously, turned, and lifted the door curtain. His heart was thumping wildly.

Laughter erupted behind him. Useless turd, she cursed. As his face reddened, he drove his fist into the wall. His thoughts were too confused to sort out. What had caused all those welts?

All this was new to Five Dragons. Maple-Poplar Village had women like this, who went into the woods with passing vendors or itinerant artists. Then in the mornings the menfolk would be out chasing their wives down the streets with scythes or clubs, the women's shrieks filling the air like the rooftop screeches of cats in heat. But that was a far-off village, where life was primitive and crude, while Cloud Weave's cleavage laid bare the decadent nature of the city in general and Brick Mason Avenue in particular.

He brooded over his humiliation. That night he tossed and turned on the mat, his body tied up in knots of sexual desire, face burning with anguish; the darkness of night concealed unrestrained thoughts; he felt deeply ashamed; he detected the odor of semen on his bedding and in the air.

Five Dragons stayed away from Elder Mistress Cloud Weave after that, afraid to look at her thin, painted mouth, and terrified to contemplate her fleshy hips, which moved so seductively. It was not a case of knowing his place; rather he feared that his look would give him away, for deep in his heart burned a flame whose light could be seen in his eyes.

One particular morning Five Dragons was in the yard fetching water when he heard a creak behind him. Cloud Weave's pale face appeared in the open window. She motioned for him to come. With trepidation he entered her room; she was seated at the dressing table, lazily brushing her hair. She did not acknowledge his presence, and the silence was broken only by the soft scraping of the brush on her permed hair. She gazed into the oval mirror and exhaled loudly.

I'm going to take you to the department store. She laid down her brush and touched up her bangs. We're getting you some shoes and socks.

Why should you buy me shoes?

Because seeing you in those plastic slippers on cold days like this gives me a chill.

Five Dragons raised his feet, one at a time. Yellow toes poked through the open fronts of the secondhand black sandals, which Proprietor Feng had dragged out from under the bed and handed to Five Dragons. I'm used to it, he said as he stared at his feet. I don't notice the cold when I work.

You enjoy being cold? She glanced at him out of the corner of her eye. If so, then forget about the new shoes. I'm not going to beg.

Please don't talk like that, Mistress, he said, quickly clasping his hands together. I know you're doing this out of the goodness of your heart. I may be poor, but I'm flesh and blood like everybody else. How could I *enjoy* being cold?

Just so you know. She turned back to powder her face. I'm not like my heartless sister. I take pity on people who suffer. Someday, if I have to suffer, I wonder if people will take pity on me.

You were born to enjoy life, Mistress. How can you talk about suffering? Five Dragons stared at the mirror, in which Cloud Weave's face seemed weighted down with genuine sorrow. This was all so new to him that he had to lower his head and try to reason things out. It's people like me who suffer, he said. Heaven is impartial. For every fortunate person, a sufferer is born. You and I are one of those pairs.

A pair? Cloud Weave cackled lustily. Moody as always, she could be sad one minute and ecstatic the next. Are you saying that you and I are a pair? Don't make me laugh.

No, I'm saying that fortune and suffering make a pair, Five Dragons explained bashfully. Fate would never smile on me like that.

Some time later, Cloud Weave and Five Dragons were stopped at the gate by Cloud Silk. Have you lost your

mind? she asked Cloud Weave. You're going out walking
with a man like him? He's got work to do. Cloud Weave
responded with a shove. Good dogs know when to get
out of the way, she said. What's your problem? Don't tell
me you're jealous. He doesn't have proper shoes, so I decided to get him a pair. With a sneer, Cloud Silk replied,
You and your good deeds. The way you give away our
money disgusts me. Cloud Weave's thin brows knitted
tightly. Shit on you! she swore. This money was a gift
from Sixth Master. What I do with it is my business. She
turned to Five Dragons. Let's go. Don't mind her, she's
jealous.

Embarrassed, Five Dragons stood right up against the
wall. The absurd arguments between the two sisters disturbed him. He despised them. Who cares about a pair of
shoes anyway? He hated their manipulative ways. Proprietor Feng walked up. That's enough bickering. He
frowned. What will the neighbors say? Let them go,
Cloud Silk. I told your sister to get Five Dragons some
shoes. He turned to Cloud Weave. Buy tough, sturdy ones,
but not leather. Remember, he's a hired hand. The comment shifted Five Dragons's anger to Proprietor Feng,
who always steered a neutral course. The idea was to let
Cloud Weave know she should buy slip-ons, since they
cost so much less. Five Dragons was convinced that no
one in the family really gave a damn about him, that their
pity and warm sentiments were like water on the street
after a rain: shallow, illusory, and quickly sucked up by
the wind and sun. They can buy me any kind of shoes
they want, but they won't own me, even if I'm less than
human in their eyes. Hatred was everlasting: Like a steel
implement, it survived fire, pounding, grinding, and cor-

rosion. Once a tool, always a tool. Hatred would live in his heart for all time.

Beginning that winter, Five Dragons wore the canvas shoes Cloud Weave had picked out for him. Cold, biting winds swept down Brick Mason Avenue from the north, turning puddles on the stones into ice slicks at night. The bone-chilling cold was worst in the early morning hours. Five Dragons, who was terrified of wintry weather, still had to climb out of bed at daybreak to buy soybean milk, sesame buns, and oil fritters for the family's breakfast. Housewives on their way to market were used to seeing him, his face pocked with chilblains, walking aimlessly around the marketplace, a basket with the family's breakfast in one hand and bunches of greens in the other. He averted his eyes as much as possible, but if the women looked closely they saw resentment and impatience on his face.

At dusk on wintry afternoons Proprietor Feng could usually be found at the Clear Springs Public Bathhouse, along with other local shop owners, where they succeeded in beating the winter cold. Sometimes Proprietor Feng took Five Dragons along so the old man could have a body rub. Perfectly at ease in the hot, steamy atmosphere, surrounded by naked bodies, Five Dragons didn't mind at all. He would strip naked, like everyone else, his and their genitals out there for all to see in the mist. Only in the gathering steam and splashing water of the bathhouse could he shed his feelings of inferiority. If we're the same, then how come I have to wash *your* back all the time? he wondered as he scoured the skin with a greasy washcloth. Why don't you ever offer to wash mine? We both have cocks, we both have oily, grimy bodies, but it's always me washing your back, washing your back, washing your back. Why? These thoughts invariably slowed his movements.

Five Dragons saw the Wharf Rats in the bathhouse one day. As he watched them dive noisily into the pool, bellies knotting up as they hit the heated water, he assumed that the pall of steam would keep the thugs from spotting him. But Proprietor Feng called out, Abao, want my helper to wash your back? Abao, who was rubbing his hairy belly, squinted to get a good look at Five Dragons. Sure. Do a good job and I'll give you a silver dollar. But do a bad job and you'll be sorry. I'll wash it for you, Five Dragons said, not even looking at Abao's fair skin, if you'll stop staring at me all the time. I've never done anything to offend you. Abao climbed out of the pool and lay face-down on the table. No promises. I was born to make trouble. Offend me? I don't care about stuff like that. I go after anyone who looks cross-eyed at me. That's what it takes to be a Wharf Rat.

Five Dragons was sickened by Abao's milky skin. His buttocks were as soft and fleshy as a woman's, with the same curves; dark curly hairs grew around the anus. Five Dragons splashed water on Abao's back, then scrubbed his shoulders, upper arms, and ribcage, his fingers brushing against flabby skin that covered a layer of cottony fat and a network of indigo blood vessels. He was gripped by a feverish impulse. All he had to do was move his hand down under the buttocks and wrap it around those two little pellets. One good squeeze and the son of a bitch would fade into history. Recalling how they slaughtered oxen back in Maple-Poplar Village, Five Dragons dreamed about doing the same thing to Abao, as if he were a crazed ox. It would be easy: Plunge the knife into the most yielding spot, then peel back the skin. His hands trembled; the moist glow of ecstasy shone in his eyes.

The emporium canopy snapped in the gusty winds of a cold afternoon. Five Dragons crossed the street from the blacksmith's, slapping the wall as he walked through the gate. Proprietor Feng was sitting in the rice shop counting his money. He looked up at Five Dragons, whose shoulders were hunched, as if from the cold, and stood up woodenly.

Old Sun the blacksmith died, Five Dragons said, his eyes flashing. Real sudden.

So I hear, Proprietor Feng replied. Typhoid, they say. Stay clear of the place. We don't want any of that around here.

They need a blacksmith, somebody who doesn't mind hard work. They asked me.

Proprietor Feng closed his cash box and gave Five Dragons a hard look. A note of derision crept into his voice. So you've learned how to move to the other side of the trough, have you? Who taught you?

They'll give me five silver dollars a month plus room and board, Five Dragons replied calmly, his fingers thrust inside his jacket, where they wiggled and made a crisp, scratchy sound. I'm no idiot. I'm going to take it.

Proprietor Feng looked surprised. But the derisive smile quickly returned. My kindness will go unrewarded, I guess. A dog bites the hand that fed it when it was sick. He sat down and reopened his cashbox, combing his fingers through the coins. How much?

Five silver dollars. What I do in the shop ought to be worth that much.

Here, take it, Proprietor Feng said as he tossed a coin

to the floor. *Clang.* Then another. He repeated the action three more times, five altogether, his expression a mixture of resentment and snide condescension. Go on, take it. Now you've become a wage earner.

Five Dragons bent down and picked up the coins, blowing on each one as if to remove some dust. The blotchy redness on his face spread to his bare neck and shoulder blades. Proprietor Feng heard his raspy breaths as he stuffed the coins into his padded jacket and walked to the door; he spun around and said, I want another pair of shoes, leather ones this time, leather shoes.

Proprietor Feng just stood there for a moment, until he realized the significance of the parting comment: canvas versus leather shoes. A minor incident, long forgotten. By them, but not by him. Finally Proprietor Feng understood Five Dragons's essential makeup: intolerant and vindictive. Until now he had pitied the man—timid and all alone in the world—overlooking each instance of rebellion and resistance. He walked to the door to watch Five Dragons hurry down the street in the quiet dusk air, shoulders drawn in, as usual, feet splayed out into a *V*, his large shaved head glinting in the fading light. He turned the corner and was out of sight.

Fucking bastard, Proprietor Feng swore from the doorway. In his state of mind he found it hard to accept some facts that were becoming increasingly apparent; they included five silver dollars and a mysterious pair of shoes.

Leather shoes? He wants leather shoes? Proprietor Feng mumbled as he locked his redwood cashbox and walked to the rear of the compound hugging it to his chest. The kitchen resounded with the thud of Cloud Silk chopping cabbage. Guess where Five Dragons is off to and what he's going to do, Proprietor Feng said. He went to buy leather shoes. He laughed. Leather shoes? Cloud Silk echoed. He just got new shoes, didn't he? Give someone like that a bamboo pole, and he wants to turn it into a roofbeam. You two wait and see. Angered by what she was saying, Proprietor Feng shouted into the kitchen, What am I supposed to do? You don't think I actually like that son of a bitch, do you? It's his muscle I like, his labor. Understand?

Five Dragons did not return until after dark. Proprietor Feng watched him enter the kitchen to eat some cold, leftover rice, squatting there stuffing his face until his cheeks puffed out; his teeth and tongue produced an awful munching noise. He had returned empty-handed. Where are your leather shoes? Proprietor Feng asked through the kitchen window. Let's see them.

I didn't have enough money, Five Dragons replied casually. He was his old tranquil self again.

I'm not surprised. Want an advance on next month's wages?

No need. He lowered his head to shovel in more rice. Actually, he said, I didn't feel like buying anything. I just walked the streets for a while to boost my spirits.

As the night deepened, Five Dragons listened to the sounds of the world: breezes gusting against the shop window, the whistling of the north wind, bamboo clappers struck by the old night watchman. Then the deathly stillness returned. Faced with the cold of winter and a dull, lonely existence, he often thought back to the freight train speeding through the wilderness. In his mind the rice emporium and all of Brick Mason Avenue turned into a gigantic train that rocked like a cradle as it carried him along. He drifted in and out of sleep; he swayed from side to side. Then he was traveling down a long, dark road that was taking him away from home. People, huts, live-stock, and vast rice paddies floated atop floodwaters. He dreamed about the man who had died of starvation in the street, his head pillowed on a gunnysack, hoarfrost in his hair. Five Dragons saw himself running madly down a pitch-black street and heard his own screams of terror swirling in the sky, desperate.

3

AS THE DAYS TURNED BALMY, CLOUD WEAVE LIBERATED her warm-weather clothes from her dresser and hung them out to air: silks and satins, woolens, velvets, and leathers competed for space in the yard, which reeked of mothballs. She treasured her fashionable clothes, the centerpiece of her youthful wealth. Over the winter she had put on a few pounds, but that only increased the appearance of voluptuousness. Even indoors she kept her chin and jowls buried in a fox muffler, like the slinky, gorgeous movie stars she read about.

Her mood was as bright as the sky. From her rocking chair she looked with satisfaction at the silk scarves and satin cheongsams. Rays of afternoon sunlight poured down past the eaves; soft silks fluttered gracefully, like waves, calming her mind. It was so quiet she could hear the gentle snapping sound. She rocked back and forth humming a northern Jiangsu tune that was popular along the wharf. It had frivolous, naughty lyrics filled with sexy teases. She stopped to giggle. That's so silly, she muttered. She couldn't remember when she'd learned the song. And as for all the new swearwords she'd begun using lately, she wasn't sure if they had come to her out of nowhere, or if she had picked them up from the

Wharf Rats, those ruffians who were taking up so much of her time these days. She had no illusions about what kind of girl she was, and about what kinds of people and events affected her uncomplicated emotions. She knew exactly what made her happy, angry, sad, or content.

Come here, Five Dragons, she called when she saw him poke his head into the yard. I want you to watch these things for me.

What for? Five Dragons walked listlessly toward her, his padded jacket and pants coated with a white powder. He patted his sleeves and pants pockets. Who'd steal them in our own yard?

Thieves on the outside, thieves in the family, one or the other, Cloud Weave replied mysteriously. I have to go out, and I don't want to leave all these pretty clothes unguarded.

Who's the thief in the family? You don't think I'd want this stuff, do you?

I didn't say you. Don't be so touchy. She pouted playfully and pointed toward the shop with puckered lips. Cloud Silk, she grumbled. She's envious of my pretty clothes, since she doesn't own any. Don't let her spit on my cheongsams.

She'd do something like that? Five Dragons asked with growing interest. She'd actually spit on your clothes?

She did it last year. You don't know how sneaky she can be. She carries her evil ideas around in a basket.

You're her older sister, why not show her who's boss? Five Dragons commented, his arms crossed. I hate the way Second Mistress lords it over the whole family.

It's not worth the effort. Father relies on her for everything. She's his little darling. Cloud Weave stopped rocking and sat up straight. You won't catch me throwing my life away over this stupid business. I can't stand to stay home two days in a row.

The yard was deserted as Five Dragons walked among the clotheslines, where the cheongsams hanging out to air took on the shape of the woman who wore them, and even retained traces of her scented powder. The sun shone on his shaved head, making it itch subtly. He scratched his scalp; the hard stubble was warm to the touch. When his finger rubbed against the sleeveless gosling-yellow silk cheongsam hanging in front of him, a silky sensation ran up his hand, then quickly spread through his body, a pool of water seeping into his bloodstream. He shivered, for some strange reason, and gazed at the cheongsam, gripped by a sudden fantasy that made him fidget uncomfortably. It was a summer dress; in it, Cloud Weave, looking shamelessly sexy, would have flounced around the shop in last summer's heat. What were they doing here then? Back in Maple-Poplar Village he was weeding the rice paddies; the mountain torrents hadn't come yet, and everyone was running around in busy desperation. As he manned the waterwheel, the sun directly overhead, he had listened to the raspy scraping of the rotating blades and watched water fill the furrows, then branch out across the field. He had sensed the coming of autumn and the changes it would bring. Worn out and sleepy, he had been visited by daydreams about the city: the factories and shops, girls in sexy gosling-yellow dresses just like this one. Full-breasted with willowy waists, they made eyes at the men, turning them mad with desire. Five Dragons thought back to all those nights he had spent in the local temple after days of exhausting fieldwork, his mind filled with crazy notions of the city, and how he had lain there physically and emotionally drained as images of one citified girl after another came into his head. The temple floor and the legs of the altar were spotted with whitish stains. One day an uncle had shown up, he recalled, and knew right off how his nephew had been abusing himself. Five Dragons, he had said sternly, you have desecrated the temple of our ancestors, for which you will pay someday.

That doesn't scare me. He reached out and crumpled Cloud Weave's cheongsam, then blushed, even though the yard was deserted. Strolling over to the spot beside the wall where he often relieved himself, he hurriedly undid his pants and stood, legs apart, as if urinating. A rat scurried past and vanished in the yard.

He heard voices in the shop. Proprietor Feng was telling the clerk Old Wang that the storeroom was nearly empty, and that the next shipment from Zhejiang was late. He would have to ask Sixth Master's help in replenishing the stock, and was concerned that Sixth Master might say no. Cloud Silk's shrill voice entered the conversation at that point. Have Cloud Weave go see him. You don't think he'd turn her down in a little matter like this, do you? What she did for him ought to be worth something. You know what I mean.

Proprietor Feng told Five Dragons to go with Abao and his men to borrow some rice at the wharf. Where does somebody go to borrow boatloads of rice? Five Dragons asked suspiciously. Who'd let you borrow that much? Proprietor Feng sputtered for a moment. Then: Don't ask so many questions. Just do as I say.

Once again Five Dragons found himself on the wharf late at night, the familiar sights and sensations flooding his mind with unpleasant memories. From a spot beside some cargo he observed his coarse companions to see how they went about borrowing the rice. A scattering of lanterns dotted the river's edge, outlining ships' masts and stacked cargo with zigzag lines and shadows. An expression of carefree confidence showed on Abao's infantile face, almost but not quite masking the evil lurking beneath the calm surface. The men quickly boarded a tanker tied up at the pier, and from there jumped onto two rice boats farther outboard, which rolled from side to side as lamps hanging from their masts were extinguished. Even from that distance, Five Dragons saw Abao fling a kerosene lamp from one of the masts into the river, and at that moment he realized that they were stealing rice, not borrowing it. Glancing quickly up and down the wharf, he wondered how they could get away with it. What about the people on the other boats, not to mention the pack of two-legged dogs in black uniforms that prowled the wharf like specters? Apparently, the only law that counted here came out of the barrel of a gun.

Abao signaled Five Dragons to come aboard. Hesitantly he made his way from boat to boat, reluctant to be in on the theft. But that fucking Abao had him in his clutches and wouldn't let go. He noticed a crewman lying hog-tied in the cabin, mouth stuffed with rags; he had seen that look of hopelessness before—grief and indignation mixed together—and felt the kinship of the downtrodden. Anyone who stood guard over a boatload of rice was asking for trouble. Didn't he realize how dark and dangerous the times were? Five Dragons gazed down at the rice in the hold, glistening a gentle white in the inky darkness. He loved the subtle fragrance and soft glare.

Can you handle a boat? Abao asked. Most country boys can.

No, he replied instinctively.

Don't lie to me. Abao cupped Five Dragons's chin in the palm of his hand. I can see it in your eyes. Now get this boat over to the pier, and be quick about it. We can start unloading it and its companion there. Do as I say if you want to keep dry.

I'm not much of a sailor, Five Dragons said as he lowered his eyes and pushed Abao's hand away, but I'll give it a try.

It took some doing, but he managed to rock the rice boat up to the pier, where men moved into the light with freight wagons, and the unloading began. Five Dragons heard a rhythmic swish as the rice was dumped into the wagons. The piracy went like clockwork: Two boatloads of rice were now on the pier. Stories he had heard about the Wharf Rats were no exaggeration. Relying upon strong-arm tactics, they always finished what they set out to do.

Splash. Five Dragons spun around in time to see the hog-tied sailor hit the water. He looked up as if to beg for his life, but no sound emerged from his gagged mouth. Five Dragons watched the pale light of despair sweep across the man's face seconds before his body sank heavily beneath the surface, the spot marked only by a few sprays of water.

Five Dragons dropped what was in his hands and reached out for the drowning man. He's in the river! he shouted. He pulled back his hands: They were wet but empty.

He was tired of living, Abao volunteered. Assholes like that are better off dead. We just helped him along, that's all. Anyone who'd jump in the river over a boatload of rice deserves to die.

Five Dragons felt his hand, which was as wet and cold

as his heart. The river flowed eastward in the faint moon-light and the glare of an occasional lantern. One year to the next, he mused, evil crawls along the earth like an army of ants. How many weak, despairing souls are swallowed up by the river as it flows along? Death had made another appearance in Five Dragons's life, this time over a boatload of rice.

Quickly the wagons transported their loads of rice down dark, narrow streets through the northern section of town. In the middle of the pack, Five Dragons helped push until the wagons stopped in front of a newly opened rice shop. A woman emerged from the doorway and had a whispered conversation with Abao, who turned and raised his hand. Unload two of them here, he shouted. Two wagonloads.

Why here? Five Dragons asked the man behind him. This rice is for Proprietor Feng of the Great Swan Rice Emporium.

Mind your own business, the man said. Proprietor Feng doesn't have a monopoly on black-market rice. Everybody wants a share, and they're willing to pay for it.

Abao counted the money under a streetlight. Then, smiling broadly, he walked up to Five Dragons and handed him one of the bills. Here's your cut. Five Dragons looked down at his hand. This is all I get for knocking myself out? Abao peeled off another bill. Don't breathe a word of this back at the shop, he warned. If anybody asks, tell them this was all we managed to get. Say any more, and you'll be feeding the fish in the river, too. Five Dragons calmly stuffed the money into his pocket. My lips are sealed, he said. Why would I tell them?

It was nearly midnight when they reached Brick Mason Avenue, but the owner and his daughters were up and waiting. Cloud Weave was first out the door as the wagons pulled up. She threw her arms around Abao's neck. A treat from yours truly, she said, planting a loud kiss on his cheek. A pretty stingy treat, Abao replied. Now go make something for the boys to eat. Meat and wine. They've worked hard tonight.

The family's fawning attitude disgusted Five Dragons, the only one whose work wasn't finished: Carrying the rice in was his job. I'd have preferred better quality, Proprietor Feng said as he scooped up a handful of the rice, but it doesn't pay to be choosy, especially since I can sell anything I get my hands on. Five Dragons wondered if he knew that the shipment had cost a man his life. Probably he had considered the possibility and figured it was worth it. Brick Mason Avenue was a dark, wicked street whose denizens coveted wealth and were blinded by greed. Snakes poisoning the world with their lethal venom. A human life meant nothing to them. Well, I guess I don't care either. He continued carrying baskets of rice out back. What's one life?

One winter night Five Dragons stumbled upon the secret that Cloud Weave and Abao were lovers. The feverish thoughts caused by this discovery, which he kept to himself, led to many sleepless nights; they were followed by mornings during which he secretly observed Cloud Weave's every frown and every smile, the light in his eyes a mixture of cunning and agony. She was oblivious to the change, for her sexual liaison brought new joy into her life. Her face glowed that winter, at home and outside; whenever Sixth Master went off to one of the elegant brothels in South City, she and Abao secretly coupled at home. She felt daringly rebellious, and loved it.

The first time Five Dragons heard stirrings near the wall he assumed that the neighbor's cat and the shop tabby were fighting. But when he went outside to relieve himself, he was startled to see Abao scale the wall; it was then that he realized that a stray dog was looking for one of the family's hens. Unaware of Five Dragons's presence by the wall, Abao cut across the yard to Cloud Weave's window, pushed it open silently, and climbed in.

Five Dragons stared at the window, aghast. A light went on, but was quickly extinguished. All he could see was the outline of window panes. He tiptoed up to eavesdrop. The conversation inside was muted and distant, but he heard an occasional suppressed giggle. Shivering in the cold, gusty wind, he hugged himself to keep warm and tried to imagine what was happening on the other side of the window. Five Dragons's heart was submerged in ice water as he stood in the cold, dark yard listening to Abao and Cloud Weave's pillow talk. Life is too easy for that son of a bitch. Five Dragons clenched his teeth. Why won't anyone stand up to a common, evil, and savage dog like that? Why don't I have the courage to burst into the room, drag him out of bed, and snap him in two or crush his balls with my knee? Loathing, dejection, and jealousy gnawed like shadowy caterpillars at his heart. He crossed the darkened yard and entered the shop, then crawled under his greasy comforter, which stank of stale sweat, and let grave and exotic fantasies of the most bizarre kind play in his head: He and Cloud Weave are fornicating in a room suffused with the fragrance of rouge and powder. A large, yellow human hide protects the copulating couple from the bare floor. As he bites down on his comforter, Five Dragons sees that it is Abao's hide, skinned and tanned to serve as a bedsheet for Five Dragons and his woman to wipe their asses on.

The next morning Five Dragons watched clouds of steam burst from a bucket of sizzling water as one of the blacksmiths quenched a bar of red-hot steel. We had a thief at our place last night, he blurted out. In Cloud Weave's room. Know what he stole?

Feminine favors, I expect, the blacksmith said with a shady smile. The other men kept on working. Cloud Weave was deflowered at fourteen, so what's to steal. She's a thief's delight, Five Dragons. Don't get all worked up.

It was that bastard Abao. I saw him scale the wall.

So? Watch out he doesn't come after you. The blacksmiths sat Five Dragons down on an anvil. Don't breathe a word of this to anyone, they warned. Pretend you didn't see a thing, or you've got big trouble.

If anyone's got big trouble, it's *him*. Five Dragons sat deep in thought for a while, until the corners of his mouth turned up in a faint smile. If he can come after me, why can't Sixth Master come after him? What do you think Sixth Master would do if he found out?

One of the blacksmiths saw Cloud Silk walking through the unlatched gate across the street, chamber pot in hand, her brow knitted, as usual. After dumping the contents at the base of the wall, she went back inside, noisily latching the gate behind her.

Do Proprietor Feng and Cloud Silk know?

All they worry about is the business, Five Dragons said. As long as the money keeps flowing in, she could become a whore for all they care.

Fine. If her own family isn't concerned about a little private dirt, then why should you be?

What do you think Sixth Master would do if he found out? Five Dragons repeated his question, a slightly deranged look in his eyes. He dragged his finger across his throat. He'd butcher the bastard, he remarked confidently. Skin him alive is what he'd do.

Maybe, maybe not. Abao's been with Sixth Master for a long time. He's his most loyal watchdog.

He'd butcher him, Five Dragons repeated, shaking his head. And he'd do it *because* he's a lowly dog. Sixth Master would never tolerate his sleeping with Cloud Weave. That's how men are.

You plan to tell him? Would you really do that?

Sooner or later, someone will. Five Dragons skirted the issue and stood up to leave. At the doorway he turned and said, You'll never know how much I hate that man.

He walked toward the intersection at Brick Mason Avenue, up to a scribe's stall outside the silk emporium. He stood there studying the ashen face of the idle old man, who was clutching a hand warmer to his chest as he leaned against the silk-emporium window and rested his eyes. The scribe sensed labored, raspy breath on his face. Five Dragons was standing so close he nearly touched the man as he anxiously looked up and down the street.

Want a letter to your family to let them know you're okay?

A letter to my family? I've got no family. *Pop pop.* He cracked his knuckles. Do you guarantee delivery of the letters you write? he asked, his head bent low.

Of course. To any living soul with a fixed address. The old scribe laid down his hand warmer, spread a clean sheet of paper before him, and picked up his brush. Who to?

I don't know his address and I don't know his real

name, Five Dragons admitted. It's Sixth Master. You must know who he is. And I'm sure the people at the post office do.

You mean Lu Piji? The startled old scribe laid down his brush. You want to send a letter to *him*? And say what? That you want to join the Wharf Rats?

Write this: Abao is fucking Cloud Weave. He'll understand.

Maybe he will, but I don't. The old scribe's eyes were glued to Five Dragons's face. Who are you? he asked uncertainly. What kind of strange letter is that? I've never written anything like it.

You ask too many questions, Five Dragons said coldly. Write what I said and I'll give you more than your asking price. I've got the money.

I know where Lu Piji lives. His creditors ask me to write so they won't have to face him, the old man muttered as he smoothed out the paper. He looked up at Five Dragons. But I can't write that filthy word. How about using illicit intercourse instead? It means the same thing.

I don't care, so long as Sixth Master gets the message. He bent down to look at the stationery, then took out a silver dollar and laid it on the writing surface. It dawned on him that this was the money Abao had given him at the bathhouse, and he appreciated the irony of letting it be the one that would cost the man his life. He looked up and down the street again. People scurried along, huddled down to keep warm in the wintry air; no one paid him any attention or could possibly imagine how he felt at that moment.

For the first time in his life Five Dragons had spent money. Blood money. He conjured up a picture of Abao's pale yellow skin being slowly peeled away. Money well spent. What better way to part with a silver dollar than to have it end Abao's life?

Three days later shop owners on Brick Mason Avenue heard of Abao's death. Reportedly his body was stripped naked, stuffed into a burlap bag, and tossed into the river by the Wharf Rats, despite their ties of brotherhood. Afterward, they went to a riverside pub, where, in a fit of alcohol-induced fury, they climbed onto a table to curse an ungrateful Sixth Master for treating them like bugs, to be squashed at will. News of the incident spread quickly, and people learned that Abao had died over his involvement with Cloud Weave. Upsetting Sixth Master's vinegar bottle had cost him his life.

No one mentioned the letter.

Word of Abao's death reached Five Dragons in the morning as he was packing oil fritters into his basket. His hand shook. He got it, he mumbled as he passed through the crowd. Sixth Master got the letter. He ran home like a man possessed, bean-curd milk spilling out of the brass decanter and splashing on the ground. He didn't stop until he was in the doorway, where he considered the possibility that the news was unreliable. So fast? Only three days. Could my letter really have done the trick that soon?

Proprietor Feng, who was sitting in the shop drinking tea, saw the look of panic in Five Dragons's eyes as he raced back outside. Where are you off to so early? he shouted. You look like you've seen a ghost.

I'll be right back. There's a body I need to see.

Now who died? Proprietor Feng stood up.

Abao! The volume and strange timbre of Five Dragons's voice shocked Proprietor Feng, but before he could get another question out, Five Dragons was gone.

Brick Mason Avenue was separated from the wharf by three neighborhoods. Five Dragons sped down wet streets and past morning crowds. The sun had just leapt into the sky from behind bulky stone pilings supporting a crane and was painting the riverside with its glare when he reached the wharf. He stopped, feeling as if his heart were about to jump into his throat; the blinding light of the world was focused on him; the deserted river and wharf, so pure and fresh, drove away the gloomy, terrifying thoughts he had brought with him.

He scoured the riverbank. There should be bloodstains. You don't butcher someone without spilling blood. He scanned the ground as he walked, but spotted only cinders, grease stains, and scraps of paper. Why were there no traces of Abao's blood? Maybe they just strapped him to a boulder and flung him into the river. I wish I could have seen how he looked just before he died. Did he get down on his knees and beg for his life? Had he guessed who was responsible for his death?

What are you looking for? An old woman in rags peeked out from behind some cargo.

A body. Did you see the man who died here last night?

Somebody dies here *every* night. Which one?

Abao. You know, the leader of the Wharf Rats. I'm here to claim his body.

You mean this one? She fished a black satin jacket out of her basket, then a pair of black trousers and a black skullcap. They're for sale.

Five Dragons looked closely. He recognized the cap as Abao's, and the black satin jacket as the one Abao always wore open at the chest. What about the shoes, the ones that ground my wrist when I was holding the piece of cold pig's head? He looked up into the sky—half red, half blue. The light hurt his eyes. A drop of icy water fell on his cheek—it was a tear. Where had that come from?

Five Dragons often woke up in the middle of the long winter nights for no apparent reason; by cocking his ear he could hear someone scale the wall and land in the compound. An oppressive, conspiratorial sound that should have died with Abao. But there it was—*thud*—in the darkness, and always late at night in the deserted yard.

Cloud Weave was as self-indulgent as ever. A perplexing, fawning smile seemed frozen on her crimson lips. Nothing could alter her nature or her interests. That winter she mastered the newest fad: the tango. She loved going into the yard to practice the crisp rhythms: *beng-cha-cha, beng-cha-cha.*

One day Cloud Weave and Cloud Silk were discussing Abao's death. Five Dragons eavesdropped. Cloud Weave was casually brushing her teeth at the sink, frothy toothpaste at the corners of her mouth. Women, he suddenly realized, terrified him. The thought that she had caused a man's death didn't faze her.

People are talking about you, Cloud Silk told her sister. They say you're a shameless bitch, and that what happened to Abao was your fault. They say he'd still be alive if not for you.

So what? Cloud Weave leaned over and spat on the ground. Seeing me wasn't the only way he offended Sixth Master. He cheated him out of money, too.

I don't suppose you've noticed how people point at the shop when they walk by. Maybe you don't care about your reputation, but I care about mine, Cloud Silk said indignantly. You walk around as if nothing had happened, while I don't dare show my face outside.

Talk all you want, but I'm not going to listen. Cloud Weave flung her toothbrush to the ground. No one cares about me. You'd feel better if Sixth Master had dumped me into the river, too. If somebody chopped me up into little pieces and cooked me, you'd eat more than anybody.

You're crazy, Cloud Silk said callously. Someday you'll get what's coming to you, then we'll see who cares.

Relations between the emporium sisters puzzled Five Dragons: They fought like alley cats. The numbing silence of the shop was often shattered by their arguments, and Five Dragons wondered why no one ever stepped up and shut their stinking mouths for them. Proprietor Feng didn't dare, he feared them more than he loved them; when things flared up between his daughters, he took himself out of harm's way, then vented his frustrations on Five Dragons and the other hirelings. Get back to work. He shoved Five Dragons. This is none of your business. If you want to listen to a vaudeville show, go buy a ticket.

Holding back a smirk, Five Dragons walked inside. What a laughable trio they were. He'd never seen a family this screwed up before. They more than anything pointed up the difference between Maple-Poplar Village and Brick Mason Avenue. His mood lightened as he scooped rice from the bins and poured it into customers' sacks.

During that eventful winter Five Dragons had discovered a series of weak links in the chain of city life, particularly on Brick Mason Avenue. It was like a wall of ice dotted with holes, and all he had to do was make himself as small as a mouse to crawl through them. I can do it, he told himself, if that's what it takes to get to the rice on the other side. The mere thought brought him such child-like excitement that he squeaked at the customers, then grinned broadly.

What are you doing, barking like a dog? Proprietor Feng asked sternly. What could possibly make anybody that playful in times like these?

I'm a squeaking mouse.

Yes, that's just what you are, a great big mouse, Proprietor Feng said. And someday, you'll steal all my rice. You're up to no good, I can see that.

The grin froze on Five Dragons's face. Out of the corner of his eye he watched Proprietor Feng work his abacus behind the counter. If, as Five Dragons believed, the comment was not frivolous, did that mean the old man was setting a trap for the mouse? Would a premonition of danger force him to kick Five Dragons out? That was the big question. But Five Dragons wasn't overly concerned, since he had already begun planning for the day he left the shop. No longer did he have to worry about going hungry, not with his youth and strength as capital. Given the growth of industry and commerce in the city, he could always find work.

Mottled wintry sunlight blanketed the cobblestones of Brick Mason Avenue, on which their bundled customers trod. And above the noise of city traffic he heard the crisp tinkle of wind chimes from the ancient pagoda. Of all the many and varied sounds of the city, Five Dragons liked that one best.

4

PROPRIETOR FENG MADE THE GRIM DISCOVERY THAT Cloud Weave was pregnant. Over the years he had developed a routine that no one ever talked about: At the end of every month he examined the contents of Cloud Weave's chamber pot. As the second lunar month came to an end he noted the absence of blood-stained toilet paper, and in the days that followed noticed to his displeasure the subtle changes in Cloud Weave's posture. Then one day, at lunch, she had the dry heaves, and her face turned bloodless white. Proprietor Feng exploded in rage, snatching the rice bowl out of her hand and smashing it on the floor. How dare you sit here and eat with us! he railed. If you must vomit, leave the table and go outside and puke all you want! Without a word of protest, Cloud Weave stepped over the shattered bowl and the clumps of rice and went into the yard. From the kitchen they heard the mewling sounds of her retching. Five Dragons, for whom this was all quite new, could not possibly anticipate the consequences of this seemingly insignificant episode.

Proprietor Feng, frowning darkly, dragged Cloud Silk out back for a strategy session. Your sister's pregnant, he said. Did you know?

I'm not surprised. I knew that someday she'd

show what a slut she really is. Cloud Silk twirled her braid around her finger. Don't ask me for advice, I'm not going to get involved in her sordid affairs. Things might have turned out differently if you hadn't spoiled her. Now, thanks to her, everybody will be talking about us.

I wonder who it was. I wouldn't mind if it was Sixth Master. But what if it was that damned Abao? He sighed. Do you know who planted the seed?

How should I know? she replied shrilly, stamping her foot for emphasis. Why not ask her? I'm not the one who had the affair.

She won't tell me. I tried to force it out of her last night, but she refuses to say. The stupid little slut. How will I ever hold my head up once this news gets out?

You never *could* hold your head up. Cloud Silk glowered at her father, before swishing her long braid over her shoulder and running back into the shop, where Five Dragons and the clerks were busy selling rice. Finish the weighing, she said. We're closing for the day. So early? Five Dragons said uncertainly. There'll be more customers. But Cloud Silk was already putting the slats up over the door. Mind your own business. We're going to the Lu home for dinner, so no more business today. We're closed.

Later that afternoon Five Dragons watched them leave. Proprietor Feng, carrying his walking stick, had changed into a new black "luck-and-wealth" padded jacket and a ceremonial cap; he was followed by Cloud Silk, who led —dragged, actually—the balky Cloud Weave by the hand. The older daughter's eyes were puffed up like walnuts. She looked pale and sickly without her makeup.

Five Dragons rushed over to the gate and watched them walk down Brick Mason Avenue, raising eyebrows with their unique styles of locomotion. Proprietor Feng, who was noticeably stooped, had a slow, heavy gait; his new jacket was already wrinkled. Cloud Silk, who held on tightly to Cloud Weave's hand, seemed to be skipping down the street. But Cloud Weave was the center of attention, for as she was dragged stumbling along, a stream of filth poured from her mouth. What are you dragging me for? Fuck your old man, fuck eighteen generations of your ancestors!

What's that all about? the blacksmiths asked Five Dragons, drawn out of their shop by the clamor.

Don't know. Five Dragons shook his head. Puzzled, he turned and went back into the shop, where he asked Old Wang, What's wrong with them? What happened?

Who knows? The clerk flashed Five Dragons a knowing smile. And I wouldn't tell you if I did. There are some things you don't need to know at your tender age.

Don't tell me, then, Five Dragons said after a thoughtful pause. But I'll know sooner or later. You can't keep it from me forever.

The Lu home, built in the Ming style, offered a luxurious contrast to the slumlike buildings of its North City residential surroundings. People said Sixth Master had spent five hundred taels of gold on the garden alone, an unheard-of show of extravagance that had townspeople making wild guesses about his wealth and background, until they learned that he had made his money in opium and gunrunning. The yardage and salt businesses, plus the gang of Wharf Rats, were merely fronts. Yet even then, his legendary enterprises were cloaked in mystery. Visitors to his garden spoke of a bunker beneath the teeming sprawl of flowers and exotic plants in which he stored quantities of opium and stacks of guns and ammunition.

The three visitors from the rice emporium stood between stone lions guarding the entrance to the Lu home waiting for a servant to open the gate. Cloud Silk, who was still gripping Cloud Weave's hand, said, You go in first, and ask Sixth Master what he plans to do. If you don't I will. He won't bite. Cloud Weave flung her sister's hand away in annoyance. You want me to ask him what? When you see him you'll know why I can't do that.

The servant led them into the front hall, where Sixth Master was standing next to a large aquarium, a concubine by his side. He was too busy dropping cracker crumbs into the water to turn around. The concubine gave the guests a chilly glance, then spun around and said, Sixth Master, your little bedmate's here again, but she seems to have grown a couple of tails.

Ignoring the comment, Cloud Weave walked over and sat on the sofa. But not Cloud Silk. Quick-witted, as always, she asked loudly, Where'd she come from, a manure pit? That would explain the shit tumbling from her mouth. She saw Sixth Master nudge the concubine with his elbow. Ouch! the woman gasped before storming off behind a screen. Cloud Silk could barely keep from laughing out loud.

Sixth Master continued feeding his goldfish, never taking his eyes off the aquarium. When the cracker crumbs were gone, he turned to look at Proprietor Feng, then at Cloud Silk, the shadow of a smile spreading across his face. After clapping his hands to dust off the remaining crumbs, he said, I don't suppose you've come about rice this time. Am I right?

I would never trouble Sixth Master over the piddling affairs of my shop. Proprietor Feng squirmed, until his gaze fell on Cloud Silk. I'll let Cloud Silk do the talking.

It's hard for a father to discuss certain matters involving his daughters.

I'll say it, if nobody else will. Cloud Silk bit her lip and blushed scarlet. Cloud Weave's pregnant. Did you know that, Sixth Master?

Of course, he replied. I can always spot a pregnant woman. I wouldn't be Sixth Master if I couldn't.

Well, we're here to ask Sixth Master's opinion. How do you think the matter should be resolved?

She's pregnant, so she has a baby. What could be simpler? Hens know how to lay eggs without being told. Now don't tell me Cloud Weave doesn't know what to do.

But she's not married. How will she hold her head up in society if this news gets out? Cloud Silk argued. Think about her, Sixth Master, think about our family.

I don't like to think. This brain of mine avoids strenuous activity whenever possible. He laughed, then looked at Cloud Weave, who was sprawled across the sofa. Maybe Cloud Weave can tell us whose seed was planted in her belly. If anyone can clear things up, it should be her. Otherwise, I don't know how I can help.

Cloud Weave, whose eyelids were drooping, suddenly doubled over with the dry heaves. Cloud Silk glared with anger and indignation at her back, then shoved her roughly. Say something, you slut! You act like this is a stroll in the park. I want you to look Sixth Master in the eye and tell him whose child it is. Hurry up, say something.

She knows better than to lie. Sixth Master flicked the aquarium with his finger and winked at Cloud Silk. Go on, Cloud Weave, tell them.

Cloud Weave looked up, ashen-faced, perspiration

beading her forehead, mucus up from her stomach hanging at the corners of her mouth. She wiped her lips with a handkerchief and glanced at Sixth Master, then lowered her eyes and stared blankly at her leather pumps. In a soft but clear voice she said, I don't know, I can't be sure.

Looks of hopelessness passed between Cloud Silk and her father; Sixth Master laughed eerily. Let's go, Father. Cloud Silk stood up, teary-eyed, and held her hand out to Proprietor Feng, who was sitting on one of the leather sofas. Now we've got no one to blame. The slut made her bed, so let her lie in it. If I get involved in any more of her affairs I'm as bad as her.

Before they reached the door something came flying at them. It was a plump red goldfish. It landed at Cloud Silk's feet, where it flapped around on the floor. Startled, she picked it up and turned to see Sixth Master groping in the aquarium for another. All my life I've been fond of goldfish and women, he said. They're so much alike. If they make me unhappy I toss them out of their aquarium. He flung a second goldfish at Cloud Silk; it was the same color. The red ones displease me these days, he said, so I'm throwing them all out.

Cloud Weave jumped up from the sofa—finally—and stumbled outside, where she wrapped her arms around a crabapple tree, heaving and sobbing loudly. The branches waved furiously in the air above her. Men emerged from buildings in the outer compound and stood under the eaves, gawking at her from a distance. Men men fucking men. She gave them an earful. They responded with knowing smiles.

Let's go home. Haven't you shamed yourself enough? Cloud Silk chided her sister.

But Cloud Weave held on to the tree and wailed, looking up into the sky every few moments. Even in this sorrowful moment her eyes sparkled like jewels.

Did you hear Sixth Master? To him you're just a goldfish, which he can toss away when he's tired of it. You think you're something special, but you're only a pitiful plaything. She looked toward the window of the main house, where she saw Sixth Master walk upstairs with his arm around his concubine, followed by an English setter. Momentarily at a loss, she quickly regained her senses and said to her father, Let's get out of this horrible place.

Leave? Just like that? Proprietor Feng could not conceal his disappointment. We didn't say all we came to say, and nothing has been decided. Shouldn't we at least try to pry some money out of him?

You want to pry money out of *him*? Cloud Silk dragged her father toward the gate. Not another word on the subject, she said. Hold your nose and swallow the bitter medicine. Remember who he is, then consider who we are. We're no match for him.

Proprietor Feng and Cloud Silk exited the Lu home under the disdainful stares of servants. On the way out, Proprietor Feng, who appeared wizened and tormented, spat on one of the stone lion guardians. Father and daughter walked single file past the dark, tile-covered compound wall, caught up in their own thoughts. They turned to see Cloud Weave's emerald shadow glide past the wall, round a corner, and vanish.

Night fell. Dinner was over, and Cloud Weave still hadn't returned. Proprietor Feng walked to the door and looked up and down Brick Mason Avenue. There were no pedestrians, and all the shops had closed for the day; yellow lamplight flickered behind paper window coverings.

Winds swept across the grimy cobblestones, sending scraps of paper and chicken feathers swirling in the air. For Proprietor Feng, every winter in recent memory had brought only troubles and vexation: such as the death of his wife, Madam Zhu; such as the time they nearly had to close down over a shortage of rice; such as all those nights with starving refugees banging on his door; such as now, when Cloud Weave's disgraceful pregnancy was about to become the talk of the neighborhood, and she still wasn't home, even at this hour.

Proprietor Feng walked into Cloud Silk's room. Go find her, he said. Maybe something happened. She's always been a foolish girl. I'm worried she might do something stupid now.

I'm not going anywhere. Do you think I'd shed a tear if she jumped into the river. Not likely. I gave up on her long ago.

You'd force me to go? Proprietor Feng asked his daughter, glowering at her back. What did I do in a previous life to deserve heartless bitches like you instead of the son I ought to have? You've given me nothing but grief.

I said I'm not going. The jade toothpick she was using gleamed in the musty lamplight. Send Five Dragons.

So Cloud Silk crossed the street and called Five Dragons's name. His hairless scalp poked out through a crack in the gate, and when he saw who it was, the rest of him reluctantly followed out into the street. She watched him clumsily hitch up his belt.

What were you doing in there?

Nothing. Just horsing around. He smiled bashfully. They had a contest to see who was biggest, and they made me join in.

Biggest what?

Biggest pecker! Five Dragons blurted out. They ganged up on me and jerked my pants off.

That's disgusting. Blushing bright red, Cloud Silk turned her face away. When you're not eating you're spending your time being an idiot. Those blacksmiths are a bad lot.

What do you expect me to do on cold, boring nights? Five Dragons stomped his feet to keep warm. What does Second Mistress want on such a freezing night?

Cloud Weave isn't home, and I want you to go find her. She gave him a stern look, then: What? She scowled. Are you balking?

You expect me to go to Sixth Master's home to look for Cloud Weave? That's no place for me.

You won't find her there. Try all the other places. She won't be seen in the halls of that demon-king again. She nudged Five Dragons and said impatiently, Stop trying to dream up excuses. Find her and bring her home.

Full of misgivings, Five Dragons slinked down Brick Mason Avenue, his crossed hands buried in the sleeves of his coat. The rice emporium was in the news again. With what he knew of the proprietor and his daughters, he quickly figured out what must have happened: Sixth Master had tossed Cloud Weave aside. He'd been expecting it for some time. That's how men are: They tire easily of their playthings, women included. Sixth Master had tired of Cloud Weave and simply tossed her aside, despite her arching breasts and full, rounded hips. Just like that—out. In Five Dragons's mind Cloud Weave became a resplendent yet tattered bundle dropped in the road, waiting to be picked up by a passing man.

A strong northern wind hit him in the face like a

bucket of ice water. The crooked street with its potholes, warped lampposts with their egg-shaped streetlamps dangling precariously, and, of course, pedestrians, individuals and little clutches of them, brushed past him. The faces of the people, dressed in their finery on that winter night, were windows to their immorality. By now he was used to city ways; as he passed a brothel festooned with red and green lanterns he peeked inside, only to have a sleepy-eyed woman reach out and grab his head. I'll show you a good time, she said in a husky voice. Cheap. Five Dragons stared at her crimson, slightly parted lips, like blood-red, dried-up leaves. He cried out softly before saying, I don't have any money. Slipping away between two overhanging lanterns, he ran a few steps, then stopped, his heart drained. Cheap whore. He felt his face—his hands were like ice, his cheeks were burning up. Cheap whore, I'll fuck you and all the others. He slapped his cheeks. North City is crawling with sluts. They're everywhere, as numerous as the rice stalks in Maple-Poplar Village. They grow out of men's crotches like weeds. His mind was churning as he walked. But they don't mean a thing to me.

The Great Prosperity Theater was letting out as Five Dragons passed by. Theatergoers poured through the darkened lobby's four glass doors; Five Dragons spotted Cloud Weave. Dressed in a dazzling emerald-green cheongsam, she was dabbing at her eyes with a handkerchief. A stranger came up and took her arm, surprising Five Dragons. How had she latched onto another man in so short a time? Still weepy, now that she was outside, the trace of a smile reappeared on her pale face.

Cloud Weave—Elder Mistress—Five Dragons cupped his hands and shouted. He drew contemptuous stares, but what did he care? He bent over, took a deep breath, and shouted even louder.

Cloud Weave walked up on the arm of the stranger. What are you doing, shouting like a ghost from hell? First a sad movie, now you, shouting like a ghost from hell.

I'm supposed to take you home. I ran my legs off trying to find you.

Find me? I'm not lost. She giggled, holding her hand over her mouth. Then she turned to the other man, You'd better go. My family's come for me. Watch out my husband doesn't decide to get rough. He's very strong.

That's your husband? The stranger looked Five Dragons up and down. I don't believe you. Where shall we meet tomorrow?

You've had your fun, now get away from me. She scuffed the man's patent-leather shoe with her toe, then turned to Five Dragons and said, Beat him up if he doesn't leave. I don't like his attitude.

Five Dragons glared at the stranger, who quickly disappeared down a dark alley behind the theater. You did it, you scared him off, she said, clapping her hands.

Maybe, Five Dragons said casually. But nobody's ever been scared of me before. Resentment showed in his eyes. Let's go. They said to bring you home. Shall we take a rickshaw?

No, let's walk, Cloud Weave said decisively. So, side by side, a foot or so apart, they walked down the street, which returned to silence once the theater crowd had dispersed in the hazy darkness. Five Dragons heard the heavy slaps of his shoes on the ground as two shadows merged and separated, slowly, like the tides. A stone deep in his chest rose and fell with each beat of his heart, making breathing difficult. He was confused by his emotions.

I thought you were crying. How was I to know it was because of a movie? I didn't realize how happy you really were, with a man's arm to lean on, and all.

Me? she slapped a lamppost. Screw his old uncle! I just wanted to show that old dog that this woman didn't need him to have fun. I don't care. Why should I?

The night air was cold and damp, with feathery snowflakes swirling around them, only to dissolve when they touched the ground. Cloud Weave and Five Dragons quickened their pace as they passed through the well-lit center of town; Brick Mason Avenue was just up ahead. Then she slowed down, gave him a look, and sidled up next to him, brushing his shoulder softly.

I'm cold, she said.

Me, too. Five Dragons looked up into the gentle snowfall. It must be the snow. It doesn't snow here often, does it?

Put your arm around me. That'll warm me up.

Five Dragons's mouth gaped in astonishment. Virgin white snowflakes stuck to the curls of Cloud Weave's newly permed hair, the glint of tender passion filled her eyes.

What are you scared of? No one's looking. And what if they were? I want you to put your arm around me, so that's what you're supposed to do.

Five Dragons hesitantly rested his hand on her hip. His lips quivered. He started to say something, but stopped short.

No, hold me here. She moved his arm up around her waist. Tighter, she said. What happened to all that strength of yours?

Five Dragons's face was burning up, although snowflakes cooled his forehead a bit. His arm tightened around her waist like a rope, until he felt her tender feminine flesh give through the padded cheongsam. Once again the stone moved in his chest, but this time it slipped toward his abdomen, inch by inch, and he knew that the front of his trousers was starting to bulge. He didn't dare look down, in fact, didn't dare look anywhere for more than a second. As he negotiated Brick Mason Avenue with his arm around Cloud Weave's waist, a mouse once again occupied his thoughts: dragging its meal toward some dark, mysterious place.

Fucking dog, I'd have dumped him if he hadn't beat me to it. Cloud Weave broke the silence as she leaned on Five Dragons's shoulder. It was more than I could take.

Remember, this is all your idea, Five Dragons managed to say. After a pause, he continued, Don't make me the butt of some joke.

The world is really strange. Men can play around all they want, but women aren't supposed to return the favor. She laughed. Well, this is one woman who's going to play by her own rules.

Five Dragons sensed what was on her mind. The look in her eyes shifted, like water, and the smile playing at the corners of her mouth had a dreamy, indefinable quality. She gently patted his hand a time or two, then, without warning, moved it up until it rested on her firm, arching breast. Five Dragons felt like a blade of grass in a gale, completely at the mercy of every gust of wind; he could barely stand.

So he doesn't want nice tits like these, she muttered. Okay then, you can have them. It's all the same to me.

Five Dragons kept walking, except that now he was holding on to Cloud Weave awkwardly. He wanted to feel and feel and feel, but his joints, seemingly frozen, would not respond. So he just pressed down on her full, wonderful breast until he sensed her heart beating beneath his palm: the slow, steady beat produced threads of hostility in him. He was holding the city's most infamous slut, one who indulged in every conceivable illicit pleasure. How could she be so composed? he wondered. The slut.

Back home they stood in the doorway looking into each other's eyes. Once again the dark, snowy sky above Brick Mason Avenue safeguarded its secrets. Five Dragons embraced Cloud Weave and sucked the warm skin of her neck, losing himself in a wonderland. Suddenly the heavy breathing stopped; he shuddered and gasped. The orgasm seemed to come from the outer edges of his body, and as soon as it was over, his crotch turned cold and clammy.

Black outlines of footsteps dotted the wafer-thin layer of snow covering the yard the next morning. Snowfalls here were a far cry from those in Maple-Poplar Village; they were actually more like winter frost. Five Dragons looked into the sky, deep blue and very bright following the brief flurry. Black factory smoke swelled into airy mushrooms, then shriveled, broke up, and disappeared.

He picked up the dull, rusty ax next to the woodpile and began to chop the damp kindling, a piece of which flew up and hit him in the hand. When he rubbed the spot, he noticed that it was smeared with light red blood. It was not the first injury he had suffered that winter, so after licking the blood off his hand, he rubbed some spit onto the wound. Inexplicably these actions evoked thoughts of the fair skin on Cloud Weave's neck. He looked toward her room; the window was tightly shut. Why didn't she leave it unlocked last night? Dimly he saw the ghostly Abao at the window, ready to spring into her bedroom. So vivid it seemed real. The image quickly soured his mood. He brought his ax down ferociously, channeling his swelling anger into the splitting of the wood.

Cloud Weave, in a pair of padded slippers, shuffled up to Five Dragons; he kept chopping wood as her foot slipped under his crotch and touched his scrotum. Ouch! he complained, grabbing himself and hopping out of the way. Don't do that, someone might be watching. But Cloud Weave, obviously pleased with herself, covered her mouth and giggled. What are you scared of? I gave you a treat last night, now I want you to see I'm not a woman you can take for granted. Five Dragons noticed the purple hickey on her fair skin, like a caterpillar crawling up her neck.

Your neck. He stared at the hickey, which was surrounded by dainty feminine blood vessels, light blue in color, and fine, light brown hairs. Did I do that?

That look in your eyes, it scares me. Like I'm being devoured. She buttoned up her robe. I feel nauseous, she said. I have a craving for pickled vegetables.

Five Dragons watched her as she stepped over the woodpile and walked into the kitchen. The ax fell from his hand and thudded to the ground. The snowy morning landscape seemed like an illusion. He heard the lid being removed from the pickle vat, then some crisp chomping sounds. He squatted down to resume chopping wood, but couldn't shake the image of the hickey on her neck. Did I really do that? He shook his head and swung the ax wickedly. Wood shavings flew.

Cloud Weave appeared at the kitchen window eating a crisp, juicy pickle, and signaled Five Dragons with her eyes to come over. He hesitated. But once he was sure no one was around, he slipped into the kitchen and rested his hands on the rim of the pickle vat to look at his reflection in the briny water. What do you want? he asked, his heart racing again.

I just love these sweet-and-sour pickles. She stuffed the last bite into her mouth and rubbed her wet hands on his pants. These make a good towel, she said.

Go ahead, he said. Why not? You treat me like a dog, anyway. He gazed up at the grease-blackened roofbeam. You're human; I'm a dog.

A great big bulldog. Cloud Weave giggled. Looking him in the eye, she let her hand linger on his leg, then moved it up slowly. A great big bulldog, she repeated. And I know what's on your mind. Men all have the shameless cock of a bulldog.

As he watched her thin, clawlike fingers close around him, his own fingers dug into the rim of the pickle vat. He stood rigid as a statue; the smell of pickles filled the kitchen, nearly smothering the fragrance of makeup that lingered on Cloud Weave's skin; the bloated image of Abao floating before his eyes demoralized him. He shrank back, freed himself from her grasp, and pushed her away. I'm no dog, he said. I'm going outside to chop wood.

Cloud Silk was in the yard combing her hair when the door flew open and Five Dragons stormed out; she spat on the ground and dragged the comb violently through her lusterless hair. You're disgusting, she grumbled as she removed strands of hair from the comb. You two make me sick to my stomach.

I didn't do anything, Five Dragons defended himself as he walked past. Ask her if you don't believe me. She knows.

I know all I need to know. I don't have to ask. Cloud

Silk kicked the kitchen door. Cloud Weave, you forget the pain before the scab even falls off. You have to be the cheapest slut on the face of the earth.

Cloud Weave rolled up her sleeve and fished another pickle out of the vat. Who did the pickling this year? she asked after biting off a chunk. I love them when they're sweet and sour like this.

Five Dragons was on his haunches chopping wood when Proprietor Feng walked outside. What's going on? he asked. Five Dragons shook his head. With me, nothing. I've been out here chopping wood all morning. You should be asking them.

War and unrest out there, and no peace at home, Proprietor Feng said with a melancholic sigh. We'd all be better off dead. He made a turn around the snow-dusted yard, then another. Stopping to look into the clearing sky, he began thumping his lower back with both fists and muttered, But since we're not, we have to go on living, then headed back to the shop. Five Dragons smiled knowingly at the old man's comment. Since we're not dead, he aped him, we have to get out of bed every morning and open up the shop. Life's a big joke.

5

THE ARRIVAL OF THE LAST MONTH OF THE YEAR INTRO-
duced a change in Five Dragons's routine: He began
to sleep fitfully and for shorter periods. At the sound
of the watchman's bamboo clappers, announcing the
third watch, he would climb out of his makeshift
bed on the floor and creep barefoot into the backyard, his coat draped over his shoulders. The passage
of time had brought changes: Cloud Weave's window was now left unlatched, so he could crawl into
her room, consumed by passion, then reemerge utterly spent when the fifth watch was sounded.
Caught up in the heady feelings of danger, like a
child at play, he would pause momentarily in the
wind-swept, icy yard and gaze at the brick wall to
reassure himself that the weeds remained undisturbed. No longer was Abao around to scale the wall
and gain entry into the yard. Now I'm the midnight
guest. In the darkness his smile went undetected. Illicit sex, he told himself, is a lot like drinking fine
wine: Guzzling it leads to a deadening intoxication,
while sipping prolongs the pleasure without any side
effects. If anything, he reflected with contentment,
my senses are sharpened; in fact, the only drawback
is the brief feeling of depletion between my legs.

Through the open storeroom door he saw the

mound of rice glisten dimly in the pale moonlight. So he strolled in and sat on a pile of burlap bags to look at the snowy mountain poking through the darkness. Even now, in the heart of winter, the autumn rice had lost neither its warmth nor its delicate fragrance. He scooped up a handful and flipped it, grain by grain, into his mouth. The lingering taste of Cloud Weave's face powder mixed with the hard raw rice produced an odd sensation; his thoughts returned to her body lying hidden beneath the satin comforter: She was a flower in full, luxurious bloom, one he could pluck but was never permitted to see. Each time he said, I'm going to light the lamp and get a good look, she responded by pinching him. No lamp. I give you an inch and you take a foot. He smiled and shook his head, then cupped his hands under his nose and breathed deeply. A merging of odors: the subtle fragrance of raw rice and the strong scent of a woman's sex, which achieved a wondrous unity on the palms of his grimy hands.

The mound of rice stood serene in the darkness. Five Dragons tried to sort out his thoughts, his hand gliding aimlessly over the grains, which rustled as they slid downward. *Snap!* A mousetrap in the corner sprang into the air with its hapless victim—a hungry rodent announcing its own death with a pitiful screech. Five Dragons's head drooped; he was getting drowsy. Oddly, he didn't feel like leaving the storeroom. Resting against the mound of rice was like lying in a big cradle. Rice must be the best sleeping potion in the world, he sensed, certainly more effective than a woman's body. And it was right there beneath him.

Before long, Five Dragons was sound asleep under a blanket of rice, shifting, illusory, fragrant, a dreamy collage busying his mind, with a series of linked images appearing and reappearing: rice paddies and cotton fields in

Maple-Poplar Village, the people and the fauna, the buildings and the flora, all being slowly devoured by an endless panorama of flowing water, and everywhere the persistent wails of anguish. He was walking barefoot on the water, as inch by inch the dismal scenery slipped past; he was being swept along by a powerful wind; in the distance rose a mountain of snowy rice, topped by a cluster of women in red tops and green trousers.

When the rooster crowed at dawn, Five Dragons crawled out of his bed of rice and pulled at his sticky underpants. Wet dreams, always those wet dreams: They were beginning to get to him. He envisioned his energy being sapped to the point where he would be unable to achieve his goals in life. Proprietor Feng, chamber pot in hand, was surprised to see him emerge from the storeroom, brushing off rice dust.

Were you sleeping in the storeroom? What's going on?

I caught a mouse. Five Dragons pointed toward the storeroom. Go see for yourself if you don't believe me. I killed me a mouse.

Those mice don't scare me. It's you, the biggest mouse of all, I'm worried about. Proprietor Feng dumped the murky yellow contents of his chamber pot on the ground. Are you sure you weren't stealing my rice?

I'm no thief, Five Dragons said as he brushed rice dust from his hair. And I get three meals a day, so why would I steal rice?

Maybe to help out your starving country cousins.

Why worry about them when I've got my own problems?

Maybe you sell it. Didn't you say you want to get rich?

I also said I'm no thief. I earn my keep, you know that as well as anybody. Workers in the dye shop get eight yuan, but you only give me five. Five yuan, barely enough to satisfy a dog. I *ought* to steal from you.

Proprietor Feng ladled some water into the chamber pot. An impenetrable smile creased his gaunt face as he crammed a brush down the neck of the chamber pot and scoured vigorously. There's more to you than simply earning your keep. I've known that for a long time, he said. My eyesight may have dimmed, but I've still got sharp ears. I hear everything that happens in the shop at night.

Then why not get up and catch whoever's stealing your rice?

Cloud Silk hears it sometimes, too, but I tell her it's her mother's ghost, still worried about her daughters. She believes me. How about you, Five Dragons, do you believe in ghosts?

Not me. Five Dragons licked his dry, cracked lips nervously as he gazed at the withered branches on trees beyond the wall. Ghosts used to be people, and I've certainly never been scared of them.

Me either, Proprietor Feng said, his eyes flashing. But they seem to be pestering Cloud Weave these days. I think she might be possessed.

Maybe it's the other way around. Hugging himself, Five Dragons took a few steps, then continued, You know your daughter better than I do.

Proprietor Feng laid his chamber pot down beside the wall, blew into it, then walked slowly up to Five Dragons. Worry, anger, and impatience showed in his bloodshot eyes as he reached out a veiny hand and closed it around Five Dragons's sleeve. Five Dragons thought the old man was going to hit him, but all he did was tug his tattered jacket.

Do you want to marry Cloud Weave? It was nearly a sob. I can arrange it.

Five Dragons stared dumbly at Proprietor Feng's prematurely wrinkled face, wondering if his ears were playing tricks on him. Things had progressed a lot further and a lot faster than he had planned, and he was caught unprepared.

I'll let you marry my daughter, but you'll not get a single grain of my rice. Proprietor Feng wiped his runny eyes. This shop has been in my family for generations, and I won't hand it over to a wild bastard like you, even though I know it's the reason you came here in the first place.

Five Dragons looked into the sky above the rice shop. It was the same steel gray he had gotten used to seeing, the morning sun hidden behind clouds that were turning dark red around the edges, like scabs drying in the wind. Someone was flying a kite off to the northwest, a series of white dots gliding in the sky like a flock of lost birds.

I don't care one way or the other. Five Dragons's voice sounded strange even to him, as a result of the exertion this seemingly casual comment had required; his throat felt as if it had been slit with a knife. He looked at Proprietor Feng apathetically. Are you sure you won't regret this? It's not too late to say you were joking. I won't be upset.

What I regret is not stuffing her down the commode the day she was born. Suddenly wracked with coughs, Proprietor Feng walked off thumping his chest. At the steps he turned around. Fate's on your side, damn you, he said. You've stumbled into the best deal of your life.

The stooped figure disappeared behind the blue door

curtain. Five Dragons shivered. Magic powers seem to be in the air this morning, he was thinking as he felt himself falling into a realm of pure fantasy, body and soul: His heart, his hair follicles, and his always vibrant genitals produced a mixture of jarring screams as they plummeted downward. The blue door curtain flapped in a gust of wind, its printed flowers blooming as if by magic. All true, all real. Five Dragons stamped every detail of that morning onto his memory. You there, rice emporium and all your occupants, are you about to change the course of my life? **Why does it have to be *you* who change the course of *my* life?**

Cloud Weave left the courtyard window of her room unlatched the next two nights, but Five Dragons failed to appear. By the third evening, her patience exhausted, she intercepted him in the yard and dragged him into the kitchen, slamming the door behind her, then wheeling and slapping him across the face. Now that you got what you were after, you probably think you're real clever! Well, I'm not about to be your plaything!

Five Dragons held his face in his hands and backed against the door, one knee bent to rest his bare foot against the pickle vat. His lips curled into a haughty, insulting smile. It was a rare sight. Cloud Weave looked at her hand, baffled by his expression.

You're going to be my wife, you slut. He casually drummed the vat behind him with his fingers, causing a rumbling echo. No need to leap into bed now, he said, since you're going to be mine anyway. I'm in no hurry.

Cloud Weave spat on the floor and laughed loudly. You can stop dreaming! Your need for sex has addled your brain.

Go ask your father if you don't believe me, or your sister. It's their idea. He grabbed her by the shoulders and forced her face down over the pickling water. Take a good look at yourself, he said. You're seeing a shoe so worn there's hardly anything left of it. Where do you think you'll find another man anywhere to marry you?

With a shriek she broke free and looked with horror into his face, her shoulders hunched protectively. I believe you, she said finally. That's the sort of thing they would do. The dullness in her eyes gave way to rekindled light. She smiled, reached out, and stroked the stubble on his chin. And you? Do you like the idea?

Yes. He looked at her lacquered red nails. It's what I want. I'd do it if you walked on four legs and barked.

You don't think you'll regret it? Take my word for it, someday you will.

Someday doesn't concern me now. He frowned and peeled her fingers from his chin. Go ask your father if he's set a date for the wedding. Since I'm marrying into the family, there will be no bridal chair and no firecrackers. But I want a full crock of rice wine. That much I know. Back home, people sneer at any man who marries into his bride's family, so he has to drink a whole crock of rice wine in front of them.

How fascinating. Cloud Weave clapped her hands. But why?

To prove he's a man.

Are you going to drink a whole crock of rice wine when we get married? A childish, not very intelligent smile appeared on her face. Fascinating, she repeated gleefully. I love it when men get drunk.

I don't drink. I hate the stuff. It puts you at the mercy

of sober people. He paused, absorbed in his thoughts, then added in a raspy voice, I know what you people want. Now you listen to me: I'm giving myself to the rice emporium, not to you people. What you get in the bargain is a strong, sturdy watchdog for all generations, a bulldog right off the farm.

Five Dragons glanced around the dark, chaotic kitchen, a look of ridicule and smug indifference on his face. Then without warning he turned his back to Cloud Weave, undid his pants, and pissed in the pickle vat. She just stood there, eyes and tongue frozen in place, and by the time she regained her senses, it was too late, he was done. Red-faced with mortification, she slapped him for the second time. Are you crazy? How do you expect people to eat anything from that vat now?

There's too much female yin in this house. It needs all the male yang I can provide, he said as he nonchalantly buttoned his pants. That's what Liu the Nearly Immortal said. Your house needs my urine and my semen.

Damn you, Five Dragons, you'll ruin this family one day. I may forgive you for your actions, but they'll never accept you as a true member of the family. You're disgusting.

They don't know anything, Five Dragons said as he walked over and pulled back the door bolt, and you won't tell them, because from now on you belong to me.

Bending over to examine the pickles in the vat, Cloud Weave saw a hazy reflection in the dark yellow water: The space between her eyes and her brows was like a void. She crinkled her nose and sniffed. The absence of a rank odor did not alter the fact that her favorite food was now steeping in Five Dragons's piss. She found it impossible to understand his little prank; he was, she felt, slightly deranged, but maybe that was because he was so happy.

The rice-emporium wedding was one of the shabbiest affairs in the annals of Brick Mason Avenue. The twenty-eighth day of the final lunar month was selected as the auspicious day, and the guest list was made up primarily of family members, most of whom came to the wedding knowing more than they let on. Barely able to control their urges to gossip and be ungenerous, they filed into the shop and the wedding chamber, seemingly having reached a tacit agreement to keep silent. The married women observed the bride with cool detachment, none of them missing the subtle thickening of her waist and the rounding of her buttocks.

Many things happened during the ceremony that evolved into barbed comments that would later characterize any discussion of the rice emporium. Item: The firecrackers didn't pop. Only a single string was purchased, and they were too damp to light. Item: A lucky red egg hidden in the bedding cracked and oozed yellow yoke when it was squeezed. It was soft-boiled. Item: The groom refused to drink a drop of wine, and when the male guests tried to pour some down his throat, he pinched his nose tightly and spat it all out. He didn't drink, he said, not a drop.

The wedding was smothered by an invisible black hand that put a damper on all the festivities. Proprietor Feng, dressed in a dark silk Chinese gown imprinted with the words *happiness* and *wealth*, paced the area, averting his eyes out of embarrassment, while Cloud Silk sat on the windowsill doing needlework, proud and composed, taking time out now and then to give orders to relatives and neighbors who were helping out; her voice had an impatient edge. Then there was Cloud Weave: Heavily powdered and rouged, she wore a lovely rose-colored gown, its train shot through with silver and gold threads as it swept languorously across the floor. But there was no joy in the bride's eyes or bashful reddening on her cheeks; only lethargy and weariness. She even yawned while she was pouring wine for one of her uncles. Emotion was in evidence, but only on the swarthy, agitated face of Five Dragons. He could not sit still, yet standing up was no better. He refused to drink, saying tersely to anyone who tried to toast him, I don't drink, not a drop. A mystifying cold glint flashed in his eyes.

Sixth Master's servant arrived as guests were clowning around outside the wedding chamber. He barged in, elbowing people out of the way, and walked up to Five Dragons. Are you the groom? Five Dragons nodded woodenly. The servant handed him a lacquer box exquisitely decorated with dragons and phoenixes. This is a gift from Sixth Master, he said. The instructions were not to open it until the ceremony was over. Then the servant leaned over and whispered something to Five Dragons, who paled visibly before spinning around, climbing onto a stool, and placing the box on top of a freestanding cupboard.

What is it? Cloud Weave asked, tugging on his arm. A bracelet? A ring? Maybe a necklace?

I wonder what he was thinking, Five Dragons said gloomily. He bowed his head and swallowed noisily. Why won't they leave me alone? I never did anything to them.

By midnight the shop was deserted, except for Five Dragons and Cloud Weave, who sat in the pale yellow lamplight observing each other. Both wore numb, weary expressions. Out in the yard someone was washing dishes—they heard water splash and the occasional clink of crockery. Cloud Silk walked up to the window, cursing; she rapped on the frame. Five Dragons, come out here and get to work. Don't think you rate a day off just because you got married.

Five Dragons sat still, ignoring the noise at the window and cracking his knuckles loudly. Suddenly he jumped up, climbed onto the stool to retrieve the lacquer box, and tossed it onto the bed. Here, he barked at Cloud Weave, take a look at the jewelry Sixth Master sent you.

The lid fell off when the box landed on the satin bedding, and out tumbled a hideous reddish-black fleshy stick that stank horribly. Cloud Weave yelped in alarm and scrambled off the bed. What is it? Her eyes were as wide as saucers. A dog's prick?

No, a human one. Five Dragons glared at her. You ought to recognize it. It's Abao's. They cut it off.

The bastards. What's that supposed to mean? Her shoulders heaved; she backed up against the wall. Throw that repulsive thing away!

I know what it means. Five Dragons walked up and turned the grisly object over with his fingertips. But I can't figure out why they gave it to me. Why doesn't anyone accept me? Why won't they leave me alone?

Throw it away, throw it away this minute! Cloud Weave stomped her foot and shrieked.

I'm going to. Five Dragons picked it up and carried it carefully to the window. Cloud Silk stood in the yard frowning and glaring at him. Out of the way, he said as he flung the thing through the window and watched it sail past Cloud Silk and over the blue tiles of the emporium roof like a night bird. It landed on the Brick Mason

Avenue cobblestones. Five Dragons smacked his hands together and said to Cloud Weave, Let the neighborhood dogs gnaw on what's left of Abao.

The wedding night slipped by amid such raucous carryings-on, with peace and quiet finally settling in shortly before dawn. A gentle winter rain fell onto the emporium eaves and windowsill, enfolding the yard in a damp, freezing mist; Five Dragons sat in bed with the comforter around his shoulders; a halo of light framed the sleeping face of Cloud Weave, who rolled over and reached out for the lamp. Not so bright, she mumbled before falling back to sleep. Slowly Five Dragons pulled back the covers to reveal, inch by inch, her voluptuous, fair-skinned body. Time to take a look, he murmured, as his hand negotiated the slippery valley between her breasts and stopped when it touched her grassy femininity. The lamplight afforded him an unobstructed view; he was comforted to note how accurate his mental picture had been. Roughly he caressed the tender bulge of her belly. His thoughts were uncomplicated: She should eat less. The slut's always nibbling on something.

Five Dragons was reluctant to turn out the lamp. The dark had never bothered him, but he was always more clearheaded in the light. Now that his life had moved in a new direction, it was crucial to gauge its likely course and future prospects. Just because you can't predict the future doesn't mean you can't think about it. Thinking is personal and private, hidden from prying eyes and ears. You can think about anything you want. The sound of rain outside lessened, giving way to the crisp but infrequent tinkle of wind chimes swirling in the lonely night air. It was the ancient brick pagoda on Brick Mason Avenue. With each gust of wind the chimes announced to all of Brick Mason Avenue the pagoda's loneliness and desolation, a sound that always made Five Dragons drowsy; cupping his hand over one ear, he sought out different sounds with the other. In the distance he heard the rumble of railroad tracks, then the wail of a train whistle; he saw a southbound freight train with a country boy, hungry and pathetic, curled atop a load of black coal; the earth shook beneath him, the rice emporium moved around him. This, too, was a train, rocking him to sleep as it crept through the wilderness. He could barely keep his eyes open.

I wonder where this train is taking me.

Over the Spring Festival Brick Mason Avenue came alive with joyous children and fashionably dressed women. The significance of New Year's was slowly slipping away from the people's lives; the holiday had grown insipid and tedious. As Five Dragons sat in the emporium doorway soaking up the sun, like other celebrants, he shucked peanuts and popped them into his mouth. Boredom showed in the way he was crumbling the shells between his fingers. A blacksmith stuck his head out the door of his shop and smirked. How's married life, Five Dragons?

Same old thing, Five Dragons replied, popping a peanut into his mouth. Five Dragons will always be Five Dragons, married or not.

Someday you'll see it's different, the blacksmith replied. Why aren't you out visiting relatives?

I'm not leaving this spot.

Weren't invited, right? The man laughed.

Don't get me started. I'm in no mood for small talk.

The sun's rays weakened as evening approached. People headed home, leaving the cobblestones strewn with melon rinds, fruit peels, and the shattered ruins of exploded fire-crackers. It had been a day of blind merriment, but for Five Dragons, the dreary holiday could not end soon enough. Proprietor Feng appeared at the intersection with his daughters; when he bowed to the butcher, he looked like a curled-up shrimp. Cloud Silk stood shoulder to shoulder with Cloud Weave, who was gnawing on a piece of sugarcane. Five Dragons stood up, suddenly troubled by a premonition that they were descending upon him like a massive specter. Instinctively he slipped inside. He shuddered. They're waiting out there to snare me. They'll stop at nothing to suck the vitality right out of me, to swallow my blood and consume my heart. Filled with anxiety over this absurd foreboding, he went into the backyard to relieve himself against the wall. But not a drop emerged, no matter how hard he tried. What's wrong with me? He looked over his shoulder—no one was spying on him, and his in-laws were still out on the street. What's wrong with me? Had all that pernicious yin energy in the rice emporium invaded his body, turning it into easy prey for them.

When Proprietor Feng entered the shop he called out to Five Dragons, who walked up to the counter, where he was met by his father-in-law's reddened face and the stench of alcohol on his breath. The old man's haughty, calculating expression disgusted him. I want you to sail to Lake Wu tomorrow. Proprietor Feng picked up his ceramic teapot; a rarely seen glint of contentment shone in his eyes. A rice shop there is closing down, and I hear they're selling their stock at half price. Bring back two boatloads; that way, if there's a spring famine, we won't have to worry.

You want me to go to Lake Wu? Isn't it awfully soon

after my wedding to be sending me off like this? You can't stand the idea of giving me a single day's rest, can you?

You're sure not wasting any time settling into the role of pampered son-in-law, are you? A taunting smile creased Proprietor Feng's face. You got my daughter for free, so don't you think a little payback might be appropriate? Besides, you get a wage for what you do, as you well know.

I know a lot more than you realize. I didn't say I wouldn't go. How could I, after having been blessed with the gift of your daughter?

You'll need some cash, Proprietor Feng said, counting out some bills. Make sure you put this where no one can find it. There are pirates out there, so don't leave the money in the cabin. The safest place is probably in your shoe.

I won't lose your money. Once something gets into my hands, that's where it stays. But can you trust me? What if I take the money and run? Then you'd be out a son-in-law *and* the money. Doesn't that worry you?

Proprietor Feng appeared shocked, humiliated, and slightly scared. I doubt you're *that* evil, he said, turning back to his cashbox. You were so pitiful once that you got down on your knees and begged me to take you in. I don't think you'll forget my kindness so easily. Especially since I gave you my daughter.

I didn't get down on my knees. I've never knelt for anyone. Five Dragons stared at Proprietor Feng. Then his attitude softened. But that doesn't matter. If you say I knelt, then I knelt.

Are you going or not?

I'm going. If your new son-in-law won't help you, who

will? Five Dragons walked to the door and blew his nose into the street. As he wiped his fingers on the doorframe he added, But let's get something straight. If I run into pirates I won't trade my life for your valuables. It's worth a lot more than two boatloads of rice. He stood in the doorway gazing out at Brick Mason Avenue as night closed in. The image of an unknown sailor sinking into the river formed in his head. The spirits of countless wronged people descend to the Yellow Springs during wars, rebellions, and famines. Stupid people. Five Dragons would not be among them. To him nothing was more important than life itself, unless it was improving the quality of that life. I'm not stupid, he reminded himself.

Late that night Cloud Silk awoke to the sound of someone banging frantically on her door. Open up, hurry! It was Cloud Weave. Let me in. Still half asleep, Cloud Silk opened the door. Her sister, a robe thrown over her shoulders, rushed past her and climbed into bed. I'm so scared! They're going to kill me. In the dim lamplight only her pale, frightened face was visible.

Have you lost your mind? It's the middle of the night. Cloud Silk climbed back into bed and nudged her sister, who was shaking like a leaf. Move over.

I keep having nightmares. They're coming to kill me. Cloud Weave pulled the covers up over her head. They chase me with a butcher knife, it's so scary.

Who's they? Cloud Silk asked with a frown.

Men. Sixth Master, Abao, even Five Dragons. He's got a butcher knife.

Serves you right! Sooner or later they'll get you, take my word for it.

I shouldn't have watched them slaughter that pig today. Cloud Weave stuck her head out and looked imploringly at Cloud Silk. I was bored, so I went out and watched them kill a pig. It's the same butcher knife—at least a foot long—blood dripping from the blade. Five Dragons is holding it.

Do you really think any of those men care about you? Cloud Silk moved her pillow to the edge of the bed to keep it away from her sister.

Cloud Weave stroked her abdomen. I've wasted the best years of my life. Once the baby comes, that's it for me. I sure didn't plan it that way.

Now what are you thinking? Cloud Silk blew out the lamp and moved to the far edge of the wooden bed. Go to sleep, she said. Just because all you do is sit around stuffing your face doesn't alter the fact that I have to get up early and slave away all day until my head swims. No one cares if I live or die.

Don't go to sleep yet, Cloud Weave said with a crack in her voice as she hugged her pillow and moved close to her sister. Let's talk. I'm so confused. It's like something terrible is about to happen. Do you think Five Dragons is in any danger out there?

Who are you afraid for, him or yourself? I think you're worried about what will happen when people learn that you're carrying the bastard offspring of a stray animal.

I don't know. Sometimes I feel like telling him everything, and letting him do what he wants to me. That way neither of us owes the other anything. I've got such a guilty conscience these days. What do you think he'd do if he found out?

Ask him. He's your husband. Don't involve me in your sordid affairs, Cloud Silk replied impatiently, shaking free of Cloud Weave's hand, which was entwined around her hair. I advise you not to tell him. He's evil and he's mean. You can see it in his eyes.

But you can't wrap fire in paper. How long can I deceive him?

Heaven only knows. Cloud Silk sat up to study Cloud Weave's face in the darkness. Let me ask you something, she said softly. What will you do if Five Dragons doesn't come back from this trip? Will you grieve for him?

What do you mean? Cloud Weave grew wide-eyed. Just what do you mean by that?

Go ask Father. Cloud Silk caught herself before saying any more. You can't control your mouth, and Father said I wasn't to tell you.

You don't have to, I can guess. Seized with terror, Cloud Weave looked at the paper-covered window. Father has hired pirates to get rid of him, hasn't he? Things like that happen all the time.

You said it, not me. Cloud Silk slid back under the covers and showed Cloud Weave her back. Don't forget, it's for your own good, and for the good name of the Feng family. This hasn't been easy on Father.

Poor Five Dragons, Cloud Weave said sorrowfully. I feel so sorry for him.

This time Cloud Silk held her tongue, and before long the only sound in the room was her slow, even breathing. Cloud Weave reached out to touch her sister's icy fingers. Terrified by the dark, cold night, she felt isolated and helpless, nearly inconsolable. A sour stench rose from a chamber pot behind the door curtain; two sprigs of wintersweet had frozen in their vase. Before she fell asleep, Cloud Weave heard icicles snap in the wind and crash to the ground.

For days on end Cloud Weave could not sit still. One morning she was leaning against the door nibbling pumpkin seeds and gazing out onto the street. Everything was undergoing subtle changes, and she was beginning to worry about her husband. The mornings were the worst; she felt like she was losing the baby all the time, and was constantly depressed. Sometimes she wished it was Five Dragons's child growing inside her; she didn't know why she felt that way, but she couldn't help it.

Suddenly she squealed with joy as Five Dragons appeared at the intersection. She ran to him, pumpkin seeds slipping through her fingers and settling to the ground with a soft rustle. She threw her arms around him and rocked back and forth, speechless. But he kept moving forward, money pouch over his shoulder. I have to see your father. Her vision clouded by tears, she followed along, still not knowing what to say.

Five Dragons entered the shop. Proprietor Feng paled and straightened up behind the counter. Good, you're back. Five Dragons said nothing as he glared menacingly across the counter at Cloud Silk and her father, then he spun around and kicked over a basket of rice.

Did you get it? Cloud Silk asked after getting over the shock of seeing him.

It's at the pier. Go get it yourselves. He looked down at the rice basket as it spiraled on the floor, and kicked it again; it rolled out into the yard. He stared Proprietor Feng in the eye, the familiar white glare back again. You didn't pay those pirates enough. For that tiny bit of money they only shot me in the foot. They said it wasn't nearly enough for a life.

I don't know what you're talking about. Go lie down, you must be exhausted. Proprietor Feng tried to keep calm. He nudged Cloud Silk. Heat some water so he can wash up.

Here, look at my foot. Five Dragons took off his left shoe, undid a coarse cloth wrapping, and rested his foot on the counter. See, one of the toes is missing. You should have seen it bleed. Take a good look, so you can get your money's worth.

Proprietor Feng turned away from the bloody foot and began gagging violently. Cloud Silk, meanwhile, was shouting, Put your foot down, put that disgusting thing down.

You're the disgusting ones, Five Dragons replied, raising his injured foot even higher, then turning to look at Cloud Weave as she cowered in the corner. First you palm this slut off on me, and now you're trying to get me out of the picture altogether. What kind of stupid game are you playing?

Don't look at me. Cloud Weave avoided his piercing gaze. I don't know a thing. Nervously she gnawed her fingernails.

You people can't hurt me. Five Dragons finally brought his foot down and, with an inscrutable smile, put his shoe back on. Five Dragons was born to enjoy a long life, so he'll be around long after the rest of you are dead and buried.

Limping slightly, he walked outside, where laundry was hung out to dry in front of the gate. Ice crystals had formed on the clothing, feeling like pinpricks when he touched it. Stubbornly he clung to images from Lake Wu: what the black-clad pirates said after they boarded the boats; the excruciating pain in his foot after a bullet had torn through it. Why won't they leave me alone? Why do they want me dead? Angrily he ripped the stiff clothing off the clothesline.

Cloud Weave watched him walk toward her with the clothing under his arm, curses spewing from his mouth. She blocked his way. Where are you going? He shoved her aside and walked out of the compound. She ran up and grabbed his jacket. Five Dragons, I asked you where you're going. He stopped at the gate, turned slowly, and looked at her impassively. The public bath, he said. Did you think I was leaving? Why would I do that? I'm your husband, the rice-emporium son-in-law. You couldn't force me to leave. He beat the stiff clothing against the wall and said with passion, **I'm not going anywhere.**

Five Dragons lay on his side, inches from Cloud Weave. When she leaned over to put out the lamp, he sat up and began plucking chin whiskers with his fingernails. It sure is dark, he said. I can't see a thing. She opened her eyes; he was right, the room was pitch black, and his seated figure looked like a stone marker. I'm not surprised, she thought. People get through long winter nights like this the best they can.

At some point she fell asleep, only to be startled awake. Five Dragons? His face—hazy, dense, shadowy—was drawn up close. He had been watching her as she slept. She climbed out of bed and groped her way to the commode. Toilet paper crinkled as she pulled back the curtain to look at her husband. Still a stone marker.

Why do you always sit there watching me sleep? What

crazy thoughts run through your head? Her voice was thick with sleep. You scare me.

I need to see deep down inside you people. You all want me dead, and I don't know why.

Don't ask me. Air escaped with a hiss from her mouth as she jumped into bed and pulled the covers over her head. I'm freezing, she complained. I need my sleep. All that matters is that you're back safe and sound.

What about the hole in my foot? He flicked the covers back to rest his wounded foot against her face. See the dried blood? he asked. Well, I want you people to lick it clean. If you won't do it, get your father, and if he won't do it, get your sister. You did this to me, and it's time you found out what my blood tasted like.

Are you crazy? Cloud Weave tried to wrench the coverlet out of his hand. If I'd known you were like this, I'd have had Sixth Master kill you. He's a dead shot. Instead of a smashed toe, you'd have a bullet in the head, on my say-so, and you wouldn't be bothering me anymore.

Your Sixth Master doesn't scare me. With a shrug of his shoulders, he slapped her viciously. Who do you think you are, you little whore? A worn-out shoe, that's what you are, one that men wear for a day or two then throw away. Sixth Master gave you to me, and I can wear you any way I want. I'm your husband.

Surrounded by darkness, she held her face in her hands for a moment before a shrill cry escaped from her mouth, and she threw herself on Five Dragons, hitting him over the head with her pillow, butting him in the chest, and swearing at him loudly: You say you're a man you think you can get away with slapping me you're afraid I won't snap off that little cock of yours! But she was no match for the stronger Five Dragons, who pushed her away until she was nearly on her knees. Grabbing his uninjured foot, she crammed the toes into her mouth and bit down. Amid agonizing cries of pain, she heard the crisp crack of bone.

Proprietor Feng and Cloud Silk were pounding on the door. Five Dragons, if you raise a hand against my daughter tonight, I'll make sure you're in jail tomorrow. Stop it right this minute! Five Dragons reached down, picked up Cloud Weave's shoe, and flung it against the door. Then, in spite of the pain, he examined the latest foot injury. What do you want? he shouted toward the door. This has nothing to do with you. Get your asses back to bed. But Proprietor Feng continued pounding on the door. Five Dragons, you've got nothing on me. You say I paid pirates to shoot you in the foot? Where's your proof? You don't have any! A mirthless, barbed laugh was Five Dragons's only response. Lifting the foot Cloud Weave had just bitten, he said, I've got all the proof I need. Your daughter has just mangled a toe on my other foot, and since I can't walk, I won't be able to work like a dog for you for a while. It's your turn to take care of me now. I'm staying put, and there's nothing any of you can do about it.

Cloud Weave ran over and jerked the door open. Like a madwoman she pounded Proprietor Feng on his chest and shoulders. Why did you make me marry that bastard? she screamed between sobs and stomps of her feet. He's a mean, heartless, peasant slob.

Proprietor Feng merely wobbled back and forth weakly. Cloud Silk raised her candle to light up the room, then abruptly blew it out and headed back to her own bed. You asked for it, she muttered. Since you agreed to the marriage, you have only yourself to blame. You get exactly what you deserve.

FOR CLOUD WEAVE THE WINTER WAS ONE LONG, TOR-
turous nightmare. She had heard neighbor women
talk about miscarriages in the past, recalling that the
fourth month was when the pregnancy was most
precarious, and that the husband was the key to
success, if the fetus was to be dislodged. She tried.
Five Dragons's rough-and-tumble after-dark perfor-
mances could have been taken for attempted murder
if she hadn't known better; but now the pain and
torment brought hope that the revolting lump of
flesh and blood inside her would wind up in the
commode. In the end nothing came of it; the fetus
continued to grow, and before long she felt it move:
the scratching of a tiny foot, the clawing of an infant's hand.

As winter passed, Cloud Weave's belly bulged
prodigiously, the fine lines in her face deepened.
Sometimes she sat behind the counter watching the
clerks sell rice, her tired, melancholic look reminding
customers of the shopkeeper's deceased wife, Madam
Zhu. But no one knew what was on her mind, or if
she had anything on her mind at all as she sat
wrapped in the fur coat Sixth Master had given her
years before, now stretched to the limit around her
middle. The local women's assessment of Cloud

Weave's appearance dripped with malice. They said she would wear anything imaginable, or nothing at all, as long as she could draw attention to herself.

The enjoyment she took in an occasional stroll remained unaffected until the day she spotted Sixth Master at the flower and bird market, where she had gone to buy a carnation plant. Surrounded by servants, he reached into a birdcage to touch the beak of a green parakeet. Stricken with a case of nerves, Cloud Weave hid her face behind the plant, torn between avoiding a confrontation and letting him see her. Shoppers surged past as she stood rigid and motionless. Before long Sixth Master picked up the cage and walked toward her, his servants lagging behind. One, whom she remembered all too well, made a face at her.

You've really started to show since I last saw you. Sixth Master looked down at the swelling abdomen straining against her cheongsam, his two gold teeth glimmering behind a broad smile. That's a girl for you, turning ugly at the slightest provocation, from lovely flower to dog shit in the blink of an eye.

What's it to you if I'm ugly or not? She looked away and patted her shoulder with a carnation sprig. I'm not your concubine and I sure am not your mistress.

I hear you married a runaway. Sixth Master's gaze rose, slowly tracing the curves of her body until it came to rest on her face. How could a girl like you give herself to one of those? What a pity.

Mind your own business. I'll marry whomever I please. I could marry a dog if I wanted to, whether you liked it or not. There's nothing more between you and me.

Sixth Master shouted over his shoulder, and out from behind a garbage heap bounded a great big dog, which gnawed playfully at his shoe. If it's a dog you want, why not mine? Anything is better than a runaway.

Cloud Weave spat loudly on the ground. You bastard. Talking to you is a waste of my time. She turned to leave, but Sixth Master blocked her way with the cage, in which the parakeet hopped onto a perch and pecked her on the breast. She shrieked and shoved the cage out of her way. Let me go. I said it's all over between us.

Sixth Master raised the cage to eye level, then looked at the red-faced Cloud Weave. Don't get so emotional, he said. Let the bird calm you. It can talk, you know. It repeats everything I say. He stuck his finger into the cage to smooth the parakeet's green feathers. Slut, he said in a pinched voice. Slut, slut.

Slut—slut—slut. The bird's mimicking cries rang in her ears while Sixth Master and his servants laughed raucously as they listened to the parakeet squawk *slut*. Cloud Weave flung her plant to the ground, her eyes flashing with anger and mortification, and threw herself on Sixth Master, trying to scratch out his eyes. But his servants quickly pinned her arms to her sides. With her puffy torso suspended in the air between two men, she ground her teeth and cursed, I wish I'd cut off that old pecker of yours and fed it to the dogs when I had the chance. How could I have let myself be defiled by the likes of you? Tears streamed down her face, which was raised to the heavens. Everyone within earshot was gaping at her.

At a signal from Sixth Master, the servants released their grip. Shaking from head to toe, Cloud Weave landed on top of her carnation plant. Sixth Master handed the birdcage to a servant and stared wordlessly at her as he reached up to straighten his hair. Then, surprisingly, he stepped up and rubbed her bulging belly, resting his hand on the crest for a long moment. She buried her face in her hands and sobbed. I hate men. I hate all you cold-blooded beasts.

Enough of that, Sixth Master said affectionately, placing his mouth to her ear. Maybe that is my seed in your belly. If the baby looks like me, I'll be responsible for his up-bringing, and I'll send a sedan chair with eight bearers to install you as fifth concubine.

Cloud Weave did not regain her senses until Sixth Master and his entourage had left the market. Hurt and hu-miliated, she pondered what Sixth Master had whispered to her. Who cares about being your fifth concubine? Not me! She dried her eyes with a handkerchief as she walked among the fresh flowers and birdcages, trying to reenact the circumstances of the pregnancy; but it didn't help, she simply could not be sure who had deposited this child in her belly. Back then she was a kitten frisking between rival masters, and now it was too late to determine which one it had been. She could only trust to luck; yet the thought that her future would be determined on the day she gave birth only deepened her mood of anxiety.

Back at the shop they were selling coarse brown rice from Zhejiang. A small mountain of it stood in the center of the room, each undersized grain nearly black in color. Yet even for such coarse fare, customers elbowed their way up to the counter to buy as much as they could. Cloud Silk, her braid coiled atop her head and held in place by a gem-studded clasp, had her hands full at the scales. It was, as Cloud Weave noticed immediately, her clasp, and in days past she would have reclaimed it on the spot. Now she couldn't care less. Tightly knitting her brows, she el-bowed her way through two ragged lines of customers. Every day, all day long, buying rice and selling rice—it's

enough to drive a person crazy. Father called to her from
behind the counter: Go tell that man of yours to get out
here. We could use an extra pair of hands. He's in the
storeroom catching up on his sleep!

The brushwood storeroom door was unlatched, so
Cloud Weave peeked in through a crack. Five Dragons
was sitting on a mound of rice, a handful of raw kernels in his hand, a faraway look in his eyes. He began
dropping the rice to the ground, one kernel at a time,
until they formed two written characters. Cloud Weave
recognized them immediately, even though they were little more than scrawls: WU LONG—Five Dragons, his
own name.

Cloud Weave opened the door and walked in. Five
Dragons didn't even look up. His bare feet were splayed
in front of him, each with a distinguishing scar.

I didn't know you could write. She ground the rice into
the floor with her toes. Let's see you write Cloud Weave.
You can write my name, can't you?

No, only my own. He curled his legs inward and rose
to a crouch, hugging his knees. Are you in heat again?
Can't you stop pestering me?

Guess who I ran into at the flower and bird market.

Who cares?

Sixth Master. Nervously she fidgeted with the door behind her, causing it to creak. The old bastard insists I'm
carrying his child.

Could be, Five Dragons said coldly, since you're the
biggest slut on the face of the earth.

What would you do if it was true? She took a few
tentative steps forward and touched him on the shoulder.
Fly into a jealous rage?

No, he replied maliciously as he scooped up a handful

of rice, flung it into the air, and caught most of it deftly in his gaping mouth. His cheeks puffed out as he crunched the rice noisily. I know everything, if you want the truth. You people think I'm some kind of fool, a stone you can roll around at will to plug the holes in your home and stop up certain people's mouths. Don't you know that you're the fools, not me?

The light in Cloud Weave's eyes dimmed. Something broke inside her. He had ripped away the last veil covering her shame, bringing raw, unbearable pain; the sense of mortification was so powerful that a shadowy moan rose from her throat as she collapsed against the mound of rice. With her face pressed tightly against bulging burlap bags, she grabbed his clothing. Please don't do that, Five Dragons, she begged. Why can't you be nice to me? Don't treat me like a bad woman. At that moment she felt completely insignificant, a sheet of flimsy paper floating woefully in the storeroom.

Five Dragons observed her calmly, his face muscles taut and rigid. Time stood still for a moment, before he went over and closed the door, returned, and began deftly undoing the hooks of her cheongsam. I'll be nice to you, if that's what you want. She knew what he meant, but lacked the strength to ward him off. Still, she held on to his shorts. Not here, please, she pleaded. Not here. He responded by ripping the clothing off her body. Shut up and close your eyes. If you so much as blink, I'll toss you out into the street.

You're a madman. What if someone sees us? But she closed her eyes, as she was told, a sudden attack of obedience that was unprecedented. Rough, cold fingers moved down her body like rivulets of water, stopping to squeeze and pinch sensitive spots. She hated quirky behavior like that, associating it with sick or crazy people.

By then he was sprinkling rice over her nude body and watching it funnel down between her breasts. The silky grains made her skin tingle strangely. What are you doing? She shuddered. What are you up to? He was too engrossed in watching her swelling abdomen rise and fall to answer. Panting heavily. Suddenly he clenched his teeth and crammed a handful of rice into Cloud Weave's vagina, then watched her eyes snap open in alarm. Have you lost your mind? Her eyes bulged. What do you think you're doing? When she tried to shift her legs, he pressed down heavily. I told you to keep your eyes closed, now close them.

You bastard. She sobbed, burying her face in her hands. What are you doing to me? Have you forgotten that I'm pregnant?

Stop crying. He kept at it, still panting heavily. Rice is cleaner than a man's cock, so what are you complaining about? You're stupid, you're cheap, and now I'm going to teach you what it means to be a woman.

I won't stay with you if this is how you're going to act, Cloud Weave complained helplessly as she pummeled him with her fists. We're supposed to be happily married, so why can't we live that way? Are you trying to kill me?

It's a little late to be talking about things like that, Five Dragons said as he spat on the floor and brushed off his hands, then walked over and unbolted the door. He turned and gave her a final contemptuous look as she climbed down off the mound of rice, her face deathly pale, crumbly rice cascading from her milky skin to the floor. No one had witnessed the little drama. And her sobs, which rang weak and hollow in the storeroom, failed to penetrate Five Dragons's heart.

Several of the bathhouse regulars witnessed Proprietor Feng's stroke. Emerging from the heated water, he had just picked up a towel to dry his chest. See this withered old body, he said to someone in the pool. Would you believe I still have to take care of everything? And not just in the shop, either. There was more he wanted to say, if only he'd had the chance; but his body stiffened, and the men in the pool saw his eyes nearly pop out of his head as a trickle of spittle oozed from the corner of his twisted mouth, just before his bony frame hit the wooden floor with a thud. As they were carrying him outside, he lost control of his bladder and sprayed them with amber-colored urine.

Cloud Silk burst into tears when they carried Proprietor Feng into the shop. All day long you soak in that steaming water, she complained. Well, you've gone and soaked yourself into an invalid. Now what? They eased him into a redwood reclining chair, from where he gazed up at Cloud Silk with eyes like icy pools. I've worked like a slave all my life, he said, his slurred speech barely intelligible. Now you can take care of me for a change. The beads of his grease-stained abacus, which lay on the counter, registered the number 58, his current age. He knew that things were progressing in accordance with heaven's will, and that he was helpless to do a thing about it, especially given the decline of his body.

When the rice emporium reopened three days later, customers no longer saw the familiar stooped figure of Proprietor Feng. The aging paralytic now spent his days immobilized in a dark room, all alone. Sometimes the smell of herbal medicine oozed through cracks in the kitchen door. A concoction was prescribed by Brick Mason Avenue's ancient herbal doctor, who said to Cloud Silk, This works on blood vessels and energy meridians. I can't guarantee it will cure what ails him. Overwork and anxiety are a recipe for a stroke. Do you understand what I'm getting at? Cloud Silk grimaced. Yes, she replied. What I don't understand is why the Feng family has fallen on such hard times. Father doesn't have to worry, now that he's laid up, but what about me? All my sister does around here is eat. She's helpless without me, so I guess I'm stuck with this broken-down shop until the day I die.

The newest odor pervading the sickroom was human waste. Cloud Weave, who was growing increasingly immobile, stayed away, leaving the disposal of Proprietor Feng's excretions solely to Cloud Silk. What sort of life is this for a girl? she grumbled as she bathed her father. I do everything around here. Three heads and six hands still wouldn't be enough. Proprietor Feng, his skeletal frame subject to the indignity of being pushed one way and rolled the other, lay in bed with tears slipping down his cheeks. Cloud Silk, he said, you can take your frustrations out on me. But who do I have? Heaven, I guess. The day of reckoning has come for the Feng family. And the worst may be yet to come. Take down the shop banner and put up a new one. Maybe that will ward off evil spirits.

But Cloud Silk was too short to reach the tattered banner, even with a clothes hanger, so she went inside to fetch a stool. There she spotted Five Dragons by the door scraping the gunk off of his teeth with a sliver of wood. Anger and resentment that had been building for days erupted. How can anybody be so thick-skinned? It must be entertaining to watch me struggle like this. What would it take to get you to flex those golden arms and silver legs of yours? Five Dragons threw down the makeshift scraper, ran up, and leaped into the air, nimbly tearing down the scarred, punctured banner. Then, cradling it in his arms, he smiled and said, There, I flexed them, okay? Feel better now? But the scowl remained on her face. Big noise, little turds. Now let's see you hang the new one. She attached a clean piece of cloth, decorated with the words GREAT SWAN COMPANY, to a wooden dowel and tossed it to Five Dragons. Amused, he sniffed it a time or two. You're just wasting your time, he said. Change banners all you want, but the days of this shop are numbered. That's what Liu the Nearly Immortal divined. Cloud Silk glowered at him. Just you wait, she said. You'll see how numbered our days are.

After hanging out the banner, with its dark calligraphy, Five Dragons stepped back to watch it flutter weakly above Brick Mason Avenue. He didn't have to be told that this simple banner signaled a juncture in the history of the emporium. Jamming two fingers into his mouth, he whistled shrilly.

Cloud Silk's haggard face was brushed with pale spring sunlight, her expression richly expressive yet impenetrable in its mixture of knowledge and sadness. She drummed the doorframe with her fingers. Five Dragons brushed past her as he walked back inside, his elbow bumping against her breast. Sensing that it was intentional, she cursed him, You're always taking advantage of people, you bastard.

He headed out to the backyard as if he hadn't heard her.

Five Dragons was struggling to come to grips with nighttime fantasies that wound tightly around his strong, youthful limbs like thorny vines, until they all but immobilized him. In the dark of night or just before dawn, as he lay stretched out on satin bedding, bronze-colored rays reflecting off his body, he thought back to the dismal days in Maple-Poplar Village. Since then he had been transformed, as if by magic. But into what? A smooth-headed cock, that's what. A decoration to hang above the rice-emporium door. No one knew how he felt. No one could see his desires rise and fall like the tides, changing subtly through the mysterious power of the moon. That was why he posed such a threat to the rice-emporium family.

It did not take long for him to tire of looking at his pregnant wife, or for his gaze to wander naturally to her sister, who had once caught him in the embarrassing act of drooling over one of her menstrual pads. Acting on impulse, she had thrown open the door, pinning him behind it. Give it a good, hard look, she snapped. In fact, why not chew on it, you slimy bastard! Red-faced, Five Dragons poked his head out from behind the door and said sheepishly, I'm just looking at it. There's no law against that, is there? Don't bite my balls off.

When Cloud Silk reported what happened, Cloud Weave merely laughed. It's your fault for leaving them lying around. They're not bunting, you know. Men are like that. They'll take what they can get. Cloud Silk was shocked. Don't you care how shameful he is? He is *your* husband. Cloud Weave's smile vanished; she chewed her nails noisily. What good would it do to care? I'm too deeply in his debt. Cloud Silk stood up with one hand on the bed and watched the pink nail clippings flutter onto the bedding from Cloud Weave's lips. Revolting. She turned away from the sight. Just revolting. You two disgust me.

Long the target of Five Dragons's flirtations, Cloud Silk steadfastly treated him with contempt and loathing. At night she slept behind not one, but two bolts on the door, and still she found no peace. Late one night she heard him outside, trying to saw through the bolts with a cleaver. Mottled reflections of moonlight on the blade sent currents of fear through her. His frenzied behavior both terrified and enraged her. She tried but couldn't find anything to knock the cleaver out of his hand, and was reluctant to scream; she didn't want to disturb her ailing father or the neighbors. At last she turned to the chamber pot resting against the wall. Hold on, I'll let you in. She walked to the door and threw back the bolts. There on the other side, a naked, slightly iridescent Five Dragons stood as if frozen, cleaver in hand. Come in, you slimy bastard. Gritting her teeth, she raised the chamber pot and emptied its stinking contents all over him. No qualms, no misgivings. The first sound she heard was his horrified screech, followed by the clang of the cleaver on the floor. She slammed the door shut and propped her body against it, as mucky, smelly water seeped back into the room under the door. She moved over to the wall, where she dissolved in loud, wrenching sobs. What's happening to me? How much torment must I endure, how much bitterness? I'd be better off dead.

Cloud Silk kept this incident from her father, partly out of shame and partly to avoid the risk of worsening his condition. She continued to hope that he would regain his health someday and resume management of the business. When she entered his room the following morning, she saw that he was cradling a rusty hatchet in his sickbed. She ran over and wrenched it out of his hands. What's this for, Father? For you, he said, shaking his head, his eyes clouded and dark. I spent half the night crawling across the floor so I could drag it back to bed with my teeth. Why a hatchet? We don't need wood in this weather. Proprietor Feng stared vacantly into the air above his bed. When he spoke, his voice was gravelly and muffled: To bury in that bastard's head. The next time he tries to get his hands on you, bury this in his head. I'd do it myself if I could.

Cloud Silk's face was ashen as she placed the hatchet at the foot of the bed, then straightened up and adjusted the old man's covers. Father, she said blankly, you're so angry you can't see straight. Don't worry about the rest of the family. There's nothing you can do, anyway. Just lie there quietly, for my sake, and let me deal with him.

He's an evil star, and if he's not gotten rid of, the Feng clan could be wiped off the face of the earth. Proprietor Feng shut his eyes, the corners all red and festery from the heat of anger inside him, and fringed by a crusty white film. This wouldn't have happened if I hadn't been such a skinflint. When those pirates asked for four ounces of gold, I only gave them two.

It's a bit late to be bringing that up now, isn't it? With a frown Cloud Silk cut her father short. Is there anyone around here who doesn't disgust me?

It's all my fault. My personal abacus failed me. I let him in the door, never imagining he'd turn out to be such a wild dog that no amount of whipping could ever drive him away. Proprietor Feng still had not purged himself of the rancor in his gut. I never dreamed he'd be such an evil star. Sooner or later this business will fail because of him. Just you wait and see.

An uncontrollable anger gripped Cloud Silk. Slamming the bedpan against the step, she shouted, If it fails, maybe things will finally quiet down around here. No one should have to live like this. Maybe I'll find someone willing to marry me one of these days, so the rest of you can hang around and watch this old family shop crumble.

A commotion accompanied the arrival of a new shipment of rice, when a dead child tumbled out of one of the stunned porters' sacks. Naked except for a pair of torn, baggy shorts, its distended belly made it look like an inflated ball. The horrified porter gaped at the corpse, half-buried in raw rice, with its purple face and flaccid skin; more rice was clutched in one of its tiny hands.

But there was no horror on Five Dragons's face when he was summoned to the storeroom. Kneeling beside the body, he pried open the child's mouth; it too was crammed full of raw yellow rice. He then pressed down on the belly, which had lost its elasticity, and announced quietly, Rice killed him. He ate until he couldn't eat any more.

What rotten luck. Cloud Silk wrung her hands and avoided looking at the corpse. How did he wind up inside the bag?

He was hungry. Five Dragons gave her a stern look. So hungry he panicked. But that's beyond your understanding, isn't it?

Get him out of there. She cast a long look at the shop as she walked out of the storeroom. Stuff him back inside the sack. The sight of him could drive away customers.

You don't understand a goddamned thing, Five Dragons said as he eased the child's body back inside the sack, since you've never gone hungry. He hefted the sack over his shoulder and walked out. Toss him into the city moat, Cloud Silk suggested from behind him. And be sure no one sees you. Anger rose up in Five Dragons, who spun around and screamed, What are you so worried about? You didn't kill him. He died from eating raw **rice**! Can you understand that?

Five Dragons headed toward the city moat shouldering the gunnysack made heavy by the child, whose corpse gave off the cold stench of death. After laying the sack down on the grassy bank, he felt the need to see the child one more time. So he snapped the tie string and rolled down the sack until the peaceful, purplish little face reappeared. A life claimed by raw rice. He might have lived in flood-ravaged Maple-Poplar Village, for all Five Dragons knew. Cradling the child's head in his arms, he bent down to scrutinize the dead face, as if to fix it firmly in his mind. Time lingered. Finally he climbed to his feet and picked up the heavy gunnysack. The moat's polluted water, with its floating garbage and filth, quickly claimed another human corpse. The rapid spring flow emptied into a river two miles downstream. Five Dragons knew that the child would, for all of eternity, be carried along by water currents or in the bellies of river fish.

Head bowed, he shuffled home, a lone figure entering Brick Mason Avenue, where he heard the crisp tinkling of wind chimes from the pagoda. A young entrepreneur was frying sparrows outside the snack shop amid a crowd of impatient customers. The thought that life went on as usual troubled Five Dragons, who rubbed his eyes with his sleeve as he walked past the grocery, where Cloud Silk was buying a New Year's pastry made of sweet, sticky rice. Five Dragons, she cried. Take this home for me. With his head bowed and shoulders slumped, he didn't hear her. So she ran outside. Take this cake home for me, she repeated. This time he looked up, startled out of his thoughts, and gaped at her. He licked his chapped lips. Do you know how many people die each day? he blurted out, catching her by surprise. Like a sleepwalker, there were traces of blurry tears in the corners of his eyes. Why ask me? she asked. I'm not the King of Hell, how would I know?

Proprietor Feng's condition remained unchanged, even after nine separate prescriptions of herbal tonic. If anything, he was worse, since his normally frail body had grown strangely puffy and bloated from chronic constipation. Increasingly dispirited, he was an old candle guttering in the wind. When Cloud Silk came in with his medicine, he managed to open his mouth, but the liquid merely dribbled down his chin, for he had forgotten how to swallow. As she wiped the dark concoction from his neck, she knew that his days on this earth were numbered.

Within the space of a single day Proprietor Feng put his affairs in order. First he handed Cloud Silk the keys to the shop and divulged the location of all the gold and silver he had hidden away. Then he summoned Cloud Weave to his bedside, where he studied her bulging figure with despair. You worry me the most, he said, since any man can have his way with you. They'll be the death of you one day. Last to stand alone beside the sickbed was Five Dragons. The death look on Proprietor Feng's face seemed familiar, strangely reminiscent of the look in the old man's face the first time Five Dragons laid eyes on him. After draping the blue curtain over a nearby hook, he gazed calmly at the dying man. Come closer, Five Dragons, Proprietor Feng said. I have something to say. As Five Dragons bent over, Proprietor Feng miraculously raised his right arm, which had been paralyzed for days. Bastard. Evil star! A curved, grimy finger shot into Five Dragons's eye socket. He jumped back in excruciating pain, as if his right eye had shattered like glass. Blood was already oozing onto his cheek and upper lip. How could he have managed? On his deathbed, no less. What had it taken to get a paralyzed arm to do his bidding? With a roar he rushed the old man and rocked his redwood bed. Again, do it again. I've got another eye, and don't forget my cock. See if you can destroy them, too.

Proprietor Feng's eyes closed while his bed shook, and an enraged Five Dragons heard the death rattle. Calmness quickly returned, as he covered his face with his hands and strode into the yard, where Cloud Weave and Cloud Silk were tearing white mourning cloth into strips. He picked one up off the ground to tie around his waist and another to wipe his bloody face. The old son of a bitch died, he said, but not before blinding me in one eye. He died happy.

The girls rushed into the sickroom, Cloud Silk dragging a strip of white cloth behind her. Five Dragons stood in the yard as familiar sounds shattered the stillness. The sisters' wails—high one minute, low the next—alarmed the shop clerks, who rushed into the yard, where Five Dragons was standing amid a pile of white strips, cupping his hand over his eye. The old shit blinded me, so the rice emporium will foot all my bills from now on.

Two bolts of white cloth that had been bought days earlier, now cut into strips and squares, lay scattered across the yard. Though equally white, cloth and rice give off different auras in the sun's glare. That afternoon Five Dragons inhaled the smell of new cotton, which he had missed for too long. It brought him warm, cozy feelings amid the mournful wailing of the two sisters. He knelt down to fondle the white cloth; subtle changes in its folds and wrinkles followed his moving finger.

ON A BRISK AUTUMN DAY THE FIRST CRY OF A NEWBORN infant broke the silence at the rice emporium. Cradling the muck-covered baby, the midwife ran into the yard and shouted, Congratulations, Five Dragons, you have a fat little son.

Five uneven rows of playing cards that he had laid out on the ground were being disturbed by gusts of wind, until he was forced to anchor them with stones. Finally he picked up the cards, one at a time, and squinted into the midwife's arms. The bloody object reminded him of slaughtered animals back home in Maple-Poplar Village. He was about to say so, but held his tongue. He was now a one-eyed dragon.

Cloud Silk was complaining about the baby's looks when Five Dragons walked in. There's something funny about him, she said. He doesn't resemble anybody. Five Dragons looked down at Cloud Weave as she lay disheveled in bed, the sunlight streaming in through the window falling on her wan face like a spectral knife. Cloud Silk was sitting on the edge of the bed holding the baby. Come see your son, she said to Five Dragons. He takes after you.

The swaddled infant was still howling, an opaque pinkness showing under the prunish skin of his tiny face and body. Five Dragons, still clutching the playing cards, bent over for a closer look. He doesn't take after anybody, he said. He looks like a newborn dog. That's exactly what they look like. I've seen lots of bitch litters. He gazed again at Cloud Weave, who removed a damp towel from her forehead. If I'd known it was going to hurt so much, I'd never have let a man touch me, not if he threatened to kill me. Five Dragons stared at her with cold contempt. You'll forget it soon enough. Pain's the last thing you'll be thinking about the next time your pants are down around your ankles.

Later that night Five Dragons had barely fallen asleep when he heard a knock at the front door. He slipped on his sandals and opened the door to a gang of men, whom he recognized in the dim light as Sixth Master and some of his servants. A hunting dog paced the ground at Sixth Master's feet, barking loudly. Doors and windows opened in the blacksmith shop and grocery across the street as Five Dragons stepped aside to let the men into the shop; the neighbors were watching.

I've come for my son, Sixth Master announced. People say Cloud Weave's baby looks like me. The women in my household don't seem to have the makings of a son in them, but your woman has given me an heir. I'm taking him home with me. You won't try to stop me, will you?

No. Five Dragons shook his head in the shadows as he turned to lead them inside. Why should I? Nothing in this shop belongs to me.

Good. You learn quickly, Sixth Master said, patting Five Dragons gently on the back. If everyone was as sensible as you, I could send the Wharf Rats packing and get rid of my arsenal. I'd become a local buddha and my men could go back to loading ships.

Five Dragons wondered why Sixth Master was telling him all this. He had never sampled the venom of serpents, as Sixth Master knew. You don't think I'm ignorant of the fact that you're a poisonous snake, do you? he thought to himself. At the bedroom door he turned up the lantern and walked in. Cloud Weave, who was sitting on the edge of the bed suckling her baby, stared at Sixth Master as he and his servants entered the room. Her face reddened from shame.

So you've borne me a son, Sixth Master said, giving her rosy cheek a friendly pinch. He pulled back the blanket to study the baby's face. He does look like me. I guess I'll be taking a son home with me.

Says who? Cloud Weave banged the bedboard with her fist. You're here for your son? After sending me away like you did? I suffered all day and all night because of this baby, and I'm not about to let you just walk off with him.

Don't give me a hard time. Sixth Master picked up the baby and handed it to a servant, then grabbed a handful of Cloud Weave's hair. Remember who you're dealing with. Calm down and give yourself a proper lying-in month.

Cloud Weave began to complain tearfully. What about me? What am I supposed to do? Your promises are like farts in the wind. You should be sending a sedan chair for me. You said you'd take me back if the baby was yours. What right do you have to walk off with him and leave me behind?

I'm as good as my word, always have been, Sixth Master replied with a laugh and a wave of his hand. His gold teeth glinted in the lamplight. I have five concubines already, he said, what's one more? But we can dispense with the sedan chair. Look in the mirror, Cloud Weave, and tell me if you are worthy of riding in the Lu family palanquin.

You won't be happy until you squash me, will you? she said, drying her eyes. Well, I'm beyond caring about face, so I guess I'm stuck with you. Yes, that's it: I'm going to stick to you like glue. Now all I need to hear is when you'll come get me.

Come get you? You can find your own way. Sixth Master walked to the door. But stay put until the month is over. If you show up any earlier than that I'll personally throw you out. I hate the way women look right after they've had a baby. Having them around is bad luck.

Five Dragons and Cloud Silk saw the visitors out the door. The baby howled. Five Dragons was surprised that a brand-new baby's tear ducts could be in such fine working order. The bastard, Cloud Silk swore from behind him. He's a tyrant and a son of a bitch. Get a wetnurse, she shouted after the men, who were leaving the rice emporium like a disorderly mob. Don't forget. There was no response. The baby's cries grew weaker, and eventually died out altogether. As she watched the retreating backs of the men in their rickshaws, she spat loudly on the ground before slamming the door shut.

Five Dragons stood in the darkened yard a while longer before returning to the bedroom, where Cloud Weave was sitting up, her satin bedding a jumble. She stared blankly at him, eyes red and swollen from crying. What are you looking at? I didn't do anything. He started taking off his jacket, but changed his mind. I'm not sleeping in here tonight, he said. The smell of you sickens me, and so does the milk that little dog left behind. He blew out the lamp and walked to the door, one sleeve hanging across his shoulder. I'll sleep in the storeroom, he said on his way out. That's the only clean place around here.

Stop right there! Cloud Weave's voice split the darkness. Only someone with the heart of a wolf and the lungs of a dog would leave me at a time like this.

You're going to be Sixth Master's concubine, aren't you? Let him keep you company. Five Dragons's eyes roamed the darkened room. His right eye always throbbed at night. He massaged it. You never give a thought to what you and your family have done to me. Fuck eighteen generations of your ancestors! You people owe me a debt you'll never be able to pay off.

One winter afternoon, as icy winds blew outside, the rice-emporium sisters had a momentous conversation. By peeping through the keyhole, Five Dragons witnessed it all. He watched Cloud Silk jump out of her chair like an angry beast protecting her young and scream at Cloud Weave, turning her normally gaunt, elongated face red and puffy. Cloud Weave stood with her arms at her sides, lips trembling weakly but insistently, tears gathering in her eyes. She, too, had plenty to say. Although he was too far to hear everything, he got the gist of their conversation. Cloud Weave's lying-in month was over, and she had begun secretly preparing her trousseau.

I know men are all alike. Sixth Master and Five Dragons are dogs that can't wait to sink their fangs in me. But between the two, I'm better off with Sixth Master. At least he's rich and powerful. I can't keep playing one against the other. It's time to choose.

I won't stop you, if that's what you want. But take Five Dragons with you. You don't plan to hand him over to me, do you?

What's wrong with that? He's strong, and you can look after him. Once I'm gone, this place is all yours. You're going to need a strong pair of hands around here.

You actually said it, didn't you? Cloud Silk stepped up and slapped her sister. You slut, she snarled, pointing threateningly at her sister. What makes you think I'm as cheap as you? Or that this beat-up shop means anything to me? I'll tell you this—if not for the dying wishes of our parents, I'd burn it down tomorrow. My sorrow is eating me up.

Then they were at each other, pulling hair and scratching faces, until the weakened Cloud Weave was on the floor bawling and pleading as Cloud Silk tossed her around like a rag doll, clothes rustling. Finally, as Cloud Silk was dragging her sister out of the room, Cloud Weave reached up and held her arms. Stop, she pleaded tearfully, you're ripping my dress. Then she held Cloud Silk's icy hand up to her own heaving breast. What happened to this family? Our mother died of a broken heart because of me, and now with Father gone, it's just us two. But instead of being sisters, we fight like cats and dogs. Why? Caught by surprise, Cloud Silk stopped momentarily, but then pulled her hand back and kicked Cloud Weave in the hip. Why? You, of all people, should know that, she said angrily. You're the family's undertaker, not to mention its shameless bitch.

On the other side of the door, Five Dragons smirked. Tired of listening, he secured the bedroom door with a chopstick. Take your time and have a good long argument, he announced to the now-locked door. To him the sight of two sisters fighting was entertaining, but held no real significance. Why don't they ask what I think? They can both leave, as far as I'm concerned, but not me. Cloud

Silk can go find herself a man, if she wants, as long as she leaves the shop and all those mounds of snowy white rice.

As he lay in the storeroom Five Dragons heard the sound of splashing water in the yard. Now that she had seemed to put her slothful ways behind her, Cloud Weave rose at dawn to wash clothes, pounding them with dull thumps. Once again Five Dragons had fallen asleep on the rice pile. Since Cloud Weave had never washed his clothes before, he had no reason to assume she was doing so now. Silence eventually returned, and when he walked into the yard, he was greeted by the sight of his dripping-wet black clothes hanging out to dry. A faint soapy smell hung in the air.

Cloud Silk, who was brushing her teeth in the corner, turned to spit out a mouthful of foamy water. Cloud Weave's gone, she said. She went to the Lu mansion, and won't be back.

I figured. He plucked the clothesline with his finger, making the wet clothes quiver. She didn't have to sneak off like that, he said. Was she afraid I'd stop her? Hah!

Maybe you should leave, too. How can you hang around after your woman has run off? Cloud Silk ladled water into a brass basin, rolled up her sleeves, and rinsed her hands nervously. Go on, get out. A real man would. Do you understand what I'm saying?

What you're saying has nothing to do with what I'm thinking. His dry, cracked lips parted into something resembling a grin. I've been thinking about how much this family owes me. He raised his legs, one at a time. See those, they ache on wet, rainy days. Then he reached up, spread open his mucus-encrusted right eye with his fingers, and walked up to Cloud Silk. Here, take another look at this. Don't shy away, take a good look. It was a nice little trick your family played on me. Now I want to see how you're going to make up for it.

Get away from me, she screamed as she backed into a corner and grabbed her enamel mug, or I'll smash that dog head of yours.

Smash away. There was no change in Five Dragons's strange demeanor. He pushed up against Cloud Silk. The others, they're either dead or they've left you here to pay off their debt to me. Don't tell me you haven't figured that out yet.

You make me sick, she screamed. Don't touch me. I'm a woman of my word, and if you don't get away from me, I really will smash your dog head.

Smash away, I said. There's always my left eye. Go for it. He lowered his hand from his eyes, pinching her nipple on the way down. Since you're going to be taking Cloud Weave's place, you might as well marry me and get it over with.

Dream on, Cloud Silk snapped with a grimace. Angered and humiliated, she banged him on the head with her enamel mug—once, twice—then watched fresh blood crawl up through his dark, ratty hair. He grabbed his head and staggered over to the window to regain his balance. He stared at Cloud Silk with a look of awareness and disbelief, his right eye cloudy and gray, the left one aglow with menace.

Now you've given me another scar. Slowly he rubbed his head, then looked at his hand in the sunlight. Blood coursed silently through the runnels of his palm, the color growing lighter and lighter, until it was nearly pink. Now all three members of your family have wounded me, he announced as he stared at his sticky palm, then reached out and smeared some blood on Cloud Silk's cheek. You won't be running away, Cloud Silk. It looks like you'll have to marry me now.

As she stood there with streaks of sticky blood on her cheek, Cloud Silk felt her sanity slipping away. Of course—the hatchet her father had told her about as he lay dying. Cursing, she ran into her father's room, where she felt around under the bed until she touched the hatchet. After blowing the dust off the icy handle, she stood her ground and cursed Five Dragons. But the realization that she lacked the nerve to use it on his dog head brought feelings of sadness mixed with despair.

Cobwebs infested the beams and furniture of the northern wing, which had lain vacant for so long. On top of the wardrobe Cloud Silk spotted some packets of medicine, which she slid around with the hatchet blade, dislodging a mass of scurrying cockroaches and other nameless bugs. The weapon fell from her hand and clanged to the floor. Thoughts of her dead father made her sob. She walked to the bronze mirror and looked at the reflection of her gaunt, tear-streaked face: It was a mask of grief. The smeared blood looked like carelessly applied rouge. She tried to remove it with a handkerchief, but only a few dried flakes glided weightlessly and noiselessly to the floor.

Father, Mother, you left me nothing but misery, she complained to the spirits of the rice emporium. I'm all alone, with nowhere to turn. What can I do? Am I going to have to marry that disgusting dog, after all?

Exhausted from crying, she fell to her knees and, through her tears, took in the once-familiar sights of the room, now dank and mildewy; she heard the scratchy sound of her withering heart; checkered sun's rays filtered through cracks in the ancient rolled-bamboo curtain at the open window; she shivered from the cold. The coming spring was a sleeping beast that had begun to stir and would eventually swallow her up: a springtime wrapped in cold, a springtime of unending darkness.

The husband swap from one rice-emporium girl to her sister was big news on Brick Mason Avenue. The complexity of the event exceeded the bounds of most people's imagination. Women talked about the rice emporium as they sat on riverside boulders, their faces a study in confusion. Men, on the other hand, gathered at teahouses and wineshops, where the central topic of discussion was Five Dragons. The version that elicited the most laughter came from a blacksmith: His tool is so long and thick it's the envy of any mortal man. The smithy repeated his observation over and over, to underscore its accuracy, and revealed that he and Five Dragons had once compared members with a measuring stick.

One afternoon a gust of wind sent a freshly laundered green bedsheet curling into the air, where it floated proudly above the compound, soared over the wall, and landed in a vat at the dyers. While the apprentice was watching a corner of the sheet soak in blue dye, he noticed traces of an oblong orange stain. The master dyer retrieved the sheet and carried it over to the blacksmith shop. Well aware that it was rice-emporium property, he asked the blacksmith to return it to its owners, with whom he had been feuding for years. Like other people, he believed that female blood brought bad luck.

When Five Dragons came to get the sheet, his face was scarred with a welter of crescent indentations—fingernail marks, by the looks of them. The blacksmiths refused to return his property without a lurid account of how the stain got there. Five Dragons nearly burst with buoyant good feelings; he shook his head and laughed. Cloud Silk bled, he said, to the raucous delight of the blacksmiths. But as he took the sheet from them his eyes underwent a transformation. Like a torch, his gaze swept the men's faces and the street outside. All women are sluts, he said. Just you wait, I'll screw her until just looking at me makes her shudder.

Cloud Silk was not in the shop when Five Dragons returned. Old Wang the clerk said she was taking a bath in the storeroom. There he found the door locked from the inside. But by peeping through a crack he could make out the lacquered date-red bathtub and the shapeless outline of Cloud Silk's bony frame. For days she had done little else but bathe; Five Dragons knew she was trying to purge her body of something. To him the whole idea was ridiculous. And yet the splashing sounds and the reflected glow of her rice surroundings aroused him; he soon had a steely erection. Rice enveloping feminine flesh, or feminine flesh wrapped around rice, always drove him into a state of uncontrollable sexual desire. Open up, open up this minute. He was pounding on the door.

It's broad daylight, now, leave me alone, Cloud Silk shouted from inside. I'm sick of you.

Five Dragons shook the door, until it seemed about to come off its hinges.

Damn you, that's all you think about, day and night. What if Old Wang and the others heard you? But the door was about to crash open. Don't do this to me, you bastard. Reluctantly she stood up, threw on her dress, and opened the door. You really are a bastard, she said. You don't know the meaning of the word *shame*. How can you do this in broad daylight?

Water dripped from her auburn hair and slid down her clinging dress to join watery footprints on the floor. As he closed the door behind him, Five Dragons grabbed his crotch. The crazed look in his eyes horrified Cloud Silk. Get over there and lie down on the rice, he demanded. Instead she tried to push him away. Not now, she screamed. I'm taking a bath, in case you hadn't noticed. So what? he replied, I want it now. You're my wife, and if I feel like screwing the life out of you, that's what I'll do. He wrapped his arms around her waist and carried her to the rice pile. Frantically she clawed at his face. If you do this, I'll kill myself. Five Dragons laughed. Is that a threat or a promise? Screwing my own wife is not against the law, so what would your death accomplish? When I'm finished, you can go hang yourself if you want. I won't stop you. He flung her onto the pile and watched her wet body make a dent in the rice, showering the area with loose grains. Stepping on the shifting rice, he towered over writhing limbs and churning torso. The scene threw him into a frenzy. Infantile moans of passion emerged from his mouth.

As Cloud Silk struggled, Five Dragons once again satisfied his deepest urges. After cramming a handful of raw rice up her vagina, his muscles relaxed, and he rolled onto a neighboring rice pile, where he lazily pulled on his pants, then lay down to crunch rice and listen to her muffled sobs and endless curses—bastard, lousy bastard, no-good bastard. He gazed at the tub. Take another bath, he said, the water's still warm. Feeling contented as never before, he stretched out on his bed of rice. Outside noises grew increasingly distant as he drifted into a realm of serenity.

His surroundings—the rice and the emporium—began to move rhythmically, it seemed, and from far off in the distance came the sound of a whistle. He was back on the train, once again moving slowly down the tracks. Train, where are you taking me?

Cloud Silk's jade bracelet was missing. She dug through her jewelry box and dresser drawers, but it wasn't there. One of a pair her mother had handed down, the other had gone to her sister. At the time Cloud Silk was such a scrawny girl that it kept sliding off her arm. So she hid it in her dresser, where it had lain undisturbed for years. Where, she wondered, could it be?

Did you take my bracelet? Cloud Silk asked Five Dragons through the window. He was standing like a statue in the yard.

Why would I want your bracelet? he replied unhappily. To twirl on my dick? You think you're so mighty, always trying to dump shit on my head.

No need to lose your temper if you didn't do it, she snapped back, not totally convinced. If I didn't know better, I'd say the place was haunted or something, she continued in a softer tone. One day we're missing firewood, the next we run short of rice. I smell a thief.

You'll get a beating if you accuse me of one more thing. He squinted with his good eye and gazed at the sky. As heaven is my witness, all I've ever stolen around here is a couple of stinking cunts. And they were gifts.

Cloud Silk spat at him and slammed the window. The only logical explanation was that Cloud Weave had taken the bracelet with her to the Lu mansion. Jaw-clenching loathing for her sister flowed into Cloud Silk's heart. What right does she have to walk off with my jewelry?

she muttered as she opened her dresser to choose an outfit to wear to the Lu mansion. She would get her bracelet back.

Men were wheeling carts piled high with cardboard boxes through the gate when Cloud Silk reached the Lu mansion. She recognized the black-clad escort: Sixth Master's insolent Wharf Rats, who showed up at the emporium for protection money on the first of every month, like clockwork. A servant rushed up from the garden and nearly knocked Cloud Silk down in his haste to close the gate on her. What kind of chicken-stealing, dog-thieving devil's haunt is this? Is that any way to treat a visitor?

What do you want? the servant asked through the gate. Sixth Master is busy with a shipment. He has no time for women. Hasn't for two weeks.

I came to see Cloud Weave. You know, Sixth Concubine.

Sixth Concubine? The servant wore a contemptuous smile as he opened the gate. Sixth Concubine is out back doing the laundry.

Cloud Silk surveyed the spacious, well-manicured compound, where people were busily moving stuff up and down corridors and in and out of side rooms. Part of Sixth Master's black-market trade, she assumed, but had neither the time nor the interest to confirm her belief. As she headed out back, she was greeted by a shot that rang out behind her left ear; she nearly jumped out of her skin. A little boy in a skullcap and suit climbed down out of a tree and waved a gun in front of her. This is real, he snarled. I'll shoot if I feel like it. She stared at the boy, assuming that it was Sixth Master's son and sole heir. She shook her head and pressed her hands against her breast.

You scared me half to death, Young Master. We've never even met, so why would you want to shoot me?

Cloud Weave was doing laundry at the well, just as the servant had said. When she saw her sister walk slowly out of the shadows, the mallet dropped from her hand. She had grown thin since leaving the rice emporium. Her stringy hair clung to her neck. But what caught Cloud Silk's eye were the jade bracelets, glinting in the sunlight above two very soapy hands.

So you finally decided to come see me. I knew you would, sooner or later. Cloud Weave's eyes reddened, but when she reached out to take her sister's hands, she noticed the angry look: Cloud Silk was glaring at one of the bracelets. Cloud Weave reached down and twirled it instinctively, her head bowed. You didn't come to see me, did you? You want your bracelet back.

Weren't you installed as Sixth Master's sixth concubine? Why are you out here doing laundry? Cloud Silk sat on the edge of the well, looking down at the fancy dresses soaking in a wooden tub.

I just do it sometimes. I can't trust the maid with my silk dresses.

You don't have to save face around me. Cloud Silk smirked. I always said you were not fated to be any man's wife. By being so cheap, you made it easy for them to treat you like cheap goods. I told you not to place your hopes in Sixth Master. He's a wolf. The last thing in the world he wants is for you to have a good life.

Cloud Weave bent down for her mallet, but attacked the laundry with little enthusiasm or vigor. After a moment she looked timidly at Cloud Silk. Is Five Dragons treating you okay?

Don't mention his name. I can't stand to even think about him. You and Father brought him into the house just so I could suffer. Thanks for ruining my life.

I dream about him sometimes. He stuffs rice into me down there. A pained smile floated onto Cloud Weave's face. He's got weird ideas.

I said I don't want to talk about him, and I meant it. Cloud Silk glanced around the deserted yard. All the flower beds could offer were some dead peonies. Sixth Master's arsenal was said to be stored in vaults beneath the flower beds. Someday they could bring death to the entire city. She shivered as she thought of prisoners executed on city streets and people who were found floating in the city moat. Getting down off the well, she squatted beside her sister. Aren't you scared to live here? she asked. Something awful will happen in this yard someday. After all the people Sixth Master has killed and the enemies he's made, doesn't he expect something to happen?

That's their business. We're women, what can we do about it? Cloud Weave dumped some water into the basin. You haven't even asked about my son, she said. Sixth Master showers him with affection. His nanny has him so plump and healthy. He's everybody's favorite. Guess what they named him. Baoyu—Jade Embrace. Isn't that strange? He's my only hope. After he grows up, things will get better for me.

Maybe, maybe not, Cloud Silk said, her eyes fixed on Cloud Weave's soapy hands. She felt pity for her sister. You're so foolish, Cloud Weave. How can you be content to live here like a dog, waiting for your son to grow up? She loosened Cloud Weave's hair and twisted it into a bun on the back of her head. But this only deepened her sadness, and she started to cry. Cloud Weave, how could you and I have come to this? I should pity you, love you. Why would I want to take back my bracelet? Who would I wear it for, anyway? They belonged to Mother, so if you like them, you should have them.

Cloud Silk walked out of the Lu compound weighted down by grief and sorrow. Wrapped in a handkerchief were some pumpkin seeds and walnuts that Cloud Weave had tucked into her hand as she was leaving. Her sister had always liked little snacks, but not her. Pumpkin seeds and walnuts fell to the cobblestones as she passed through North City's grimy lanes, but she didn't bother to pick them up. By the time she reached the muddy river and its forbidding wharf, only an empty white-silk handkerchief remained in her hand.

The wharf was a gathering place for idlers on the lookout for would-be suicides. The men would drag jumpers out of the river and escort them to their homes, where they were usually given a modest reward. On this particular afternoon they saw a slight young woman in a blue cheongsam plunge into the water, a white handkerchief floating gracefully above the surface like a tiny bird. After tossing down a mouthful of rice wine, for luck, the men jumped in after her.

They brought the woman back to solid ground, where one of them flung her over his shoulder and ran until river water gushed from her mouth. It's Cloud Silk, another said when he examined the pale, water-soaked face. I know her. She's the second mistress of the rice emporium over on Brick Mason Avenue.

A SECOND MAJOR FAMINE HIT SOUTH CHINA IN
1930, while far off to the north fierce battles raged.
Refugees and wounded soldiers, their clothes in rags,
jumped off trains with steaming engines and poured
into the city by the river like swarming locusts. One
day on Brick Mason Avenue Five Dragons spotted
two young men who made a living from boxing ex-
hibitions, and he knew from their accents and man-
nerisms that they were from Maple-Poplar Village;
he joined the crowd of spectators, holding his five-
year-old daughter Little Bowl with one hand and
his eight-year-old son Kindling Boy with the other.
The boxers did not recognize Five Dragons, who
tried to guess which clans they likely belonged to;
silently, but with uncommonly powerful emotions,
he watched the demonstration by his fellow villagers,
whose movements were clumsy, primitive even, and
whose faces were a mass of purple welts. The bout
ended with both fighters sprawled on the ground
near a chipped bowl at the spectators' feet. Five
Dragons emptied his pockets of copper coins and
dropped them in the bowl. He stopped himself from
speaking to the young men, although he was
tempted.

You gave them money, Daddy, Kindling Boy said, but you never give me any.

Five Dragons, whose brow was more creased than a young man's ought to be, stood with a distant look on his face and said nothing. Finally he turned and headed home, squeezing the children's hands so hard that Little Bowl kept tripping over her feet and crying, You're hurting me, Daddy!

That afternoon Cloud Silk insisted on closing up shop to celebrate Rice Boy's tenth birthday. So when Five Dragons and the two younger children walked into the front room they found the table covered with an array of tantalizing food, which Rice Boy was cramming into his mouth with both hands as he knelt on a stool. Turning to look fearfully at his father, he let one leg dangle off the edge of the chair. I'm not sneaking food, he said. I'm supposed to see if it's salty enough.

More of your lies. Five Dragons walked up and slapped the back of Rice Boy's head. You're like a little rat that doesn't know when to quit stealing food.

Cloud Silk walked in with two heaping platters. Who are you to teach him manners? You're two peas in a pod, if you ask me. Have you forgotten what you looked like when you first showed up? Well, I haven't. You were the reincarnation of a starving ghost. She banged down the platters. It's our son's birthday, she went on, a happy day. If you want to walk around with a long face, as if everybody owes you something, that's your business. But tell me, just who owes whom in this house?

Five Dragons turned and went into the southern wing, slapping Rice Boy on the way, and sat in a wicker chair to rock back and forth, images of the two boxers in his head. Having wandered so far from home all those event-

ful years ago, he was suddenly overwhelmed by home-
sickness, a feeling so intense it acted like a sedative. But
when he closed his eyes, a vast yet hazy panorama of
floodwaters spread out before him, closing itself around
the rocking chair, around the tiled buildings of the rice
emporium, and around his exhausted body, floating silently and aimlessly. More scenes followed: the paddies of
his youth, the cotton, throngs of famine victims, all moan-
ing in desperation.

The clatter of a dish resounded in the front room, followed by the ear-splitting wails of Little Bowl. Cloud Silk
was ranting, as she usually did when she scolded the children: I told you to quiet down, but you wouldn't listen.
Don't you know it's bad luck to break a rice bowl on a
day like this? You could have broken everything else in
the house, and we'd be better off. But you had to go and
knock the bottom off a rice bowl. She flung the offending
vessel into the yard, where it hit the ground with an ugly
clunk. You're as crazy as your aunt, Cloud Silk said sadly.
The old man in heaven must have gone blind. Why else
would he have given me children who take after everybody in the family except me? What do I have to look
forward to in life with you people around?

Shut your mouth! Five Dragons said as he stormed into
the room, a look of disgust on his face. The only way to
handle a chatterbox like you is to stuff a cock into your
mouth. Bitch and moan, that's all you ever do. Well I've
had all I can take.

You've had all *you* can take? What about me? I'm busy
from sunup to sundown, but you sit around doing nothing. Cloud Silk removed her apron and rubbed some ashes
off her face. Why don't you just pass up dinner, she said
angrily, and lie down to think more of those crazy

thoughts of yours? All you ever do is scowl. With all those notions in your belly, I'm surprised you have room for food.

She stopped in midthought, as if struck dumb. For there, walking into the yard, carrying a cloth bundle, was Cloud Weave. She had come home for Rice Boy's birthday. She was alone.

Where's Jade Embrace?

He didn't want to come. He's such a strange boy. He hates going out. Cloud Weave, her face heavily rouged, her green velvet cheongsam reeking of mothballs, looked around the compound, vacant, tentative.

Won't he do as you say? Cloud Silk asked. It doesn't matter to me, but the children have been asking to see him. He's the only kin they've got, after all.

Ignoring the comment, Cloud Weave walked inside and sat down to open her bundle. Out came a ball of peach-colored yarn, which she placed on the table. It, too, reeked of mothballs and was darker than it should have been. This is for Rice Boy, she said. Knit him a sweater, and consider it a gift from his aunt.

A single glance told Cloud Silk that it was yet another item Cloud Weave had taken when she left. For years it had lain at the bottom of their mother's trunk. You shouldn't have gone to so much trouble, Cloud Silk remarked, unable to pass up a chance for sarcasm. It's a wonder moths haven't claimed it, after all the years you've held on to it.

Embarrassed, Cloud Weave smiled weakly as she hugged the children and planted a kiss on each little cheek. Where's Five Dragons? Shouldn't the birthday boy's daddy be here running the show?

Him? He's dead! Cloud Silk turned up the volume.

Five Dragons coughed, but stayed in his room. Not until the lamps were lit and the children emerged from the kitchen carrying a bowl of longevity noodles for Rice Boy did Five Dragons make an appearance. Ignoring Cloud Weave, who turned her back on him, he chatted away with Cloud Silk; muted, dispirited slurping sounds set the tone around the table, as the rice-emporium family shared Rice Boy's longevity noodles in the dim lamplight. The birthday boy, having been slapped by his father, looked just like another gloomy adult. It was his tenth birthday, and he couldn't have been more unhappy. Meanwhile, his brother and sister were spilling soupy noodles all over the table, keeping Cloud Silk busy mopping up after them.

I saw Jade Embrace a few days ago, Five Dragons said without looking up from his food. The comment was clearly meant for Cloud Weave's ears. He was out taking a walk, like any other little mutt. He doesn't look a thing like Sixth Master. I think he takes after Abao, even in the cocky way he walks. I'm betting our little Jade Embrace grew from Abao's seed.

Cloud Weave put down her bowl and chopsticks and paled noticeably. Glaring at Five Dragons's greasy lips, she picked up her bowl and flung the remaining noodles in his face. Liar! she screamed hysterically. Stop spouting that shit.

Pandemonium broke out among the terrified children, who were incapable of understanding this sudden, violent confrontation. Five Dragons, the epitome of self-control, wiped the noodles from his face. Don't get yourself in an uproar, he said. I won't tell Sixth Master. It's just a reminder not to confuse the false with the real. Take me, for instance. The me in this shop is false. The real me is steeping in the floodwaters of Maple-Poplar Village. Which means *I'm* not real.

Your head is filled with crazy notions, and I won't listen to them anymore, Cloud Weave said hoarsely. My life's bitter enough as it is. The next person who tries to take advantage of me will see what I'm made of.

Rice Boy's tenth birthday broke up in disarray, with the children going outside to play and Five Dragons taking Proprietor Feng's purple-fired teapot over to the blacksmith shop across the street. For years he had maintained an amicable relationship with the rough-hewn blacksmiths, who were his only friends on Brick Mason Avenue. Cloud Silk hurled curses at his retreating back: Why not live out your life at the blacksmith shop? There's no need to come home—ever. Her fingers flew as she cleaned off the table, driven by anger and resentment. I don't know how I've made it this far, she remarked to Cloud Weave. Rice Boy is ten years old already.

After washing up, Cloud Weave reapplied her makeup, until the woman in the mirror was again red-lipped and nicely powdered. But crow's feet at the corners of her eyes were an unmistakable sign of a woman whose beauty was on the decline. She touched the reflection of scarlet lips with her fingertips. How old am I? she asked. I don't even know my own age. I must be in my thirties.

You're a girl of eighteen, Cloud Silk remarked, drawing out the words to ridicule her sister. Plenty of time left for you to marry three more men.

This stinks. Being a woman really stinks. Cloud Weave followed Cloud Silk into the kitchen to do the dishes. There she informed her sister of late-night visits to the Lu mansion by a ghost. Her disjointed tale revealed that while she herself had never seen it, the domestic help talked about it in whispered conversations. Cloud Silk, her interest growing with every sentence, kept interrupting so as not to miss any details. Her white-faced sister ended the revelation with the most important detail: The ghost bore a striking resemblance to Abao.

They say it looks just like him. Terror crept into Cloud Weave's eyes. But how could it? she wondered aloud. Sixth Master sent Abao to the bottom of the river to feed the fish long ago.

Didn't you say you never actually saw the body? Maybe he's not dead, after all. Maybe he visits the Lu mansion for revenge. If so, that's bad news for all of you.

No, Cloud Weave replied with an insistent shaking of her head. I'll tell you something you don't know. They lopped off his you-know-what at the time, so even if he wasn't dead then, he sure would be by now. I know enough about men to assure you that they can't live without their you-know-whats.

Then it must be Abao's avenging spirit, which is the same thing. Cloud Silk was unable to hide her smug satisfaction over Cloud Weave's dilemma. After a lifetime of tyranny, she said, it's time Sixth Master got what was coming to him. I say let the ghost do its business and bring down the whole family. What right does he have to dine on delicacies while other people have to make do with chaff and wild grass?

You're awfully spiteful, Cloud Weave said unhappily. You're talking about my new family now, which includes Jade Embrace. If anything bad happened at the Lu mansion, we'd suffer right along with the rest of them. And that would have an effect on business here.

Are you saying that Sixth Master has become our patron? Cloud Silk laughed; the dishes in her hands clattered. A dog-shit patron! Why should he give a damn about us when he doesn't even worry about you? The Wharf Rats come for their protection money every month, without fail, even though he knows that the shop belonged to your father.

Cloud Weave stood in the kitchen a while longer, feeling awkward, then went out into the night. Simple reminders of a carefree childhood saddened her unbearably. So without even saying good-bye, she picked up her bundle and left. Her visits always ended unhappily. Maybe the enmity between sisters was too deep ever to be resolved.

Out on the street she saw Five Dragons leaving the blacksmith shop. Instinctively she turned her face and pretended she hadn't seen him. Clutching her empty cloth bundle, she had taken only a few steps when he shouted out, Be very very careful. She spun around. What's that supposed to mean? What should I be careful of? With one leg propped up against the wall, he grinned. Ghosts, of course, especially Abao's!

You're the ghost around here, Cloud Weave said weakly. How, she wondered, had he learned this secret? The Lu family lived a life of excess behind high walls, ever the envy of Brick Mason Avenue residents, who delighted in spreading stories of what went on in the forbidden inner sanctum. She took comfort in that, and with her vanity soothed somewhat, the spring in her step returned. She walked home feeling quite smug.

Over the years, subtle changes had come to the shops lining Brick Mason Avenue: people still observed the late-night comings and goings, but the young clerks who now watched the graceful passage of Cloud Weave had no idea who she was.

The three children who lived in the rice emporium often played hide-and-seek in the dusty northern wing, which had gone unused for years, following the departure of its former occupants—the maternal grandparents whose portraits stood atop a bulky, black-lacquered trunk. They gazed out through the dimness of yellowing glass picture frames at future generations of Fengs. None of the children had ever seen either of the deceased elders in the flesh; thus the concept of death usually held no reality for them at all, while at other times it scared them out of their wits.

Rice Boy was hiding under his grandfather's redwood bed one day, making himself as small as possible, when his hand bumped into the damp, moldy wall, and one of the ancient bricks fell to the floor. He reached into the hole and removed a small wooden box and a little book.

After crawling out from under the bed, he impatiently opened the box. Gold objects shone in the weak light. He immediately summoned Kindling Boy and Little Bowl. Know what this is? It's gold. That's enough hide-and-seek, he said. Let's take this stuff to the store and trade it for candy. But don't tell Mommy or Daddy. It'll be our secret. Kindling Boy asked, How much candy can we get from this little bit of stuff? Lots, Rice Boy said as he replaced the lid and hugged the box to his chest. I'll let you two split half, but don't ever tell Mommy and Daddy. Little Bowl, meanwhile was flipping through the thread-sewn book. The paper, old and brittle, crackled. What's this? she asked. There's writing. Rice Boy snatched it out of her hands and flipped it under the bed. Just a book, he said. It's worthless.

The children sneaked out of the compound and went straight to the Brick Mason Avenue grocery store, where Rice Boy stood on his tiptoes and laid the wooden box on the counter. There's gold inside, he informed the owner, and I know it's the same as money. We want lots and lots of candy. A surprise awaited the woman when she opened the box, and it took time for her to sufficiently regain her composure and walk out from behind the counter to close the door. I'll give you a great big bag of candy if you promise not to tell any grown-ups, she said in a hushed voice. Promise? An irritated Rice Boy said, I won't tell anybody, and they wouldn't dare. They know I'd beat them to a pulp. So let's have it. The woman looked warily at each child before going back behind the counter and taking out a large bag of candy, which she thrust into Rice Boy's outstretched arms.

Over the next several days, the three rice-emporium children went around sucking on hard candies from early in the morning to late at night. Rice Boy even took candy to school to trade for slingshots, marbles, and cigarette boxes. The adults were too busy taking care of business to notice their children's odd behavior. But then one day Little Bowl broke a teacup, and when she was being scolded by Cloud Silk, she tearfully pleaded her case: You always scream at me. How come you never scream at Rice Boy? He stole the family's gold and traded it for candy.

Cloud Silk reacted as if thunderstruck. Her first thought after regaining her composure and learning what had happened was to go see the proprietress of the grocery store, gathering quite an audience as she cursed the owner; a few people even elbowed their way inside to get a better look. Back and forth the shouting went, each outburst bringing the spectators that much closer to learning the whole story. Everyone within earshot agreed that the rice-emporium family was playing a cruel joke on itself. At last they saw the grocery-store proprietress toss a little wooden box onto the counter; Cloud Silk's back blocked their view as she inventoried the contents. When she looked up she hissed through clenched teeth, A pair of earrings is missing. But keep them if you want them so badly. You can count it as a coffin gift.

Rice Boy knew something was wrong as soon as he stepped in the door after school that day. But by then it was too late to turn and run. Five Dragons grabbed his frail little body and had him hog-tied in no time. The next thing he knew he was hanging from a rafter in the back room, twisting painfully in the air, as his father stood below, a murderous glint in his eyes and a thick carrying pole in his hand. Kindling Boy and Little Bowl cowered behind their father and looked up at Rice Boy. Who squealed? he shouted furiously as he began to twist and squirm. Who let the secret out? He saw his sister cringe and run to her mother. I didn't tell anybody, his brother whimpered. Don't look at me.

Cloud Silk was sitting in the dim light of a corner, pale quivering lips the only sign of movement. Suddenly she pushed her daughter away and stood up. Beat him! she snarled. You can kill him for all I care. I don't want him anymore.

Rice Boy saw his father's pole slice through the air toward him, menacingly cold, whistling. At first he bore the pain stoically, saying over and over: I'll kill you, Little Bowl. Then he passed out. The dull thud of the pole against his body, like shifting sand, faded until he could no longer sense it. He was punished often, but this beating was special, and when he came to, he was lying in bed, with his mother sitting beside him sewing cloth shoe soles under the lamp, her eyes red and swollen. She came up and wrapped her arms around his head, sobbing as she said, How could you be so stupid? The gold in that box is what keeps this family from the poorhouse. How could you trade it for candy? Tears flowed from Rice Boy's eyes, too, but he squirmed out of her embrace and stared through holes in the canopy, directly at a little bed at the other end of the room. It was where Kindling Boy and Little Bowl slept. Rice Boy said, Little Bowl let the secret out, and she promised she wouldn't. She didn't keep her word, and I'm going to kill her.

Rice Boy was ten, and his need for vengeance was abnormally keen. In this he was the image of his father. He was determined to avenge himself against his sister no matter how long it took.

He watched Little Bowl's braid sway and leap as she jumped rope in the yard, the incident of a few days earlier apparently forgotten. Big Brother, she shouted, want to jump rope with me? He was standing in the storeroom doorway staring darkly at her dirty, snotty little face. He shook his head. I don't feel like it. I've got a better idea. Let's play here on the rice pile. Little Bowl jump-roped her way across the yard, but the look of raw ferocity in his eyes, reminiscent of their father, frightened her. You won't hit me, will you? Again he shook his head. No, I won't hit you. Come on, let's play hide-and-seek in the rice.

Holding his sister's hand, Rice Boy crawled to the top of the pile, where he pushed her deep into the rice. You

hide in here, he said, and don't make a sound. I'll get
Kindling Boy to find you. But he won't be able to, nobody
will, he said, winded from all the effort. Not even Mommy
and Daddy. Obediently, she scrunched way down, until
all that showed above the rice were her little face and her
braid, which stood straight up. Hurry up, she said. I can't
breathe in here. If he can see your face it'll be too easy,
Rice Boy said as he picked up a half-full sack of rice and
poured its contents over Little Bowl's head. He watched
the snowy white kernels quickly cover her face and braid.
For a moment the surface of the rice shifted and created
little sink-holes—signs of Little Bowl's feeble struggles—
but all movement stopped before long, and the storeroom
was eerily quiet.

Rice Boy knew exactly what he had done, and how
serious it was, but he had already figured out what to do.
First he bolted the storeroom door from the outside, then
he ran out of the compound with his schoolbag. As he
passed the shop, he saw his father and a couple of the
clerks weighing out rice for some men in military uniforms; Mother was sitting behind the counter knitting a
sweater from peach-colored yarn. It was for him, he knew,
and he couldn't bear the thought of wearing it.

That afternoon Five Dragons and Old Wang went out
to move some rice into the shop. No more than a few
spadefuls had been removed from the pile when a tiny
braid tied with a red ribbon poked up through the top.
A little avalanche of rice revealed Little Bowl's coiled
body, which then tumbled to the floor. Her face was a
hideous purple. Five Dragons picked her up and put his
finger under her nose—not a breath of air. He saw she
was clutching a jump rope.

This staggering tragedy nearly sent Cloud Silk over the

edge. Through strength of will she had forced herself to bear up under everything else, but now the facade crumbled. Cradling her daughter's icy body in her arms, she sat in the doorway waiting for Rice Boy to return from school; none of the neighbors knew of Little Bowl's death, so they naturally assumed that she was ill, and that her mother was sunning her; they did not hear her weep.

But there was no sign of Rice Boy. Two days later Five Dragons placed Little Bowl's body in a flimsy, hastily constructed coffin. As he was nailing the lid shut, Old Wang came up and told him he had seen Rice Boy down at the wharf, eating a rotten orange. When I called to him, he threw a rock at me and ran away. Cloud Silk walked up and pounded on the coffin lid. Get him and bring him back, she shrieked between sobs. I want him sleeping alongside Little Bowl. Get rid of both of them at the same time. And throw in Kindling Boy while you're at it. I don't want any of them. I won't suffer over you people any longer.

Five Dragons spat the nails in his mouth into his hand and glowered at his wife. What are you screaming about, you heartless bitch? Let's make it a clean sweep and send you along, too! I'll personally nail the coffins shut.

Eventually Five Dragons nabbed his son, who was fast asleep in an empty oil barrel, his face so black and oily he barely looked human. Five Dragons studied his son's features. You take after me, that's for sure, he said. But how could you think of murder at your young age? How could you bury your own sister alive?

Breaking Rice Boy's leg was Cloud Silk's idea. For the second time in only a few days, Rice Boy hung from a rafter. But this time, Cloud Silk shouted tearfully, Beat him, cripple him. Teach him a lesson he won't soon forget. Five Dragons picked up his oily carrying pole. Remember, you said it. If he wants revenge one day, he'll come looking for you. Cloud Silk shuddered, then turned her face away and said with a low sob, Go ahead, do it while I'm not looking. Yet even cupping her hands over her ears, she still heard Rice Boy's agonizing screams and the *crack* when his leg snapped, sounds that would later haunt her in her dreams.

Rice Boy was bedridden for a full month. Then one day the family watched nervously as he took his first feeble steps; now he was a true and permanent cripple.

Cloud Weave made a rare trip home to pay rather perfunctory condolences. There she and her sister sat in armchairs conversing stiffly and listening to the occasional bickering emerging from the shop. They had nothing to say to one another. Cloud Weave's thoughts drifted to recollections of Little Bowl, with her hearty pink face and lustrous black eyes, then shifted to the backyard at the Lu mansion and the ghost that frequented the place. One night, she said, she heard rustling sounds outside her bedroom window, and when she threw open the shutter, she saw the specter—all in black—walking toward the peony beds.

It was Abao. I actually saw him. Fear showed in her bulging eyes. He looked the same as when he was alive. He even swaggered the same way.

Cloud Silk hadn't heard a word. Her barren gaze rested on Cloud Weave's moist, reddened lips, as she continued to dwell in her private grief.

They said he was flesh and blood, not a ghost, an avenging Abao coming after Sixth Master. But I don't think so. Remember, I saw his severed you-know-what. That means he has to be dead.

That's enough, Cloud Silk broke in. I don't want to hear any more.

Maybe Abao was saved by some magic spirit. Cloud Weave fumbled with the jade bracelet on her wrist. Sixth Master won't sleep at night without half a dozen servants around his bed. Everybody but me is scared to death. Abao and I had feelings for each other. He might go after the others, but not me.

You're exactly who he'd go after, Cloud Silk said hatefully. **You are the source of this family's misfortunes.** If not for you, I wouldn't have fallen so low that life is meaningless and death an impossibility. I've even run out of tears.

Cloud Weave was used to hearing her sister complain about the past, but this time it was different. She could take it no longer. With searing anger in her eyes, she flicked her sleeves back and swept out of the room, muttering, I'll never darken your ratty door again. I'm through letting you take your frustrations out on me. Well water and river water don't mix. I no longer have a sister, and don't you dare come asking me for anything. She walked into the shop, where Five Dragons blocked her way. What's the hurry? he asked. Why not stay for dinner? His fingers glided over to pinch one of her nipples. She slapped him. You bastard! Flirting with me at a time like this. What kind of man are you?

Once again, Cloud Weave left in a sorrowful mood. And an oath made in anger would prove to be prophetic: She would never return to the rice emporium on Brick Mason Avenue. For years she had lived a cloistered life in the Lu mansion, her youth floating out of the walled compound like a scrap of paper. Everyone on Brick Mason Avenue knew she had become Sixth Master's sixth concubine, but none could have imagined the demeaned existence she led in his home, none knew of the pipe dreams that formed her future or the humiliation that composed her present. Only Cloud Silk knew how despised she was by the others in the mansion, high and low. She learned that Jade Embrace even refused to call Cloud Weave Mother.

Several days later the residents of North City were jolted awake by a series of explosions that shattered the midnight stillness with heavy rumbles and loud pops. Coats draped over their shoulders, men rushed outside to look northward, where the pink sky framed an enormous column of smoke. Faint smells of sulfur and charred metal hung in the air. Everyone assumed that whatever it was, it involved the Lu family, that something momentous had occurred at the mansion.

News of the explosions spread quickly up and down Brick Mason Avenue. An eyewitness reported that someone had blown up the arsenal in the backyard, at least half of which was destroyed by the blast. Many died; the survivors piled into a truck to be driven to the train station. Five Dragons stood in the crowd. Who else got out alive? he shouted. The man, an apprentice tanner who knew all about Five Dragons's relationship with the Lu family, said, Not a hair on Sixth Master's head was singed. He was standing on the truck shouting and giving orders. And, of course, Jade Embrace, he got out fine. But I didn't see Cloud Weave. Maybe she died in the blast, the man surmised. Do you know who did it? Five Dragons asked him. The apprentice hesitated, then replied uncertainly, People say it was Abao, but he's been dead ten years, so that's impossible, isn't it? Could it have been Abao's ghost? No, that's impossible, too. A ghost can't blow up an arsenal. The apprentice knitted his brow in what passed for deep thought. Finally he announced to the gathering, I think there's something strange about all this.

By the time Five Dragons and Cloud Silk had rushed over to the Lu mansion, the dead had been removed to a makeshift outdoor morgue. The compound, once a show-case of the family's wealth and status, was now little more than a pile of rubble. Trees and shrubs had been incin-erated; as Cloud Silk walked numbly through the debris, she spotted something green and shiny on the ground. She gasped: a jade bracelet! As she picked it out of the rubble her face turned white. The bracelet, once hers, was singed in places; she wiped it clean with her sleeve; tears wet her cheeks. I knew Cloud Weave would die tragically, she sobbed, but I never thought it would be this bad. She didn't deserve it. With his foot, Five Dragons sent a piece of steel pipe flying. It was, he saw, a rifle barrel, so he chased it down. We all have to die sometime, tragically or not, he said, so what are you crying for? Cloud Weave's lucky she doesn't have to worry anymore.

Cloud Silk slipped the jade bracelet onto her wrist, but quickly took it off—somehow it seemed unlucky—and wrapped it in a handkerchief. That was when she heard Five Dragons ask from far off, Do you know who did this?

They say it was Abao, that he's still alive.

Would you believe me if I said it was me?

Cloud Silk stared at him, speechless. He was sitting cross-legged on the only stone bench left standing in the yard, fiddling with the rifle barrel. He looked like a little boy who's been caught in a lie and a vicious killer at the same time. Cloud Silk stared at him for a long moment. I believe you. If anyone's capable of something like this, it's you.

While Cloud Silk was cleaning out the northern bedroom—her father's room—she found the family genealogy under the bed. The paper was still damp from the moist air, the pages of family history mildewed and water-stained. As she flipped through the book, the names of Feng ancestors crawled and wriggled past her eyes, until she reached the last one—her father. Obviously no one had bothered to record her generation in the genealogy; probably he had seen no need to continue the history. The empty pages at the end of the book immersed her in a chilling sadness. She laid the book on the windowsill to dry out, suddenly caught up in a desire to bring the history up to date.

The following day the local grade-school teacher appeared at the emporium, as requested, bringing with him a writing brush and some calligraphy paper. She waited until he had finished a bowl of date-and-lotus-seed soup, then sat down to watch him mix ink on an antique clay inkslab, after which he flipped through the genealogy, with its fifty-three generations of the Feng clan, and asked the question: Since there are no male descendants, what shall I enter for the fifty-fourth generation? After a thoughtful pause, she replied, I guess we'll have to let the no-good bastard keep the Feng line going. Write Five Dragons Feng under my father's name. For better or worse, he's a man, and since you can't put my name in there, it will have to be his. As the teacher was writing, he heard Cloud Silk sigh remorsefully.

The fifty-fifth Feng generation was easier: Rice Boy and

Kindling Boy. But below the entry for Rice Boy Feng the teacher added a footnote: one crippled leg as punishment from his father. He knew Five Dragons couldn't read, so there was no reason to be apprehensive. For a moment he thought about telling Cloud Silk what he had done, but then he heard rapid footsteps out in the yard, and knew that Five Dragons had come home.

Cloud Silk watched Five Dragons slip into the storeroom dragging two empty rice baskets behind him; she followed him in. There's plenty of rice in the shop, we don't need any more. But he kept pouring rice into the baskets. The Wharf Rats have a new leader, he said, and they'll let me join if I give them a bushel of rice. I won't allow you to take my rice! Cloud Silk protested. You can go into the mountains and become a bandit for all I care, but I will not allow you to take my rice. Five Dragons ignored her, and once the baskets were filled, he hoisted them onto his shoulder with the carrying pole. Cloud Silk grabbed one of the baskets and held on desperately, cursing over and over, You spendthrift bastard, three meals a day isn't enough for you. Now you want to give food away. I said I forbid you from taking a single grain of rice out of this compound! Five Dragons laid down his load, picked up his carrying pole in both hands, and glared at her with white-hot loathing. I've told you to stay out of my way. I'll do as I please, and you won't try to stop me, if you know what's good for you. With that he swung his pole in the air and brought it down hard on her hand, then picked up his load and strode out of the compound, leaving Cloud Silk crying on the ground. He bounced as he walked.

The grade-school teacher had witnessed the entire episode through the window. So once Five Dragons was safely out of the compound, he sat down at the table, reopened the revised family genealogy, and drew a question mark beneath the fifty-fourth-generation entry of Five Dragons Feng. Then he added a footnote in the right-hand margin: Member of the Wharf Rats.

9

AS FIVE DRAGONS ENTERED THE PRIME OF HIS LIFE AND gained a reputation up and down Brick Mason Avenue as a local tyrant, the rice emporium no longer held the appeal of "home" for him. Together with the Wharf Rats, he spent most of his time in bars and whorehouses in South City or at hangouts belonging to other gangs; he had managed to fulfill the fantasies of all Maple-Poplar Village men in a strange and distant land. Yet even in bars, Five Dragons, still a teetotaler, preferred the coarsest, bitterest tea he could find. Whoring was his great pleasure. And wherever he went he carried a small cloth bag filled with raw rice; at the critical moment, he would take out a handful and cram it inside the woman. Talk of this vile obsession spread among South City prostitutes, who condemned his low-class, uncouth ways; his cruel little rice trick demeaned their bodies.

One day, as he was lounging in a whorehouse, surrounded by music from an array of instruments and recalling how he had turned a bushel of rice into a life of prosperity, he babbled along, utterly distracted by thoughts of the past. Revenge was usually his favorite topic of conversation, especially all the different ways it could be exacted. As he sipped thick, blackish tea, he said, You don't need a knife or a gun to get revenge. You don't even have to kill with your own hands. There are times when vengeance requires calling in ghosts and spirits. Have you heard how Sixth Master was driven away by a ghost? With a glint in his good eye, he gazed at the prostitutes seated around him, then stuck the grip of his pistol under the chin of one of the younger ones and raised her head. Know who that ghost was? Me. It was me, Five Dragons.

Then one drizzly morning, as he and two fellow gang members were passing a dental clinic, his attention was caught by a set of gold teeth and a pair of chrome-plated tweezers on an enamel tray in the window. A wild idea popped into his head. I want new teeth, he announced as he opened the door and walked in.

Toothache, Master Dragons? asked the local dentist with an ingratiating smile.

No, I want a new set of teeth. Five Dragons sat down in the swivel chair and spun around—once, twice—before pointing to the gold teeth in the shop window and saying, Pull mine and put in those gold ones.

The dentist looked into Five Dragons's mouth. Your teeth are fine, Master Dragons. Why pull teeth that are still good?

Because I want the gold ones, that's why. Now do as I say. He spun around with irritation. You're not afraid you won't get paid, are you? No? Then get to work.

All of them? The dentist walked around the chair to study the expression on Five Dragons's face.

Yank them all, and put in the gold ones. Five Dragons's tone of voice left no room for argument.

I can't replace them right away. You have to wait at least two weeks after your real teeth are pulled.

Two weeks? Too long. Five days. Five Dragons grew

thoughtful for a moment, then clapped his hands and said with perverse determination, Come on, let's get on with it.

It's going to hurt, Master Dragons, even with an anesthetic, the dentist said as he readied his tools and picked up a little hammer. I have to knock them out one at a time with this. The pain is indescribable.

You don't have a very high opinion of Five Dragons, he said as he leaned back in the chair and closed his eyes. With a slight grin, he added, I'm no stranger to suffering. I'll pay you double if I make a sound, how's that? I'm a man of my word.

Full-mouth extraction was a long, drawn-out, monotonous process. His two companions waited patiently outside, listening to the thumps and clangs emerging from the clinic as the dentist extracted every one of Five Dragons's natural teeth with hammer and pliers. Yet not a single groan from the patient, as promised.

Blood filled Five Dragons's mouth as he floated in a sea of exquisite pain, dimly aware of his Maple-Poplar Village home, which was engulfed in water. Puny rice shoots and withered cotton plants were swept by as pitiful, desperate villagers ran along the water's edge, their hopes for a bountiful harvest shattered. He even saw himself, ragged bundle over his back, fleeing in panic, two muddy feet stumbling down a dark refugee road. All I ever see are corpses—the dead man by the railroad tracks, the rice-choked child who fell out of the sack. Why don't I see familiar faces, like those of my children? A large, turbid tear oozed unsummoned from the corner of his eye. He tried to reach up for it, but his hands were bound. Does it hurt? I told you it would. The dentist paused to observe the progress of the solitary tear; Five Dragons shook his head and shut his eyes, then swallowed a mouthful of blood; with great difficulty, he spat out a single, mystifying word: Pity.

Several days later Five Dragons stood in front of a dental-clinic mirror admiring his new gold teeth. Once sallow cheeks glowed with renewed vigor. Rubbing the teeth lightly with his finger, he turned to the dentist and said, Perfect. Back in Maple-Poplar Village this was the stuff of dreams.

Once again a light rain fell, so his companions held an oilpaper umbrella over his head. In spite of the dentist's admonition to avoid talking until the new teeth were firmly anchored, Five Dragons would not be put off. Know why I wanted gold teeth? I'm not one to throw money around just to impress people, as you know, so why spend so much on a set of gold teeth? The men exchanged glances, but did not dare guess, since they invariably misinterpreted Five Dragons's behavior. It's simple, he said. When I was poor, people treated me like a subhuman. But from now on my gold teeth will do the talking, and it'll be the speech of a man.

The dentist came running up just then, and thrust a paper packet into Five Dragons's hand. Here, take your real teeth. They were a gift from your parents, so you should keep them.

Five Dragons opened the packet and looked at the snowy white teeth with their bloody roots. These are my real teeth? He picked one out, held it high, and gazed at it fixedly for a long moment before, unexpectedly, flinging it away. Real teeth? Hah! They're false. Why? Because anything I throw away is false. They may have chewed on grains, munched on greens, and chattered in the dead of winter, but I don't want them. To hell with you all!

he shouted like a little boy as he flung the packet at a nearby trash bin. Go on, to hell with you all!

Few people were out on the slick streets that day, and those who were willing to brave the weather showed little interest in the strange objects gleaming white in the rain. Five Dragons's discarded teeth lay in disarray in puddles, in a muddy ditch, and all around the trash bin.

A light rain had been falling for some time, yet the sun persisted stubbornly, even through the heavy mist, and managed to warm Brick Mason Avenue. Once the long, meandering cobblestone road was washed clean, it turned sober and dark. The plum rains—those late-spring drizzles common to the South—were on their way.

Rice Boy grew fidgety with the advent of the rainy season; moss growing in a frenzy at the base of the wall seemed to climb up his twisted left leg to cover his grim spirits. He entered the shop, dragging his crippled leg along, and from there hobbled out into the yard; the women of the family were playing mah-jongg in the back room. Not surprisingly, Mother's habitual complaints filled the space above the board. At the moment she was inveighing against her lack of luck at the table. Why do no decent tiles ever stick to my hand? Nothing comes easy for me. I was born under an unlucky star. On and on she complained. This is the last time I'm ever playing this game.

Rice Boy's wife, Snow Talent, was keeping her mother-in-law company, since she herself wasn't much of a player. It had taken Rice Boy two years of married life to realize that his wife was a clever, quick-witted woman who had a disposition he found loathsome. In large measure their relationship was based upon a misunderstanding: Two years earlier, as she stood in the gateway selling magnolia blossoms, Rice Boy naively assumed she was a timid girl, one to be pitied, a flower peddler whose rosy cheeks and dark, sad eyes made his heart race. She reminded him of his dead sister, Little Bowl, and he was smitten. So he scooped a handful of magnolia blossoms out of her basket, tossed them onto the shop counter, and handed her some coins from his pocket, letting his hand linger on hers as he did so. You look like Little Bowl, he said. She was five when she died. Her brother suffocated her. At the time, Snow Talent failed to catch his drift, but there was no denying the look of affection in his eyes, and she sensed at that moment that someday she would marry into this well-to-do family of rice merchants.

I'm short of money, Rice Boy, Snow Talent shouted from inside. I'm losing.

Then stop playing. Enough's enough. Standing beneath an overhanging eave, he looked skyward through the curtain of rain and mist. He was not in a good mood.

Why so glum? Snow Talent asked. Just because I've lost a little money? She studied his face. I'm keeping Mother company, trying to make her happy.

Who cares about you and your pious good deeds? Tell me, is she happy? My mother doesn't know the meaning of the word. Once you're in her debt, you can forget about ever clearing the slate. Rice Boy glared at his wife. Why not spend a little time trying to make *me* happy? On a rainy day like this, you could lie down with me for a change.

Snow Talent laughed and tweaked his ear playfully, then headed back to the tableful of people waiting impatiently for her. Kindling Boy's bride, Redolence, was drumming a tile on the table. Well? she asked. Did you get it? No, he didn't have any. But I'll see if there's some behind the counter, all right? She looked at Cloud Silk for a reaction. Don't you dare touch the money behind the counter, her mother-in-law said. That's one of the rules of the shop. I told you that a long time ago. Snow Talent slipped into her chair. Then I'll have to play on credit, she said. Once again tiles clicked across the table-top. The fourth player was a woman who ran a bamboo crafts shop. Your husband has always been a tightwad, Cloud Silk remarked. Don't waste your time waiting for some money to slip through his fingers. I've raised two worthless sons. Rice Boy will do anything to keep from spending money, Kindling Boy spends all his time stuffing his face and having a good time, no matter how much it costs. The shop would go out of business within days if I had to rely on those two.

Rice Boy, who overheard every word his mother said, cursed under his breath and swept his hand across the windowsill, knocking a ceramic vase to the floor and send-ing a hush across the room, broken only by the clacking of mah-jongg tiles. He went to his room, head down and dragging his crippled left leg along, the sound of his moth-er's complaints rattling around inside his ears. It was a sound he had grown up with, ever since the time he had done that terrible thing as a ten-year-old. But there was more to it than what had befallen Little Bowl. He was convinced that a core of darkness lay at the center of his family, darkness that thrived in an atmosphere of anger and insult.

In a flash the atmosphere inside the room grew tense and confrontational; as the four women mechanically scooped up tiles, the level of hostility rose. After a while Redolence pushed her tile rack away and complained, If you don't have any money, why not just quit? This is no way to play. Snow Talent's face reddened. I pay my debts, she said with a quick glance at the others. Why do you have to be so picky with a member of your own family? But by then Redolence was already on her feet. You've got it wrong, she said with a contemptuous snort. Don't you know the saying, Never give an IOU to your own brother? I believe in being honest. I hate things that aren't black and white, straightforward and clear. Snow Talent's face paled as she took out an embroidered coin purse, removed a bill, and flung it at Redolence. You'd actually question your own sister-in-law's character over that little bit of money? Snow Talent looked over at her mother-in-law. I was just keeping you company, she said on her way out. For that I go into debt and get ridiculed at the same time. Who needs it!

Rice Boy was sitting on the bed playing his harmonica when Snow Talent stormed into the room and slammed the door behind her. She was biting her lip, clearly about to cry.

Just because you're mad at somebody doesn't give you the right to slam my door.

She's the most calculating bitch I've ever known. Snow Talent sat down beside Rice Boy and directed her loud comment to the window, so everyone could hear. Who does she think she is, lording it over others because her family owns a coffin shop and makes a living off a bunch of dead people?

Had a blowup, did you? Rice Boy smacked his harmonica against the palm of his hand to clear out the spit. Good, I'm glad. That should make everybody happy.

To say that Rice Boy played the harmonica badly is an understatement. He seemed to be trying to test the limits of everyone's endurance, including his own. Stop that before I go deaf. Snow Talent tried to snatch the harmonica from him, but he pushed her hand away and directed his atonal squawks to the yard, then listened as Mother came running up fuming. Stop that maddening noise. It'll kill me one of these days. Finally he put down his harmonica and announced to the window, I don't like the sound any better than you do, but a little noise once in a while might breathe some life into this dead compound.

On average Five Dragons returned to the rice emporium once a week to take a look around, rest briefly on the rice in the storeroom, and eat dinner with his family. His appetite, like his general health, was on the decline, but his fondness for rice was undiminished. Invariably, when he had finished eating and was picking his teeth, he examined the others' rice bowls. Not long after coming into the family, Redolence drew a malignant stare from her father-in-law, and when she asked Kindling Boy why his father was so obsessed with her bowl, Five Dragons flew into a rage. Lick your bowl clean, he said darkly. Every grain.

Redolence didn't know whether to laugh or to cry. As the daughter of the coffinmaker from South City, she was used to being pampered, and during her early days at the rice emporium, looked disdainfully upon her surroundings, holding the other family members in contempt; that included her husband, on whose profligate ways marriage seemed to have no effect. Day in and day out he roamed the streets, cricket jar in hand, looking for worthy opponents for his pride and joy—the king of fighting crickets, to hear him tell it. He kept an assortment of clay and sandstone cricket jars beneath the bed at home, and although their occupants turned noisy after the sun went down each day, Redolence thought it was kind of fun having them down there—for a while. Then one night she climbed out of bed, opened every single jar and turned the occupants loose, to hop freely around the room. But when that succeeded only in upsetting her more, she picked up a sandal and began eliminating them one by one. By the time Kindling Boy reached a groggy state of wakefulness, thanks to the slapping sounds, the floor was littered with the broken bodies of crickets. He jumped out of bed, still half asleep, and pounded Redolence's head and face. Killing you wouldn't make up for what you've just cost me, he screamed as he pummeled her.

Redolence's first beating at the hands of her husband thus came a scant few days after the wedding. A proud, vain woman, she refused to make the customary trip to her parents' home with her face all swollen and marred with welts. Instead she pleaded her case to Cloud Silk. That son of yours, she complained, would you say he's a man or a son of a bitch? Look what he did to me over a bunch of crickets. Cloud Silk reacted to her daughter-in-law's boorish behavior with noticeable displeasure. Clean up your speech in front of me, she said, refusing to take note of the bruises. That's just the way he is, and there's nothing I can do about it. You're his wife, it's up to you now. Redolence walked off, Go ahead, protect him. You figure he'll kill me one of these days, but you're wrong. If he thinks he's free to do what he wants to me just because it's his house, he's dead wrong.

Redolence fought constantly with Kindling Boy practically from the day she crossed the threshold; at times they were at each other's throats in the middle of the night, earning shouts of disgust from a sleepy Cloud Silk. Rice Boy and his wife, on the other hand, ignored the disturbances, showing no interest in trying to mediate. So during one of Five Dragons's periodic visits to the emporium, Redolence cornered him in the yard to plead her case, showing him her bruised and battered face. With an impatient look at her long, ugly face, he said, I work to keep food on the table and clothing on your backs, just so you can bother me with your shitty little problems. He shoved her out of his way. I'm sick to death of your cockbite affairs.

That night the stillness of the rice emporium was again shattered by screams from Redolence, punctuated by a highly vocal enumeration of family scandals. Kindling Boy, wearing only his underpants, was chasing her around the room, a door bolt in his raised hand. Finally, she crawled under the bed, without a pause in her litany: Your aunt was a whore, your father's a one-eyed dragon who murders for fun, and your brother's a cripple who suffocated his own baby sister. There isn't a decent human being in the family. The words were barely out of her mouth when the door opened with a bang and Five Dragons was standing in the doorway. Where is she? he demanded of Kindling Boy. Get her out here.

After being dragged out from under the bed, Redolence looked at her father-in-law, who was still standing in the doorway, his face menacing. Something in his hand, which was partially hidden in red satin, gave off a blue metallic glint; it was, she was shocked to discover, a Mauser pistol.

Are you finished? Five Dragons asked as he raised the pistol and took aim at her forehead. You're right, I'm a one-eyed dragon who murders for fun. But you neglected to mention my target skills. If I hear another word out of you, I'll shoot your clit off and feed it to the dogs. Slowly, steadily his arm rose until the pistol pointed at a dim lightbulb. A loud pop sent minuscule shards of glass flying in all directions and threw the room into darkness.

There's nothing worse than a bawling, bitchy woman. How can your petty complaints compare to what we men have to put up with? Five Dragons's white satin pants and shirt seemed to create their own light in the dark room. He kicked out at Kindling Boy, who stood frozen to the spot. Throw that woman of yours down on the bed and give her a good, hard fuck. Do it often enough and she'll start listening to you. Women are all sluts.

Redolence sat stunned on the floor, her hair a mess. Kindling Boy picked her up and carried her over to the bed. Now you know what it means to be scared, he said. You can yell at me all you want, but what made you think you could get away with cursing my father? Everyone knows what he's capable of. Get him mad, and anyone can expect a bullet in return. Including me. Redolence was gasping for air. With her back to Kindling Boy, she sobbed hoarsely. You're bastards, all of you. She bit down on her fist. But by then her husband was snoring loudly. She heard the night watchman's bamboo clappers draw closer out on Brick Mason Avenue. She would never forgive her parents for marrying her into the rice-emporium family. From now on, she believed, her life would be one dark unending nightmare.

A ship steamed upriver with its load of cotton, table salt, and industrial oils, plus contraband of opium bricks and illicit arms hidden in the hold and beneath deckboards. The Wharf Rats were on hand when it pulled up to the pier, where Five Dragons supervised the unloading, as sailors passed on news from downriver. One of them said that Lu Piji—Sixth Master Lu—had been stabbed to death at a Shanghai racetrack. The Bund was abuzz with the news, fueled by a front-page photo of the body, which showed seven stab wounds in the back. Master Dragons, he said, handing him the newspaper, your worries are over. But Five Dragons barely glanced at the blurry photograph before tossing the paper into the river. I hate newspapers, he said. The smell of printing ink makes me sick.

He stood motionless on the riverbank, thinking back to his arrival in the city years before, when he had been humiliated near this very spot. He could still see the faces of Abao and his gang, and could still feel the sting of their drunken insults. Memories of calling them Daddy just so he could get his hands on some leftover pork conjured up a raging sorrow, which he tried to purge by running up and down the gangplank and flapping his outstretched arms. That helped. Then he jumped down onto the pier, narrowed his good eye, and fixed it on a young man dozing against a stack of cargo. He walked up and plucked a whisker from the man's chin with two silver coins. The fellow's eyes snapped open. Call me Daddy and these coins are yours. His voice oozed tenderness. Go ahead. One word, and you won't have to work for days. The astonished porter gaped at Five Dragons, not sure what to do. Finally he uttered a timid Daddy, and Five Dragons tossed the coins down at his feet, a benign look on his face. You really did it, didn't you? he muttered as he stepped down on the hand that had reached out to pick up the coins. Spineless creature, he cursed, whacking the man's head with his carrying pole. There's nothing worse than a coward. All it takes to get you to call somebody Daddy is a chunk of pork or a couple of coins.

The other men on the pier watched this savage episode

in silence. Over the years they had grown accustomed to Five Dragons's odd behavior, and were painfully aware that such acts were merely rungs up his psychological ladder. It was the unpredictability that intimidated most people. Finally he dropped his carrying pole and watched the blood drip through the man's fingers and onto the ground. I see hatred in your eyes, he said. That's good. I was more craven than you once. Want to know how I managed to become what I am today? By nurturing that hatred. It's the prize of human capital. You can forget your mother and father, but you must never relinquish your hatred.

When police whistles shrieked through the air from the direction of the chemical plant, Five Dragons and his gang made a quick departure with their contraband. The police arrived on the scene, only to find deathly silence surrounded by the blackness of night. A subtle vestige of criminality floated in the now peaceful atmosphere. They had grown used to being one step behind their quarry, and were well aware that the germs of countless criminal acts gravitated naturally to North City. Unbridled forces of darkness sought out the wharf to carry out everything from smuggling to murder. On that particular night, for instance, they spotted a pool of blood on the ground and a young stranger seated atop a stack of cargo, staunching his injured head with scrap paper and gaping at them. They asked what was wrong, but all they got was the barely audible response: I hate.

I hate.

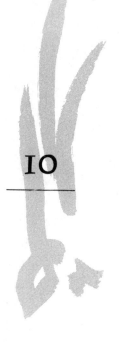

10

THE POSTMAN STOOD IN THE RICE-EMPORIUM DOORWAY
calling out Cloud Silk's name, then handed her a
letter, probably the first mail she had ever received.
Too many years had passed since her last contact
with the written word, so she asked Rice Boy to read
the letter to her. It's from Jade Embrace, he said after
scanning it quickly. He wants to come visit. Cloud
Silk sighed and counted on her fingers. The poor
boy's mother has been dead twelve years now. It's a
wonder he remembers he even has an aunt. How
about you, do you remember your cousin? He was
a hundred times smarter and handsomer than you
two. A boy with a real future. Rice Boy crumpled
the snowy sheet of paper and stuffed it into her hand.
How could I forget him? he grumbled. He used to
ride me around like a horse, whipping me on the
rump with a branch.

Three days later a stylish, handsome young man
in a Western suit and leather shoes came to Brick
Mason Avenue. Old-timers and neighbor women
took special notice as he strode into the rice emporium. When she saw what a gentleman he had become, the grocery-store proprietress, who knew the
rice emporium's history as well as anyone, blurted

out, It's Cloud Weave's son. Cloud Weave's boy has come home.

Rice Boy and Kindling Boy, who had been sent to meet their cousin, returned empty-handed from the train station. By then the help was already killing chickens and ducks; Snow Talent was plucking a freshly killed rooster. Your cousin's here, she gleefully announced to Rice Boy. How could you miss him like that? Where is he? Rice Boy asked with a scowl. Inside, talking with Mother. Go on in. Rice Boy glared at her. And demean myself? He should be greeting me. He hobbled into his room.

But Kindling Boy went inside, where Mother and Jade Embrace were sitting in redwood chairs. The cousins sized each other up as they greeted one another. Jade Embrace's cold, darting eyes and easy, refined manner filled Kindling Boy with admiration. After taking a seat, he joined the conversation by asking about the gaming setup in Shanghai. Are you a cricket fan? If so, I can help you lay your hands on a champion. Jade Embrace just smiled and said in practiced northern Mandarin, I used to be, but I've moved on. Now I mainly invest in real estate, or ship northern coal south.

See what useless sons I raised? Cloud Silk complained sadly. This one never does a lick of work, and all his brother knows how to do is gripe. Sooner or later they'll put us out of business.

That's because Uncle is still in charge. Flashes of wisdom showed in Jade Embrace's eyes as he took out a packet of cigars and flipped one into his mouth. I was just as lazy as they are when Father was alive, he said. But things have changed. Now it's up to me to take care of certain matters, which include settling old scores dating back to my father's era. I've got so much on my mind sometimes I can't make sense of any of it.

Cloud Silk gazed tenderly at her nephew, whose head was framed in a cloud of blue smoke that could not quite obscure the cold glare hidden in the angular recesses of his face. Hardly a sign of his rice-emporium origins remained. Recalling the frightful calamity that had befallen his family all those years before, and how Cloud Weave had perished in a ball of fire, Cloud Silk could not hold back the tears. Jade Embrace, she said as she dried her eyes, if your father had died in the explosion it would have been retribution for his evil deeds. But your poor mother came to such a horrible end all because of the Lu family. There wasn't enough of her left to bury. What did she do to deserve that? I know that her fondness for men was her undoing. She offered them her body, and wound up giving them her life.

Funny you should mention my mother. You know, I can't recall what she looked like. Jade Embrace shrugged. I was raised by a nanny, you know. They wouldn't let me near my mother. I honestly can't tell you what she looked like.

People always forget their origins, so I'm not surprised. Cloud Silk went inside to fetch a small red bundle, which she handed to Jade Embrace. I found this in a pile of rubble that day. It's the only thing your mother left behind. Take it and give it to your wife.

He picked up the bracelet and held it to the light for a moment, then put it back and returned the bundle to Cloud Silk. Poor-quality jade, he said. Little more than green stone. Besides, without a mate it's worthless.

So? It belonged to your mother. Sadly she stroked the

fire-scarred bracelet, and more tears came. Poor, poor Cloud Weave, she mumbled, her silent tears turning to sobs.

If it's that important to you I'll take it, Jade Embrace said with a smile. He stuffed the bracelet, red bundle and all, into his pocket. I hate to see people cry. Please stop.

I'm not just crying for your mother, I'm crying for me, too. Why have we suffered so? What in our family history caused it?

Jade Embrace and Kindling Boy slipped out of the room. Don't let her get to you, Kindling Boy said to his cousin. She can cry at the drop of a hat. I know, Jade Embrace replied. I know all about your family. From where they stood in the yard they could see Snow Talent and Redolence working in the kitchen. The sound of a harmonica drifted out of the southern wing. Who's playing? Jade Embrace asked. Rice Boy? Kindling Boy nodded. He's strange, he said. All he ever does is blow on that old harmonica. A knowing smile played across Jade Embrace's mouth. He spread a pile of chicken feathers with the tip of his shoe. I know, he said. And I know he suffocated my cousin, Little Bowl, in the rice.

Dinner was laid out on the dining table, but before anyone could eat, Cloud Silk lit candles on the ancestral altar and had each member of the family kneel on a rush mat to pay respects. The visiting cousin's turn came last. Jade Embrace, Cloud Silk said reverentially as she sprinkled a jar of rice wine along the base of the living-room wall, pay your respects to the spirits of your mother and maternal grandfather. Ask them to protect you against misfortune and evil influences. Looking embarrassed, Jade Embrace replied, I've never paid respects to anyone but ancestors at the Lu mansion. I'm an outsider here. But since it's you, Auntie . . . After placing a silk handkerchief on the floor, he knelt on one knee and bowed toward the ancestral tablets. The others stood off to the side and watched. Snow Talent giggled. Cloud Silk glowered at her. Grow up, she said. What's so funny?

Five Dragons chose that moment to return home. The room fell silent, a hush broken only by the thin crackle of red candles burning in brass holders. He fixed his good eye on Jade Embrace and loudly blew his snot onto the floor. So you've come back. I figured you'd show up sooner or later. He walked up to the altar and blew out the candles, then knocked the offerings and tablets onto the floor with one swipe of his hand. I see you're up to your old tricks, he said to Cloud Silk. Well, I don't like it. Whose help are you asking for? If you can't get it from the living, what good will the dead do you? Without waiting for a response, he sat down and looked over the faces around him. Let's eat, he announced. That's one thing everybody can do.

He began gnawing on a pig's knuckle, shoveling two bowlfuls of rice into his mouth between bites. When he was finished he showed Jade Embrace the clean bottom of his bowl. This is the respect I show food. Now you know how I made my fortune. With his eyes fixed on the rice bowl, Jade Embrace smiled. You don't need to explain, Uncle. I've heard how you made your fortune. In my view, making it is all that counts, not how you make it. Five Dragons nodded and laid down his bowl. Then he wiped his greasy mouth with his sleeve. Know what I said to myself when I was young and struggling to get by? When I make my fortune I'll treat myself to the meal of a lifetime: a whole pig, half a cow, and ten bowls of fluffy rice. But now that I'm there, my appetite's gone. All I can manage at any meal is two bowls of rice and a pig's knuckle. Know what I mean? Jade Embrace laid down his bowl and chopsticks, spread his hands over his bulging paunch, and, uncharacteristically, laughed long and hard, until he noticed that no one else was even smiling; that included Five Dragons, one of whose eyes was dark and devoid of expression, while an angry white glare seethed from the other. Jade Embrace looked away evasively and shifted his leg, which bumped into a soft, warm thigh; he knew without looking that it belonged to Snow Talent. When he rubbed it gently— once, twice—it stayed put. If anything, it pressed up closer. Out of the corner of his eye he saw her cheeks redden, and in her face the hidden promise of a bud about to open.

The older you get, the more you look like Abao. Five Dragons stopped Jade Embrace in the yard, rudely letting his gaze linger on the wrinkled crotch of his nephew's white trousers. He picked his teeth and continued, You don't look anything like Sixth Master, you know. You're the spit and image of Abao.

Abao? Never heard of him.

A ghost. Five Dragons picked a yellowing piece of meat from his teeth, then squinted to examine it. Sixth Master cut off his cock and sent it to me. That's funny, don't you think? Yes, Sixth Master could be pretty funny sometimes. But Abao was even funnier—he wound up feeding the fish in the river with most of his body and the dogs in the street with his cock.

What you're saying, I guess, is that he's long dead, Jade

Embrace commented cooly. Dead people bore me, just like they do you. Only the living interest me.

When Snow Talent awoke, she was struck by how unbearably hot the morning was—a common phenomenon during the plum-rain season. The boards in the partitions and the clothing in her wardrobe all reeked of mildew. After climbing out of bed she tried on every summer outfit she owned, settling on a sleeveless red cheongsam with a white print. Then, seated on the edge of the bed, she put up her hair and set it off with a magnolia blossom. But after studying her appearance in a hand mirror, she decided to let her hair down after all. One of Rice Boy's feet poked out from under the blanket as she sat absorbed in the task of combing her long, wavy hair. He pulled back the blanket, revealing little by little his mangled left leg.

Stop it. You know that sound makes my teeth stand on edge, he said as he rolled over, altering the angle and position of the leg; it looked like a broken tree branch. You wake me up every morning with all the noise you make.

And you make life miserable for me every day, she replied. If I so much as pass wind you scream at me. She walked over to the window to resume combing her hair. Once it was nice and straight she'd tie it with a satin ribbon, like the girls at the normal school did. She had been thinking about changing her hairstyle for a long time.

I know who you're doing all this for. Rice Boy sat up in bed. Put your hair up, you slut. I forbid you to let it down like that. I said, put it up. Like it was. Do you hear me?

Snow Talent's hand, and the comb it held, froze in

midair. Her round, bronzed shoulders heaved. You never let me do anything, she said, staring at the comb. I can't even comb my hair without your permission. I might as well be a puppet.

You don't plan to disobey me, do you? He climbed down off the bed, hobbled up, and wrenched the comb from her hand, flinging it out the window. Then he began putting her hair up himself, fashioning a crude bun at the back. There, like that. He let her go. That's how a slut like you is supposed to wear her hair. Don't try it your way again. We'll see if that son of a bitch wants you like this.

So Snow Talent stood inside the kitchen doorway, cleaning celery, her hair a mess, her mood as sodden as the skies. Cripple! she cursed her husband under her breath. I hope you die a death as twisted as your leg. Then, to her surprise, she discovered that Jade Embrace had sneaked up next to her. Why did you throw this out the window? He held the comb out to her. When she reached for it, he pulled it back and ran it through his own hair. It's a good one, he said. She lowered her head and busied herself with the celery. Keep it if you like it. Jade Embrace laughed and stuffed the comb into his suit pocket. Then when he withdrew his hand, he was holding his mother's jade bracelet, which he gently placed atop the bunch of celery. I don't like taking gifts from women. You can have this, but don't tell where you got it. Wear it after I've left. Her face already red as a beet, Snow Talent took a furtive look around and quickly covered the bracelet with celery stalks. I understand, she said. Why should I tell anyone?

While they were chatting, the sun's blistering rays baked the stones of Brick Mason Avenue and drove away any chance of rain; the air turned even more stifling, even stickier. Sounds of bickering between the first customers of the day and shop clerks emerged: A woman complained shrilly, What dynasty did this black rice come from? A rat wouldn't eat it. Great Swan Rice Emporium is getting worse all the time. In response to the commotion, Cloud Silk emerged from her room and spotted Jade Embrace and Snow Talent in the kitchen doorway, one standing, the other seated. She gave them a long look. Jade Embrace, she said, I thought you had business to take care of. The earlier you wrap it up, the quicker you'll be back home. Don't trust this weather. The sun may be out now, but it could start pouring anytime.

He grunted a reply and watched his aunt's thin, slightly hunched figure disappear through the beaded door curtain. He winked at Snow Talent. I'm going out. Come with me. We'll have a Western lunch and see a movie. After that we can stroll in the park and have a nice talk. I love spending the day with a pretty woman.

I have to wash this celery.

What are you worried about? With a smile he watched her clean the vegetables. It's Rice Boy, isn't it? Why be afraid of anyone with only one good leg?

Snow Talent nodded indecisively, then shook her head. Finally she picked up her grocery basket and carried it inside, shutting the kitchen door behind her and leaving a surprised Jade Embrace on the outside looking in. Then he heard her whisper through the door: Rice Boy's a late riser. The rice storeroom is deserted in the morning.

Shoes in hand, Snow Talent sneaked into the darkened, secluded rice storeroom, where Jade Embrace was seated on a mound of rice, his expression showing he had been confidently expecting her to show up.

I can't live like this, she complained as she crawled up the mound. I'm suffocating. She reached out to caress Jade Embrace's sleek, firm face and neck. Her labored breathing mirrored her chaotic emotions. As she let her head drop listlessly into Jade Embrace's lap, strands of hair fell loose from the ragged bun and fluttered in front of him. Hurry, please hurry. Somebody might catch us. I'm so scared.

Not so fast. Some things can't be hurried. He patted her softly on the hip. A cool medicinal odor clung to his skin. This is truly amazing, he said. I came to take care of important business, never dreaming I'd get caught up in the snarl of family matters. The idea that I'd be lying with you here on a mound of rice seems preposterous.

Hurry, she urged him in a choked voice, wrapping her arms around his waist. Stop talking. They'll hear you. You don't know what keen ears they have, or how sharp their eyes are. Hurry, I beg you. I'm scared to death. My heart's about to leap out of my body.

Slow down. I said I never hurry things like this. He laughed. My pistol is missing, he said. It was in my suitcase. Did you take it?

No, she replied, puzzled by his question. Seeing the absence of sexual desire in his eyes, she knew she had made a terrible mistake. You tricked me, she said, moving toward a neighboring rice mound. Just what are you up to?

A little of everything, he replied as he dropped his pants. Where do you think you're going? He looked down at his exposed genitals and grinned. Come on. I'm the best at everything I do.

The door creaked open just then, and the occupants froze. It was Kindling Boy. He walked over to the corner, where he hid something in a vat used for rubbish. Then he looked up and spotted two people on the rice. At first he thought they were thieves, but before he could scream, Snow Talent came rolling down and wrapped her arms around his legs. Don't shout, she pleaded. For my sake, as your sister-in-law, you must help me. Then he realized that the second party was his cousin, Jade Embrace. There's always a stray dog in this family's henhouse, he said with a forced laugh. We're rotten from top to bottom. While the neighbors are bragging about my sister-in-law's virtue, she's screwing her own cousin on a mound of rice. So choked with sobs she could hardly speak, Snow Talent held on to Kindling Boy's legs. Promise me you won't tell, and I'll serve you for the rest of my life. I'll even make your clothes and shoes by hand. He bent down and pried her hands loose. I've got all the clothes and shoes I need, he said. But money is another matter. I won't tell on you, but if I'm short of cash from time to time, I'll expect you to come through. He turned and walked out, pulling the door shut behind him.

Jade Embrace slid down off the rice after hitching up his trousers. Carefree as ever, he grabbed a handful of Snow Talent's hair. You can stop crying, he said. It looks like romance wasn't in the cards for us. Go on back to Rice Boy, and we'll just count this as my little game. I like to play games with women.

Snow Talent glared at him through her tears and spat in his calm, genteel face before picking up her shoes and nearly flying out the door.

On the day of Jade Embrace's departure, Cloud Silk told her sons to see him to the station. Rice Boy refused. I wouldn't mind seeing him to his grave, he said, but not to return to Shanghai. Faced with such intransigence, she decided to see her nephew off herself, even though she hadn't been out of her neighborhood for years.

Their rickshaw negotiated the narrow lanes and alleys of North City after turning off Brick Mason Avenue. Cloud Silk noticed the unsettled look on Jade Embrace's face; he was constantly looking behind them. What's the matter? she asked. Lose something? In the noonday sun he looked pale as he drummed his fingers nervously on his suitcase. We're being followed. Cloud Silk turned to look, but all she saw were crowds of people and an array of vehicles on that early-summer day. Don't think such strange thoughts, she said. Who in his right mind would dare raise a finger against Five Dragons's nephew? Jade Embrace smiled mirthlessly. What if *he's* the one who's out to get me? For that she had no answer. Again she turned, and this time she saw some men in black, well behind them. He wouldn't dare, not with me sitting beside you. If he so much as harmed a hair on your head, I wouldn't rest until he was dead. As the rickshaw puller threaded his way between two melon stalls at an intersection, Jade Embrace ordered him to turn around and go to the steamship pier. Cloud Silk gave him a puzzled look. What business do you have there? Aren't you returning to Shanghai? Of course I am, Jade Embrace replied. I'd rather go by boat, that's all.

The pier was a scene of filth and chaos. Cloud Silk stood in a rare spot not covered with chicken coops or duck shit, sweating as she waited for Jade Embrace to buy his ticket. That was when she saw the men in black run past the gate. They were, she saw, the thugs known as the Wharf Rats. The sons of bitches. Jade Embrace was right. When he walked up with his ticket, she held his head in her hands and said, Don't worry, if that son of a bitch tries anything, he'll have to kill me first. What do I have to live for, anyway? Jade Embrace scraped his jutting chin with the steamship ticket and looked around. I'm not particularly eager to die, he said. Especially not now.

Thunder rolled heavily in North City, announcing a deluge. Even with the sun shining brightly, raindrops pattered loudly on oilpaper awnings and the wooden flooring of the pier. The stench of poultry, sweaty bodies, and cheap cigarettes filled the crowded, ramshackle waiting room, where Cloud Silk and Jade Embrace held their noses before braving the rain on their way out to an old rustbucket. They stopped at the gangplank. I'll say goodbye here, Cloud Silk said. I have a terrible headache, and with this rain, I'll be lucky if I don't catch my death of cold on the way home. Suddenly something blocked the sun's rays and the mist above her. She looked up, and was shocked to see two umbrellas, held by men in black, above her and Jade Embrace. What do you think you're doing? Who asked you to follow us? The men turned to look at a black automobile parked at the foot of the gangplank. Master Five Dragons told us to see Young Master Lu off.

Five Dragons emerged from the automobile, a pistol in his hand. When he was close enough, he tossed it to Jade Embrace. I'm returning this to its owner, he said, and giving you back your life, while I'm at it.

I knew it was you, Jade Embrace remarked as he took a silk handkerchief from his pocket and wiped the handle clean. He dropped the weapon into his case.

At first I was going to kill you with your own pistol, Five Dragons said as he removed a handful of rice from a small cotton pouch. But I changed my mind. He flipped the rice into his mouth and began chewing it raw. How could you be stupid enough to come gunning for me on my own turf? Not to mention the fact that I'm your uncle. A rabbit doesn't eat the grass around its own burrow. What made you think you could pull it off?

You've got me all wrong. I told you I came to see the family and take care of some business.

Who are you trying to fool? Five Dragons spat out some rice husks. His broad smile radiated with forgiveness and goodwill. I know everything about you, even what you looked like when you came out of your mother's womb. I've crossed more bridges than you've walked roads. You can't fool me. I may have only one eye, but with it I can tell in a minute what a person has on his mind. No one pulls the wool over that eye.

Jade Embrace looked up. The mist and soft sunlight peculiar to the plum rains covered his fair skin and delicate features with a patina that highlighted the grime and wrinkles of his white suit. Half of his face had a golden sheen, the other half was immersed in darkness. He brushed the soot off his sleeve and looked into the sodden sky. What strange weather, he commented as if lost in thought, then picked up his case and headed up the gangplank. Among all the people scurrying about on the pier, only he had any spring in his step. An air of mystery enveloped the outline of his retreating figure.

See how the son of a bitch's shoulders slump to the right, Five Dragons remarked to Cloud Silk. He even walks like Abao. By letting him go I've passed up the chance to uproot a vicious weed.

She said nothing as she turned away from the steamship and wiped her eyes, overwhelmed by sorrow. With three blasts of its whistle, the aging steamship slid away from the pier, leaving Cloud Silk feeling drained. Good riddance. From her handbag she removed a tin of cooling salve and dabbed some on her temples. They can all stay away, she said. I don't need any of them, good *or* bad.

Five Dragons turned to his companions. If anything happens to me, he said, that son of a bitch will be the cause of it. **I saw it in his eyes.** He hates me like poison. Just like I once hated Abao and Sixth Master. Rivers flow east for one generation and west for the next. It's a strange world we live in, strange and funny. And, of course, dangerous.

After walking on eggshells for days, Snow Talent began to relax a bit, once it appeared that Rice Boy knew nothing of her infidelity. On rainy days his sexual appetite increased dramatically, so, burdened with feelings of pity and guilt, she brought him to a state of total arousal. By giving themselves over to sexual indulgence throughout the long rainy season, Rice Boy and his wife grew haggard and drawn. One morning Redolence met Snow Talent in the yard while she was washing some underclothes. What's going on in your room? she asked. Every night I hear cat screeches. They give me goosebumps. The look of suppressed mirth on her sister-in-law's face told Snow Talent what lay behind the question. Your room isn't exactly quiet. Why make such a fuss over a few cat screeches? Wrestling is less jangling on the nerves than boxing. Maintaining her mocking grin, Redolence skirted Snow Talent and the washtub on her way to the kitchen. Her waist and hips were hugged by calico shorts that were losing their shape. Her pregnancy had begun to show. In the kitchen she searched for something to eat, but the thought that Snow Talent had humiliated her stung badly; she went to the window to get in the last word. Kindling

Boy may cuff me around, but at least the baby I'm carrying is his. I'm no hen that cackles without laying eggs. He could beat me to death, and still I'd keep my pride.

Snow Talent's hand stopped in midair above the washboard. Her only response this time was a hateful glare toward the darkened kitchen window. Over the rainy season there had been a decline in meaningless squabbles with her sister-in-law, since her thoughts seldom strayed from Jade Embrace. She lived in fear of Kindling Boy telling Redolence what had happened in the rice storeroom, but so far her worries appeared unfounded—Redolence was still in the dark, it seemed. Maybe Kindling Boy was keeping his promise, and then again, maybe he spent so much time gambling that the incident was forgotten. She examined her soapy hands; the red, chapped fingers were like tiny eels squirming amid the folds of wet laundry. The disturbing sight reminded her of Jade Embrace lowering his pants on the rice.

The jade bracelet was locked away in her dresser in a bamboo basket under some old clothes. The same basket from which she had sold flowers as a girl, so beautifully woven she couldn't bear to throw it away. Hiding the bracelet there symbolized the state of her emotions: Anyone could easily crush such a fragile container. Each time she peeked at Jade Embrace's casual gift, her insides knotted up. The sharp teeth of transgression mercilessly devoured her virtue, her reputation, and a host of fantasies that remained concealed to her.

Snow Talent closed the door and slipped the jade bracelet over her wrist for the first time. Ignorant of its origins, her only worry was that Rice Boy might spot it. The fear that his jealousy would erupt into violence was constant. She leaned against the door and slowly raised her arm to watch glitters of green swirl through the air; an enormous penis took shape in her imagination, emitting a green glow as it rose magically to float in the air; she closed her eyes to shut out the sight, and her ears detected a pattering noise; it was raining again. The moist air carried an odor from her past: the smell of rotting magnolia blossoms.

II

ONE DAY IN JULY JAPANESE WARPLANES FLEW IN OVER the river and bombed the northern section of town. One of the bombs landed at the base of the ancient pagoda on Brick Mason Avenue. As the thud of the explosion died out, residents of Brick Mason Avenue watched the structure wobble and collapse like a dying old man, until all that remained was a heap of shattered wood and crumbled brick. A few bold youngsters ran over to search for the brass wind chimes that had hung from the pagoda for generations. They lugged the ones they could find home.

Feeble old men taking shelter in the pagoda died in this act of aggression, and the atmosphere all along Brick Mason Avenue was of terror and panic. People closed up shop and fled with their families to the countryside. Rice Boy stood in the doorway of the shop watching his neighbors flit in and out of narrow byways like swarms of buzzing flies, suddenly aware of how vulnerable his crippled leg made him in such circumstances. He went back inside the deserted shop. The rest of the family was out gawking at the bodies of bombing victims, except for Cloud Silk, who was in the front room drinking a medicinal broth made of wolfberry and mountain ginseng, which she hoped could cure her headaches. How about casualties? she asked. I heard the woman who ran the grocery store died. Rice Boy nodded. And she wasn't alone, he said. Cloud Silk laid down her bowl. She got what was coming to her. I always said women like her are destined to be struck down by lightning. I figured you'd say something like that, Rice Boy remarked. You won't be happy till every person on earth is dead, except for you, of course.

Superheated air covered the area in the wake of the bombing. With waves of heat washing through the shop, Rice Boy nervously paced the floor, his bare back beaded with sweat. Maybe we should hide out in the countryside until it's safe, he said. People say the Japanese airplanes will be back tomorrow. After mulling the suggestion over for a moment, Cloud Silk replied, Our lives are controlled by destiny. If the heavens want us dead, nothing can save us. I won't subject myself to the miseries of life in the countryside. If I need to hide, a coffin's as good a place as any. Dying there would be a blessing, since you wouldn't have to bother about a funeral. Rice Boy cast an icy glance at his mother and mopped his sweaty brow with a rag. What a load of crap, he said. You know I can't get far on this leg. I'd be the first to go if we took a hit. Pushing her medicinal broth to the side, Cloud Silk stared at his gimp leg and said, Just the sight of you makes me sick. Keep your opinions to yourself. I'm not interested in anything you have to say. Only your father is a match for the evil you represent. Now I've got a headache and I don't feel like talking. Rice Boy balanced the wadded-up rag on the back of his hand, then snapped it into the air. Why don't we get him to break my other leg? He snapped a ceramic vase with the soggy rag, knocking it off the table to shatter on the floor, one stray shard landing next to his mother's foot.

By the time Snow Talent returned home, Rice Boy had calmed down; he was lying in the shade playing his harmonica. You should see all the people who died on the north side of the avenue, she reported. They're hideous. Unnerved, she shook him by the shoulders. How can you play that at a time like this? What if the Japanese airplanes come back? He pushed her sweaty hands away. What do you think? We lie here and wait to die. No one can bitch if we all go together.

The signs of war in North City let up after a few days. No longer visited by the terrifying specters of Japanese airplanes overhead, shop owners on Brick Mason Avenue cautiously reopened their doors; once in a while a clerk stood on the steps and looked up into the air, but all was calm in the light blue sky, where the blazing sun baked the ground until it shimmered; the smell of rotting garbage drifted up and down the ancient street, drawing swarms of flies amid clusters of people rushing about on cobblestones as hot as molten steel. It was a sweltering, miserable summer, and old, experienced clerks talked of little but the weather, convinced that the hottest summers were usually the most dangerous.

At the time of the air raid Five Dragons was relaxing at Emerald Cloud House. When he heard the drone of engines in the sky, he ran naked onto the porch and fired several shots at the aircraft overhead. It was, he knew, a futile gesture. Some of the prostitutes and their customers, in various stages of undress, laughed nervously. Five Dragons lowered his clouded gaze from the sky and banged his pistol on the carved bannister. What's so funny? If I was up there, I'd drop a bomb right on your heads. I'd like to see you laugh then. He took aim at a balloon lantern hanging from the eave and fired, putting a blackened hole through it. Then he walked off amid bulging stares, rubbing his groin with the barrel of his pistol. I hate the way you people stand around gaping and giggling. I wish I knew how spending a little money on rotten cunt makes you so happy. Or getting a free view of my cock. Nothing's worth getting *that* happy about.

He parted the beaded door curtain. The prostitute Little Beauty was gazing out the open window as she removed kernels of raw rice and laid them out on the windowsill. What was that all about? Somebody get killed? Almost, Five Dragons said as he dressed. Nothing but calamities and death. Well, dying is about the easiest thing anybody can do. He surveyed the fair curves of Little Beauty's body, and had a wonderful idea. Scooping up the sticky kernels of rice, he held them to her lips. Eat these, he said menacingly. Instinctively she squeezed her lips tight. You're not normal, she said after a moment. I've never had a customer like you before. He grabbed her as she squirmed to get away, then pried open her mouth with the muzzle of his pistol and stuffed the rice in, a kernel at a time. His cold expression soon began to thaw, and the hint of a smile appeared. Go on, eat it. He watched the rice vanish without a sound between Little Beauty's red lips and down her throat. Now *that's* worth getting happy about, he said.

Emerald Cloud House was close by the city moat, where Five Dragons liked to bathe in the late afternoons, when the heat was most oppressive. Now he watched excitable people scurry back and forth in the spaces between buildings; off in the distance a bombed-out factory burned, filling the air with the pungent smell of gunpowder. Meanwhile, inside Emerald Cloud House, reed pipes and flutes made a reappearance; southern melodies sung by the courtesans were like the monotonous drone of an old machine; Five Dragons ˙floated willfully in the dark green water, which was coated with an oily scum, thinking about war and the effects it would have on his life. But answers were elusive, so he stopped looking for them. Spotting a scooped-out melon rind floating toward him, he swam up and put it on his head like a cap—once again he was a boy in Maple-Poplar Village. The past always found a way to wrap its tendrils around his wide-ranging thoughts. After all these years, I'm still floating on water. Why is that? As he surveyed the water enfolding him, a nameless fear gripped him; jerking the rotting melon rind off his head and flinging it away, he swam as fast as he could to the bank, where he sat on a stone step and looked out at the summer floodwaters, dwelling upon thoughts of Maple-Poplar Village, and of how water that seemed to cover the earth had carried him to this private beach below Emerald Cloud House. It was at that precise moment that he felt the first prickly sensation in his genitals; he reached down to scratch himself, immediately transforming the stinging pain into an unbearable itch. The coarse, ruddy skin of his penis was covered with strange little blossoming sores.

One of the Wharf Rats came running down the beach with news of the bombing of Brick Mason Avenue. Five Dragons didn't seem to hear him as he stood up with a perplexed look, holding his baggy shorts in one hand. Come over here and tell me what these things on my cock are. It's some foul disease, he concluded after a closer examination. Those rotten fucking whores, he snarled through his clenched gold teeth. How dare they infect me with their filthy disease, like a bunch of assassins?

That night a gang of black-clad men swept through the brothels in South City, hiring out every whore Five Dragons had ever been with, handing over payment for a three-day engagement. No one gave it much thought at the time, except, maybe, for the brothel owners, who congratulated themselves on an unexpected windfall. Until three days later, that is, when an elderly housemaid from Emerald Cloud House went down to the river to wash out chamber pots. Her brush touched something soft and matted in the water, and a gentle nudge brought the thing to the surface: a white, bloated corpse. Even amid her horror she recognized it as the body of Little Beauty, one of the girls who had been hired out of the brothel.

News that eight whores had been found floating in the moat created a furor in the city that summer, quickly becoming the most frightening, the most mystery-clouded topic of conversation among residents as they cooled off in the night breezes. Unique riddles always accompany unique events. In this case, the discovery of raw rice in all eight corpses baffled the women, who condemned the sinful flesh markets of South City. Men, on the other hand, focused on the questions *Who did it?* and *Why?* A growing number of people guessed that Five Dragons and his gang were responsible, and residents familiar with the unsavory history of the area began circulating tales of Five Dragons's unusual background and strange habits, emphasizing his keen sense of revenge and the methods with which he exacted it. That was when people learned that a single bushel of rice had gained him entry into the local underworld. The name Five Dragons appealed to locals like a block of ice on a scorching summer day. They went out of their way to buy rice at the Brick Mason Avenue emporium, just to get a glimpse of him. But he seldom rewarded them with an appearance, and they had to settle for the other adult members of the family, with their gloomy expressions and sluggish movements: Cloud Silk, the proprietress, lounging in a reclining chair, sipping medicinal potions, for instance; or her elder son, the crippled Rice Boy, who did little all day long but fume and curse; or her younger daughter-in-law, Redolence, who walked around with a scowl and a swelling abdomen.

The rumor mills had a field day when a black paddy wagon pulled up to the Great Swan Rice Emporium, and out poured a squad of policemen. People expecting to see Five Dragons hauled off to jail emerged from neighboring shops and crowded around the doorway to get a good look. They were surprised to see the police come out loaded down with sacks of rice, followed by Five Dragons himself, who bowed them out the door. Clerks helped the police load the rice into their paddy wagon, then watched them speed off in a cloud of dust. With his hand clutching his crotch, Five Dragons shouted to the blacksmiths, Come over for some mah-jongg. I've just been cleaned out. Maybe I'll have better luck at the table.

Not long afterward, newspapers put forth a new theory on the deaths of the eight prostitutes: The countless dead left in the wake of the Japanese bombs included eight prostitutes who were swimming in the city moat at the time.

Five Dragons's unmentionable disease forced him to stay home to regain his health. To avoid the summer heat, he spread a rush mat on the ground under a shade tree and slept all day. Cicadas in elm trees beyond the wall chirped without respite, but members of his family made a point of tiptoeing past him so as not to disturb his long summer naps.

In reality, Five Dragons lay suspended in the twilight zone between sleep and wakefulness, and as he dozed, imaginary sounds drifted in and out of his consciousness. He heard Cloud Weave sing a provocative folk song as she sat in a far recess of the yard; he heard the ghost of Abao thud to the ground from the compound wall, his black leather shoes seeming to brush the edge of the rush mat; he even heard the raspy coughs of Proprietor Feng on his deathbed and the pop of his own eye as it was gouged by the old man. The sounds robbed him of any chance for peace and quiet, and the passage of time increased the painful itching in his groin. The indescribably exquisite torture surpassed all the bullet wounds, bites, and gouges he had suffered up till then.

Five Dragons flew into a rage over the itinerant physicians who were summoned, suspicious of their healing arts and herbal remedies, and convinced that his condition actually worsened under their care. In a final act of exasperation, he drove away every last one of them, with their claims of infallibility, and undertook a regimen of self-treatment. He thought first of the folk remedy for boils back in Maple-Poplar Village: plantain seeds and burdock, crushed, then mixed into a medicinal plaster from Zhenjiang, and affixed to the sore after being heated to a tacky consistency. He completed his preparations in private, standing naked in front of a full-length mirror in the center of the room. There was no getting around it—he cut a strange and comical figure: long, thick limbs; a still-hard abdomen; and a penis swathed in a red plaster.

He was like every other man, yet different, for he was no longer whole: The light had gone out in one eye, he was missing a toe, and his life was threatened by the ravages of a dark disease. But his depression was only temporary, for now it was time to reflect on the mistakes he had made. He had always been contemptuous of the city and of city life, yet was drawn irresistibly to it, and thus powerless to resist its temptations. He realized he had come to grief not because of women, but as a result of the lifestyle he had chosen and the dream he had pursued.

Cloud Silk walked into the room fanning herself; she scowled at Five Dragons. That won't do any good, she said. No medicine in the world can cure your filthy disease. I always said you lived a charmed life, no matter how it stank, and that the only person who could bring you down was you yourself. Five Dragons replied sadly, You were right, and that just proves you're a witch. What are you doing here, waiting to remove my corpse? Cloud Silk's face showed no emotion as she walked to the window and raised the bamboo curtain. I'm not going to remove your corpse, and I won't wait around for people to remove mine either. I'll spend my old age in a convent. That way I won't be dependent on you or your sons. I've already bought a plot inside the convent. Five Dragons smiled. You're not as stupid as I thought, he said. But then neither am I. Now listen to me. If I die, it will be back in Maple-Poplar Village. Want to know why? Because I'm afraid you'd chop my body into pieces. You'd do it. You're all scared of me now, but that will end the moment I die.

Having nothing more to say, Cloud Silk shooed a fly with her fan and walked out. Wind whistled through the southern window, carrying the chirps of cicadas from the elm trees along with the late-afternoon heat. Five Dragons walked to the window, where he was greeted by the sound of splashing water. Rice Boy was helping Snow Talent wash her long black hair, which looked like seaweed floating in a brass tub. Off in the northern wing, Kindling Boy and Redolence were cranking up their newly bought phonograph: The unnatural croaking of a man's voice faded in and out. There they are, my family, my heirs. The only family I've known since the age of twenty. Suddenly Five Dragons felt surrounded by strangers, and wondered if any of this family business was real. Maybe the rice emporium was nothing but an illusion; maybe the only reality was his penis, germ-infested and itchy. He had shed his identity as a pitiful young clerk in a rice emporium years before, only to suffer **new forms of torture** now. He shut his eyes, a return to the feel of night; devoid of emotions and trapped in an envelope of hot air, he listened for the wind chimes. He had not forgotten that the pagoda had been reduced to rubble, but in his imagination the crisp tinkle of chimes still echoed in the summer sunset. And there was more: a distant train whistle and the rumble of railroad tracks.

In his mind he had never left the inside of a railroad car. It bounced and it shook, until he experienced a sudden attack of light-headedness; he took a few shaky steps, holding his heavy head in his hands, walking the way he had when sneaking aboard the freight car all those years ago. He slapped himself to clear his head, and a strange noise rose to his ears: The two rows of gold teeth had broken loose and lay loosely on and beneath his tongue. The gold felt uncommonly warm and silky against his skin when he pressed it with his finger, and at that moment he sensed that those gold teeth were the greatest single comfort of his life. Even after years of drifting like smoke, the blood of Maple-Poplar Village still flowed through his veins, globs of sweat still oozed from his armpits, and his feet still stank when he slipped them out of his shoes. But now he had a set of sparkling teeth made of pure gold. That may have been the only true change in his life; yes, they were in fact his greatest single comfort.

Snow Talent was jittery as a bird around an archer. Thoughts of the aborted tryst in the storeroom still sent nervous prickles down her back. Jade Embrace's unannounced arrival and sudden departure now seemed like a frightful dream, or a yielding pit from which she viewed a discomfiting pale yellow sky. Shadowy dangers were everywhere in the shop, embodied most menacingly in Kindling Boy's violent nature. Seeking refuge from the blistering summer heat in frequent cool baths helped her control her fragile emotions as she considered her predicament and her options. The key to everything, she knew, was Kindling Boy, and at times she wished he would never emerge from the gambling halls and opium dens, until, as so often happened in such places, someone buried a knife in his chest. That alone guaranteed release from her peril.

But Kindling Boy was not about to let her off the hook. One day he slipped into the kitchen as she was rinsing vegetables. His grin told her he brought bad news. He asked for a hundred yuan to pay off an urgent gambling debt.

Don't drive me to suicide, Snow Talent implored, her face reddening as she tried to control her rage. Give me a few days. You know Rice Boy controls the purse strings. He'd never give me that much money without good reason.

Make something up. Say your father died and you need money for his funeral.

But he didn't die. Anger crept into her voice, yet she quickly softened it, fearful that Redolence might overhear their conversation from her room in the western wing. Kindling Boy, you and I are kin. I've even made shoes for you. Don't hound me like this. I have no money, except for a pathetic monthly allowance and the grocery money. I've never been able to put any aside for myself. Take a look in my purse if you don't believe me.

So you're going to hold out on me. Well, that's all right, I won't force you. He pushed the purse away and started out the door. People who say that women are long on hair but short on sense know what they're talking about. I'm not forcing your hand, you're forcing mine.

Dropping her purse and the eggplant she was holding, she ran after him. The combined look of panic and forced seductiveness was not becoming. She clutched his hand and raised it slowly until it rested on her breast. I don't have any money, she said, trying to gauge his reaction. But you can have this.

Kindling Boy kept his hand on her breast for a moment, but when he finally let it fall, he shook his head. That won't do. I need something I can spend, I need money. Since you don't have any, I'll settle for jewelry. I can always pawn it.

Each one of you Fengs is worse than the next, and greedier. Snow Talent sighed out of despair. But his comment had jogged her memory. I can give you a jade bracelet, she said. It's worth a lot more than a hundred yuan.

But you have to promise, no more blackmail. If you come to me again, I can only give you my life.

The bargain was sealed there in the kitchen, but as they emerged, single file, they were spotted by Redolence, who was leaning out her window. What funny business have you two been cooking up in the kitchen? she shouted. There was a rat, Snow Talent replied, maintaining her composure. I asked Kindling Boy to kill it for me. Redolence eyed them suspiciously. A horny female rat, I'll bet. She sneered. You've got a husband, so why ask your brother-in-law? Pretending not to hear, Snow Talent hurried across the yard to avoid a scene. But her sister-in-law's epithets followed her like a swarm of angry hornets. Shameless slut. Redolence walked into the yard and spat contemptuously on the ground. Even your brother-in-law isn't off limits.

Safely back in her room, Snow Talent could still hear Redolence's voice, and she was quaking uncontrollably. Rice Boy, who also heard the curses, yanked his wife out of her chair and glared at her. What the hell have you been up to? Do you honestly need a screwing so badly you go looking for Kindling Boy? Wracked with sobs, she stomped her foot and cried out, I didn't do anything. If you take their side, the only way I can prove myself is to die. Fuming by now, Rice Boy slammed the window shut, cutting off the sound of Redolence's voice in the yard, then grabbed his wife by the hair and stared at her tear-streaked face. If I find out you did it, I'll personally fetch the rope for you. There's plenty around, and our eaves are high enough.

The yard was peaceful again, at last. Redolence said nothing when Five Dragons walked outside and stood silently in the middle of the yard, his hands on his hips as he stared into the sky; a strange odor rising from the crotch of his white satin trousers sent Redolence running into the house holding her nose. Having shed her anger, she dragged her thickening body over to the hidden side of the bed and carved a mark in the wood with a knife; it joined four similar notches, each representing a family squabble she had engineered, five so far, in accord with her mother's unique premarital advice: The only way to avoid being bullied in the Feng home is to cause a scene from time to time. People oppress the weak and fear the strong, so if anybody makes trouble for you, raise a stink. Do it ten times and they'll stop picking on you.

A few days later the owner of the Prosperity Pawn Shop showed up; Five Dragons was puzzled by the visit, until the man laid a jade bracelet on the table and said, Your younger son pawned this. I gave him a hundred yuan, but wouldn't think of keeping it, in case it's a family heirloom. I'd feel better if Master Dragons bought it back. Five Dragons scooped up the bracelet and examined it briefly before tossing it back onto the table. He frowned impatiently. I've never concerned myself with piddling matters like chicken feathers and garlic peels. Go talk to Cloud Silk. There was something familiar about the bracelet, but he couldn't recall who he'd seen wearing it. Cumbersome, useless things like women's jewelry disgusted him. But Cloud Silk's reaction to the news confirmed the pawnbroker's suspicions and affirmed his professional intuition. She handed over the hundred and five yuan required to redeem the bracelet as soon as she saw it, and as the pawnbroker counted his money he heard her cry softly and mutter, Poor Cloud Weave, if your spirit is still intact, come back and see what unfilial bastards the Feng family has produced. Having dealt with the rice-emporium family for years, the pawnbroker had known Cloud Weave and knew of her death at the Lu mansion. In the doorway he tried to recall what she looked like, but, unhappily, her face had vanished from his memory. She had been dead for so long that her beauty and her sultry ways had slipped away in the stream of time and no longer held any significance for flesh-and-blood men.

At first Kindling Boy denied he had pawned the bracelet. But Cloud Silk's questioning eventually wore him down, and the truth came out. All but the part about the adultery in the storeroom. Either he glossed over that part because Snow Talent was in the room, or he was thinking ahead to more blackmail down the line. Whatever the reason, he pointed to Snow Talent and said, Sister-in-law gave it to me, then picked up his cricket cage and walked out.

Although he had revealed only a portion of the truth, what the rest of the family learned was enough to stun them. Redolence reacted first. Fully intending to provoke Rice Boy, who was sitting next to her, she turned and said, Did you hear that? She gave him a bracelet. You call yourself a man, placing her on a pedestal while she's out cuckolding you? With a throaty growl, he stormed out of the house, picked the ax up from the woodpile, then stripped the hemp cord from a load of kindling and walked back inside. Cloud Silk tried to block his way, but was pushed roughly aside. You're going to kill again! Rice Boy tossed the cord at Snow Talent's feet and said hoarsely, Shall I do it, or will you? It's your choice. I've killed before—my own sister—and if I have to pay with my life, so what? They can only kill me once. Snow Talent's head drooped until she was looking at the rope. She bit her lip as she wrestled with ways to save her own skin. Then the answer came. I didn't give Kindling Boy the bracelet, he *stole* it from me. **He stole it.** Why would I give him a bracelet? Rice Boy paused to consider. Then: One of you is lying, he said as he tested the edge of the ax with his finger. Maybe both of you, and I might as well finish you off together. Then I'd be two up on the executioner. A real bargain.

With the room thrown into confusion, Cloud Silk managed to keep her head; she persisted in asking Snow Talent how the bracelet had wound up in her hands. Snow Talent stuck to the story that she had found it on the storeroom floor, but Cloud Silk fixed her daughter-in-law with a hard stare and said, Snow Talent, don't be a victim of your own cleverness. Jade Embrace may be far off in Shanghai, but rocks emerge when the tide goes out. Be very, very careful. Don't offend the bodhisattva and get struck down by one of her thunderbolts. With her face set, Cloud Silk took Rice Boy and Redolence by the hand and led them out of the room, shutting the door behind them. After a sip or two of medicinal broth she said to Snow Talent, I used to think you were a clever, filial girl. But I guess that was all an act, further proof that this family does not attract people of strong character. Maybe that's the Feng clan's fate. Snow Talent had nothing to say, having been beaten down by the vicious battle that had just ended. I know Jade Embrace gave you the bracelet, since I was aware of your squalid relationship from the very beginning. It shames me to talk about all the scandals this family has witnessed. Snow Talent shut her eyes, only to be transported back to the events of that day in the storeroom, and to the sight of Jade Embrace, trousers down around his ankles, looking so superior. Her heart was breaking. **I've been wronged. Every member of this family has wronged me.** Her defense came out sounding like sickly moans.

Cloud Silk responded to the accusation by splashing Snow Talent with the broth in her bowl; the brown liquid spread across her daughter-in-law's pale face, reminding her of rivulets of blood, an association that took the edge off her savage mood. The men in our family are born killers, she mused, the women shameless sluts. That, too, is our fate. Why should I try to keep things going all by myself?

Snow Talent, as we have seen, was jittery as a bird among archers. The rest of the family, sensing she had been indiscreet, pressured her in a variety of ways. The tirades and indirect attacks by Redolence didn't bother her, nor did Rice Boy's brutal beatings and violent sex. Only Kindling Boy scared her. She lived in constant fear that he would reveal what he had witnessed in the storeroom.

I underestimated you, he said through clenched teeth one day. I never thought you'd squirm out of it like that. Now I must punish you, to the tune of a hundred yuan.

Don't be angry with me, Kindling Boy. I didn't mean for it to come out like that. She knew how weak her defense sounded. A little scandal now and then can't hurt a man. But a black mark or two can make a woman's life miserable.

I can't believe you're so wrapped up in yourself, he sneered. You and I still have business to take care of. If you don't come up with a hundred yuan, I'll stand in the middle of Brick Mason Avenue and broadcast your ugly infidelities for all the world to hear.

She looked at him with a desperate, pleading expres-

sion, holding a pale yellow magnolia blossom in her hand.
Tomorrow, she said. Give me till tomorrow. She plucked
the petals of the flower and let them fall to the ground,
one at a time. I'll find a way to settle up with you people
someday.

That night she didn't sleep. The suffocating heat and
stagnant air in the shop drove everyone outside, where
sleep was made impossible by mosquitoes that swarmed
out of the storeroom to attack them on the ground, on
bamboo cots, and in rattan chairs. Apart from Five Dragons, who was snoring loudly, they cursed the weather and
the flying scourge. Cloud Silk lit a mugwort mosquito coil,
but was disappointed to find that the aromatic smoke had
no effect on the insects; they continued to buzz and whirl
in the air above the yard. Amazing, she said under her
breath as she looked into the dark red summer sky. We're
not even into the dog days, and the heat is already unbearable. This year is different somehow. I see calamities
ahead—heavenly or human.

Immersed in her private thoughts, she noticed dark
clouds filling half the sky. But no rain. Weather like this
kills off the old and the sick, she murmured, fanning herself frantically as she looked at the faces arrayed around
her. Snow Talent was not in the yard. Where's your wife?
she asked Rice Boy. How can she stand it inside the
house?

Don't ask me, he said sleepily.

You don't think she'll take the easy way out, do you?
She hit her son with her rush fan. Go check. But he didn't
move. Who cares what she does? he said.

I don't want anybody dying inside in this weather,
Cloud Silk grumbled as she stood up and walked to the
window of the southern wing, where she raised the cur-

tain and peered inside. Snow Talent was sitting on the edge of the bed in dim lamplight, oblivious to the swarming mosquitoes landing on her glossy skin. She looked like a yellowing paper cutout. A delicately woven flower basket was on the bed beside her; her hand lay buried beneath fresh red flowers inside. Cloud Silk recognized the basket as the one Snow Talent had brought along when she married into the family. The flowers rested on a bed of snowy raw rice. The pitiful dowry now seemed to symbolize Snow Talent's miserable fate. But for the moment Cloud Silk was unable to fathom Snow Talent's thoughts as she sat quietly in her room, the picture of peace and tranquillity, while everyone else was in a terrible mood caused by the withering heat.

Just before daybreak a light breeze swept in from the factory area off to the northwest, carrying with it a strange odor. Snow Talent, dressed in her favorite, peach-colored cheongsam, emerged from the house and stepped lightly around sleeping kinfolk on her way to the kitchen to wash rice for the morning meal. She lit a fire in the oven. What are you doing? Cloud Silk asked, awakened by the crackling sounds. Making porridge, Snow Talent replied from the kitchen. Isn't that what you told me to do yesterday? Her soft response was framed in a husky, distant voice. Make it sort of soupy, Cloud Silk said, then lay back down again. Some time later, groggy with sleep, she caught a hazy glimpse of Snow Talent walking through the gate, flower basket in hand, her peach-colored silhouette briefly visible past the shop before she vanished from sight.

Snow Talent still hadn't returned by breakfast time, but no one seemed overly concerned. She went to the market. We'll start without her, Cloud Silk suggested as she dished out the porridge, which was thin and sticky, just as it should be. She had to admit that her daughter-in-law wasn't all that bad around the house, after all. First to sample the porridge, Five Dragons took a big slurp, and spat it right out. What's this? He laid down his bowl and chopsticks and crinkled his brow. It tastes funny. Who made it?

Maybe the rice wasn't washed thoroughly, Cloud Silk offered as she tasted it. Or maybe there was a trace of rat poison in the bottom of her basket. But it does have a funny taste.

Don't eat that stuff. Five Dragons stood up. Bring me the cat. But the family's yellow tabby was nowhere to be found, and no one else had any ideas. Suddenly Rice Boy picked up the pot and dumped its contents at the base of the compound wall. His lips were quivering. It's arsenic, he said. Last night she threatened to take arsenic. I never dreamed she'd put it in our porridge instead. Everyone turned to look at the spilled porridge. She tried to kill us, Redolence shouted, breaking the spell. In the ensuing clamor, Five Dragons alone held his tongue; he walked over and scooped the porridge into the pot. When she comes home, I'll make her eat every last drop.

But Snow Talent never came home. Someone told the brothers that she had been spotted walking with her flower basket toward the train station.

Where do you think she was going? Kindling Boy asked.

Who cares? It just means I'll have to buy a new wife. He bent down and picked up a piece of brick, which he thumped against the trunk of a roadside umbrella tree. If I'd known it would come to this, he said, I'd have buried a knife in the slut long ago.

I bet I know. She's gone looking for Jade Embrace in Shanghai. As he gazed off at the cinder-colored train station building, a grin appeared on Kindling Boy's hollow face.

12

FIVE DRAGONS'S PHYSICAL CONDITION WORSENED IN THE blistering heat. Festering sores on his genitals spread down to his thighs and up beyond his navel. Houseflies buzzed around his midsection, even daring now and then to fly up through the wide legs of his satin shorts. Frantically he tore at the rotting skin with his fingernails, and there were times, as he raged desperately, that he heard the footsteps of the Angel of Death prancing around the rice emporium.

And still he insisted on being his own healer. After trying and discarding Zhenjiang balm and Asian plantain, he switched to a folk remedy of bathing in slow-aged, hand-distilled rice vinegar. It lessened his physical agony, yet did little to ease the fears and anxieties he had experienced ever since the lesions began erupting on his skin. Ripples of vinegar from his diseased body and tortured soul reached the outer edges of his wooden tub, and as he floated in the dark red liquid, he realized how little meat he had on his bones; he was like a dislodged branch being carried along atop flowing red vinegar. He pictured a young man fleeing Maple-Poplar Village through an expanse of rotting rice shoots and cotton plants on the surface of vast floodwaters, then across raucous roads choked with refugees. The young man had strong limbs and a pair of radiant eyes filled with the bright light of hope—how I envy that young man, and how I miss him. Five Dragons splashed some vinegar on his face and exposed parts of his body; the puckery odor made him cough violently, and it was all he could do to force back thoughts of death that surfaced with the wrenching hacks; he concentrated on the refugee-packed road as it slowly disappeared in floodwater. Everywhere he saw the victims and perpetrators of death; all around him were poverty and looting. Penniless people hunted desperately for distant stores of rice. Me, I found one, an endless supply of snowy rice, but with such a long road ahead, I wonder when and where I'll find rest in the grave.

Rice and wicker baskets were still stacked on the floor, customers and clerks were still doing business. The world continued to spin on its axis, carrying with it all sorts of shops and trade centers; the old, reliable emporium flourished as never before. With farmers on the banks of the Yangtze reaping bumper harvests, people no longer had to worry about famine or hoarding or speculation. But the terrifying fires of war spread to the southern bank of the river, and squat Japanese soldiers with stubbly chins materialized in town and on the wharf, omens that drove people back to the shop to stock up on rice, the key to survival, as everyone knew. Seated behind the counter, Cloud Silk was in an ambivalent mood—a mixture of joy and anxiety—as she watched people crowd the shop. An anguished, raspy cry came from the rear of the house, alarming everyone but Cloud Silk, who turned a deaf ear; she was used to it.

He's screaming again. Should I look in on him? the clerk Old Wang whispered to her.

Don't worry about him. With what he's got, you're miserable if you don't scream and miserable if you do. She went back to counting the bamboo markers for rice purchases. I knew he'd wind up like this, she said. People who embrace evil seldom die of old age.

While Five Dragons lay sick in bed, complex territorial struggles snarled gang relations in North City. The Green Gang aligned itself with newly bivouacked Japanese, and the Wharf Rats, as Red Gang affiliates, were cut adrift; one day they made a pilgrimage to the home of Five Dragons, who was lying in his tub of vinegar when they arrived. Looking contemptuously at his unhinged henchmen, he said, All I care about is getting better. Do what you want about that other stuff. Anything's possible as long as you stay alive.

As August came to an end, the situation grew increasingly chaotic. One day a bullet from a Japanese watchtower at the chemical plant ripped through a thick fir plank in the shop. Cloud Silk demanded that Five Dragons go look at the hole. It's all your fault, she complained. We could be killed while you soak in your tub. As he rubbed his suppurating belly, nonchalant and distant, he said, It was a stray shell, nothing to get upset about. Save your concern for bullets with eyes. If one of them has me in its sights, it'll never visit you. Women know how to lace porridge with poison, but there are more ways to kill people than that. She flipped the spent bullet into his vinegar bath. Do you really think I'm going to die, damn you? he demanded angrily, grabbing the Mauser lying on the floor behind him. Stop hovering over me, waiting for that to happen. He splashed dark vinegar on her and waved his pistol. Any more trouble from you and I'll put a bullet right in your cunt.

Five Dragons refused to go anywhere without his new Mauser; it even lay beneath his pillow when he was in the yard cooling off, attached to his finger by a red string as a precaution against the covetous eyes of his sons. The chaotic, constantly changing state of affairs, plus the aging hero residing in him, put him on his guard, as he carefully considered every possible contingency. One night he startled the household by shooting the family cat: The old tabby alit from the top of the wall with a piece of fish in its mouth, and Five Dragons shot it dead. Cloud Silk jumped out of bed. Have you lost your mind? she screamed. What's the idea of shooting that off? Five Dragons pointed to the dead cat. I thought it was Abao, he said. I was sure Abao had come back. You've really met the devil this time, Cloud Silk said. Why not kill the rest of us while you're at it? But Five Dragons put away his weapon, closed his eyes, and, with difficulty, rolled over on his rush mat. I thought it was Jade Embrace, he mumbled, hugging the pistol to himself. I thought I saw Jade Embrace jump down off the wall. They're my mortal enemies. Sooner or later they'll all be back.

The old yellow tabby had been Cloud Silk's favorite, so the next morning she laid it in a basket and carried it over to the city moat. She flung it into the green-tinged black water, with its fishy smell, she then watched it float off in a pile of garbage. She stood on the bank holding her now-empty basket and cried silently, wondering if she'd have been quite this sad if the same fate had befallen one of the emporium's human residents.

Five Dragons hadn't heard from the Wharf Rats for a long time, and he was growing concerned over payment for some smuggled tobacco. As his patience wore thin, he sent Kindling Boy to the hangout. Remember, he told his son, I want every cent they owe me. Don't let them hold anything back, and don't you get any funny ideas on the way home.

Later that day Kindling Boy returned home with a bloody nose and a bruised, swollen face. He burst into his father's room. See what they did to me! Now, slow down and tell me what happened, Five Dragons said to his son as he stood up in his vinegar bath. Who did that to you? Kindling Boy pointed angrily in the general direction of the window. That gang of men who used to hang around here. And they said they'd do the same to you if you showed your face. Five Dragons stood in the tub for a moment, covering his nakedness with his hand, before sitting down again and dismissing his son with a wave of his hand. Go on, get out. I understand now. Go clean up. What's a little blood? That's one of the risks of being a debt collector. It comes with the territory.

Suddenly the vinegar bath seemed to sear the very skin it was supposed to heal; he felt as if it were being torn from his body, like mud peeling off a damp wall, or willow leaves curling up as they baked in the sun. He screamed in agony and clawed his way out of the vinegar bath in which he had soaked for half the summer. Looking down at the spreading ripples, he saw his face, darker than usual, reflected in the deep red liquid, distorted by shifting waves.

A volley of crisp popping noises arose in the yard. It was Kindling Boy smashing empty vinegar pots against the base of the wall. Venting anger over his humiliation, apparently. One after another he raised the pots high over his head and flung them to the ground; he stopped at five.

Everyone pitches in to push when the wall's about to

topple. Why get so worked up? Five Dragons walked out into the yard, his skin mottled by clinging drops of red vinegar. He stepped barefoot on the broken pots without feeling anything; by the time Cloud Silk had come out to see what was going on, he was standing alone in the yard, shielding his eyes with one hand and mumbling as he looked into the sunset.

How long since I've gone anywhere? I'm going crazy in here. I'll bet the world has already forgotten what a man called Five Dragons looks like, he said to the heavens.

What *do* you look like? Cloud Silk began sweeping up shards of broken pottery, banging the tip of her broom against the wall. With oozing sores all over your body, don't you think people will laugh at you?

What's the highest spot on our property? he asked. I don't have to go out, but I want to see what's changed outside.

Nothing's changed. People still come to buy rice, and the streets are as noisy as ever. Japanese soldiers killed a pregnant woman on the bridge—one bullet, two lives, Cloud Silk muttered. Chaos rules out there. People who should die live on, and those who should be spared are killed off.

I'll ask you one more time. What's the highest spot on our property? Where can I get the best view of the changes outside?

Climb up onto the storeroom roof. You can't get any higher than that. Cloud Silk walked off to dump the broken pottery. Five Dragons's temper was getting harder to predict and even harder to understand. When his incurable VD finally sent him to hell, would she give him the kind of send-off expected of a spouse? she wondered. She shook her head. No, she would not wail like other wives.

Most likely she would simply take out the Feng genealogy and cross out his name. Better, she concluded, for the Feng clan to skip the fifty-fourth generation than for him to stain the reputation of a name that had graced the rice emporium for so long. If nothing else, she would sever the thousands of ties binding him to the Feng clan and give the spirits of her father and generations of his forebears the peace they deserved.

As dusk fell, Five Dragons climbed onto the roof, and once again the sights of North City spread out before him. On that summer evening the sunset painted the horizon a spectacular orange; waves of heat scorched the layers of clouds from behind, gradually turning them to cinders. Chimneys in the factory district and the unusual buildings that made up the chemical plant dwarfed everything around them as they sent black columns of smoke into the air, where they dissipated over densely packed homes in North City, with their roofs of ceramic tile or black sheet metal or gray cement blocks. At ground level he saw people moving slowly through narrow, winding streets and lanes—from his perch, they seemed like animated puppets. He looked off toward the horizons: The east and the west were marked, one by a gleaming railroad track, the other by a mist-shrouded river. A train rumbled across an arched span; a cargo ship, whistle shrieking, nestled up to a pier. This was the city. Or, as Five Dragons would have put it, an obscene, sinful, huge, fucking trap ready to lure the unwary. For a handful of rice, or a few coins, or a moment of pleasure, pitiful people poured into the city by train and by boat, all bending their efforts toward finding paradise on earth. If only they knew it didn't exist.

The world hadn't changed much. Five Dragons sat on the roof licking his wounds as heat rose all around him.

He had expected to be cast aside by the Wharf Rats, but not so soon and not so abruptly. A pack of miserable bastards. He tried to remember how they looked and acted. Amazingly, all he could recall were their trademark black clothes—that image, at least, was stamped on his memory. A far-flung sadness brought tears. He reached up to rub his eyes, first the useless one on the right, which was covered by a colorless secretion, then the left one, in which tears he never knew he had were pooling. He examined his body, starting at the bottom, where his left foot, with its broken toe, rested on a green roof tile, the dark purple toothmarks as ugly as ever. Then he looked over at the right foot, twisted and misshapen by the pirate's bullet. Slowly, painfully, his gaze moved up past his legs and torso, where oozing lesions crawled like cockroaches. He was racked by violent shudders. They've left scars all over my body. **They are cutting me up, slowly but surely, limb by limb.** Maybe I'm already a slab of salted meat lying in their frypan. Suddenly he was unable to hold back the hysterical rage inside. He stood up, cupped his hands like a megaphone, and damned the world beneath him: FUCK YOU ALL!

His voice carried so far that residents up and down Brick Mason Avenue heard the desolate curse and its echoes as they cooled off outside. Turning their heads toward the scream, they saw a figure perched atop a building in the rice-emporium compound; everyone recognized the long-absent Five Dragons.

Out on the street Redolence heard news of Snow Talent. Women had crowded round a young clerk from the local silk shop to hear about his encounter with Snow Talent in Shanghai. Redolence shouldered her way up front, nervous and joyful at the same time.

Well, I was carrying a bolt of cloth past a brothel, when three whores ran out and grabbed me. One of them held on to my shorts and wouldn't let go. Guess who it was. Snow Talent. He tapped the glass counter with his yard-stick for effect. It was Snow Talent, he repeated with a broad smile. She recognized me and didn't so much as blush. In fact she dragged me to the side to ask me some-thing. Know what it was? She asked if anyone had died at the rice emporium. I said no, but she didn't believe me. Not a single one? she said.

Once the shock had passed, the women burst out laugh-ing. Then came the conjectures and opinions. You're her sister-in-law, someone said to Redolence, tugging on her sleeve. You should know something. But Redolence turned, hoisted up her belly, and walked proudly out of the shop, leaving a single comment for the curious women left behind: Talking about women like that makes my mouth feel dirty. One of the listeners, who wanted to con-firm rumors of what went on in the rice emporium, fol-lowed her outside. Did Snow Talent really lace porridge with arsenic? Redolence ignored her and walked home, sucking on purple dried plums. She had already decided that her brother-in-law would be first to hear the news.

Rice Boy was perched on the windowsill of his southern-wing room playing the harmonica, his crippled leg hang-ing limply, the other banging nervously against the wall. He watched Redolence enter, her thickening middle mak-ing her sway slightly. She offered him the bag of dried plums. He didn't move. Redolence disgusted him, and so did the sour smell of dried plums.

Know what Snow Talent's doing these days? she asked as she spat out a plum pit. Then, with her eyes glued to his face, she said, drawing out each word, **Working as a prostitute in Shanghai.**

Rice Boy laid down his harmonica and looked indifferently at her mouth, with its dribbles of plum juice.

She drags customers in off the streets. One of them, as it turns out, was the clerk at the local silk shop. She laughed as she untied the handkerchief on her wrist and dabbed at the corners of her mouth, somewhat disappointed by his indifference. With undisguised contempt, she stared at his crippled leg before turning to go to her own room. Stay right where you are, came Rice Boy's menacing voice.

What else would you like to know? If you want the juicy details, go ask the clerk at the silk shop. That is, if you've got a strong stomach.

Your filthy mouth sickens me, he screamed at her. But not as much as your sow belly. He picked up his harmonica and flung it at her bulging abdomen. The sound of her frightened yelp as it thumped against her belly cheered him, so he climbed down, picked up the harmonica, and blew a few notes. She's a whore, he said. And so are you. Women are shameless, stinking whores.

Instinctively, Redolence held her hands protectively against her belly and backed up slowly to the door of her room, where she lifted up her blouse to inspect the offending spot. What do you think you're doing? You can't plant your own lousy seed, so you want to destroy ours, is that it? I'm telling Kindling Boy. He'll fix you real good.

The ensuing brawl had long seemed inevitable. Their eyes red with rage, the two brothers armed themselves with axes, clubs, and stones from the pickling vats, and by the time it was all over, nothing in the yard would lie undisturbed, having crashed or thudded against one thing or another. Redolence stood in the doorway egging her husband on. Go for his good leg, she screeched, break his good leg. Meanwhile, Five Dragons, who watched the savage battle through a window, shouted, Put down your weapons and go outside. Don't fight in the yard. At length it was Cloud Silk and a couple of the shop clerks who ran into the yard, where they tried, but failed, to stop the fight. In desperation, she ran to get help from the blacksmiths, a half dozen of whom eventually separated the battered and bloodied combatants. Rice Boy, who was resting on one knee, edged over to pick up his hatchet, and when no one was looking, he flung it at his brother's back; it sailed harmlessly past Kindling Boy's ear and shattered a window.

What's this all about? Cloud Silk asked after retrieving the hatchet. The dogs are always barking and the chickens forever squawking at the Feng house. This family has no face left.

Ask her, Kindling Boy muttered, pointing to his wife with his chin as he toweled his bloody face. She said the cripple hit her in the belly, and demanded that I whip him. I had no choice.

I should have known you were behind all this, Cloud Silk seethed at Redolence. What has the Feng family done to deserve this from you? You'd like to see me die of anger, wouldn't you?

Why does all the shit get dumped on me? Redolence asked with a mocking grin. I'm supposed to be the big sinner in this family. What a joke. She stepped back into her room and slammed the door. But it quickly reopened just enough for her to poke her head out. By the way, a blessed event has occurred in the Feng family. I won't say what it is, because I don't want to steal anybody's glory. Ask Rice Boy if you want to know.

Rice Boy sat stunned on the ground, cupping a dislodged tooth in his hand. It could have been Kindling Boy's, it could have been his own. His bloody lip oozed bright red. Cloud Silk walked up to help him to his feet, but he shoved her away. In agony she squeezed her eyes shut, her deeply creased brow set above a ghostly white face. As she massaged her temples she said, You've been a troublemaker since the day you were born. Have you forgotten how your leg was broken? You killed your own sister, isn't that enough? Now you want to murder your brother.

Sure. Why not? And I wouldn't mind including you in the process. Rice Boy slowly climbed to his feet and looked down at the solitary tooth in the palm of his hand. He whirled and threw it onto the storeroom roof, where it clattered on the tiles for a moment before disappearing.

Not long afterward, a gun battle erupted between the Wharf Rats and the Long Guns from the Green Gang, sending shock waves through the city. Men in teahouses on Brick Mason Avenue talked about little else, surmising that it was a territorial dispute. All night long residents of Riverside Avenue heard gunfire, but it died down around sunrise, when the curious came out to look around. They found black-clad corpses strewn among piles of cargo and under the arm of a dockside crane, from which a severed and very bloody head hung. Most of the dead, they saw, were Wharf Rats; someone took it into his head to make a body count, of which there were more than thirty. Obviously, a lopsided victory for the Long Guns.

The Wharf Rats had controlled the dockside for as long as old-time residents of North City could remember; all that time they and the Long Guns had stayed clear of one another. Well water and river water do not mix—that was the policy of local gangs. The old-timers suspected a hidden conspiracy behind this odd outbreak of violence. Before long their suspicions were confirmed when word of a land deal circulated among the teahouses. A Long Guns survivor of the battle revealed that someone had sold title to Lane 11 of Third Street in the wharf area to the Long Guns, and when the Wharf Rats denied its validity, the battle began. The seller's identity was not revealed but teahouse customers thought they knew anyway: It was not Lu Piji, Sixth Master Lu, who had died on the Bund in Shanghai, and it certainly wasn't the new gangleader Little Shandong, whose head hung from the crane. No, it had to have been Five Dragons.

On the morning following the incident, Kindling Boy rushed over to the wharf. Many of the dead were men he knew—he pointed them out by name and nickname to curious bystanders. When he returned home, his father was sitting alone in the yard enjoying a cup of tea—thick and dark, as always, the only difference being the addition of a chunk of wild ginseng.

You escaped with your life this time, Father, Kindling Boy reported, gasping for breath. Your gang brothers are lying dead on the wharf. Blood all over the place. Long Guns did it.

Five Dragons's face showed no emotion as he sipped tea and reached down to scratch his crotch. See that, he said to his son, holding up blood-and-pus-streaked fingers. I'm bleeding, too. Have been all summer long.

Want to go see? Kindling Boy shivered as he recalled the carnage on the wharf. It's horrible. Yesterday they were swaggering up and down the street, today they're face to face with King Yama of Hell.

I don't have to go see. I calculated their life spans myself. None of them stood a chance of living through the summer. He raised his fingers to the sunlight to get a closer look at the foul matter clinging to them. Smell that? he asked Kindling Boy. That's what death smells like.

Kindling Boy looked away from the rotting flesh in disgust.

I've learned lots of ways to murder and wreak vengeance in my lifetime, Five Dragons said. He climbed out of his rattan chair and hobbled a few steps across the yard, until the pain from angry sores on his thighs rubbing together made walking nearly impossible. He looked up into the morning sky. Another scorcher, he noted. How can it get so hot? If not for all those dead men, the weather would never start to cool off. **Summer is the season of death.**

Kindling Boy walked into his room, where Redolence was sitting on the commode embroidering baby clothes. Her rounded belly rested in her lap. Where were you off to so early this morning? she asked as she closed the curtain around her.

Off looking at dead bodies, he replied, holding his nose. Everywhere I go it stinks to heaven. Blood and guts at the wharf, and smelly shit in my own house.

Who died this time? It seems like somebody dies every day. She bit off the thread and shook out the red baby jumper to get an appreciative look. She had crudely embroidered a pattern with words like "good luck" and "wealth." You know I like to look at dead bodies, she said. Why didn't you take me with you? You have no idea how stifling it is in this house.

You'd have been terrified. There were more than thirty. Blood and gore covered the wharf. He held his thumb and finger out with an exaggerated showing of the thickness of the layer of blood. Who died? The Wharf Rats, all but Father. That shows how strong his grip on life is.

A hissing sound from behind the curtain was followed by the emergence of Redolence, commode in hand. See how big and clumsy I am? she grumbled. And still I have to clean the commode every day. You people don't care about me. You count every coin as if you had to dig it out of your assholes. It wouldn't bankrupt you to hire a maid, would it?

We don't have any money. Haven't you heard my mother complain about how poor we are? The old skinflint holds on to her beat-up cashbox for dear life.

Your father has money, Redolence said, as if it had just dawned on her. She put her mouth up to Kindling Boy's ear and whispered, He just sold some land, sold it to the Long Guns and made a potful of money.

Who said so?

My brother-in-law. He works for the Long Guns. He said your father drove a hard bargain, but wouldn't tell me how much was paid. My guess is at least a hundred ounces of gold.

Don't pin your hopes on *his* money, Kindling Boy sneered. I've lived in this house all my life, and he's never given me any of it. Of course he's got money, but who knows what he plans to do with it? I've never been able to figure out what goes on in his head.

Say what you like, but he'll die before we do, and then his money will be ours. Redolence carried the commode outside. She had enough common sense to know the benefits of death—someone else's—which raised her hopes and confidence level. As she crossed the yard she saw Five Dragons sitting at a low table slurping a bowl of porridge, straightening his neck with each painful swallow and making little popping noises. A face that had once inspired fear now looked sickly and sad, and as she walked by, she gave the commode a provocative shake, sending ordurous little splashes over to the porridge pot. There was no reaction from Five Dragons, whose breakfast progressed in an atmosphere of private grief. Redolence drew a simple conclusion from the sight: The old man's rotting away in front of us.

Somehow it never occurred to Kindling Boy and his wife that the bodies strewn across the wharf and Five Dragons's sale of land were somehow linked. But even had they made the connection, it would have held no particular significance for them; they were too obsessed with Five Dragons's diseased body (or, more accurately, his imminent death) to be concerned.

One afternoon, following a rainstorm, Five Dragons took advantage of the cool weather to leave the compound. Brick Mason Avenue residents saw him ensconced in a rickshaw, a wide-brimmed straw hat hiding his face from view, a loose-fitting black shirt and black trousers flapping in the wind; the sight called to mind the unforeseen fall of the Wharf Rats. Now only he wore the black clothes, and people stared as the rickshaw moved down the street until it was only a tiny speck.

Five Dragons had long wanted to check out the changes at the wharf for himself, observe how the Long Guns went about governing this valuable piece of land, and see if the storm had washed away the blood of thirty-eight Wharf Rats. There it was. The muddy water flowed swiftly along, and fewer ships were under way than usual; the faint smells of grain and lumber issued from the docks, where cargo was scattered around a newly erected block-house; puddles had accumulated in the indentations of oil-cloth tents. From the rickshaw, Five Dragons quickly surveyed the area. He saw no Long Guns, nor anyone wearing a red sash, although from beneath his straw hat he did see a lone helmeted sentry atop the blockhouse, his head thrust out the window as he shouted at a parade of stevedores. His rifle was strapped across his back, a red sash dangling from the tip of his bayonet and fluttering with each breeze. It was a Long Guns sash, and Five Dragons could only guess how it had wound up as an adornment on a Japanese bayonet.

It's the Japanese. They've been running the show on the docks for the last five days, the rickshaw runner volunteered.

Too bad, Five Dragons said as he took one last look at the wharf, a self-mocking tone creeping into his voice. After all that fighting, neither side wound up in control of this place. Who'd have guessed it would be occupied by the Japanese?

They're in control of all the good places these days, the runner said. Who knows how long they plan to stick around?

Let's go, there's nothing more to see here. The weak smile on Five Dragons's face showed his sadness. He pulled the hat down to hide his weary face and said, Everybody's scared of the Japanese, including me. You can take me back to Brick Mason Avenue now.

Five Dragons at last felt he had taken care of this unfinished business. On the way back they encountered a column of wagons piled high with rice moving slowly down the street. The distinctive smell suffused the moist air in a natural and moving way, and Five Dragons felt as if a warm and gentle apparition were floating in the air around him. Raising his arms in an empty gesture as he sat in the rickshaw, he thought back to that earlier time when he had walked down Brick Mason Avenue behind a line of rice-laden wagons just like these. He had been following them ever since.

Those wagons will lead us home.

The command sounded to the rickshaw puller as if it had been spoken by someone who was talking in his sleep.

13

A STRANGER WITH A MONEY POUCH OVER HIS SHOULDER burst upon the scene at the rice emporium. Introducing himself as Five Dragons's cousin, he said he had just made the long trip from Maple-Poplar Village. Hushed discussions between the two men behind a closed door aroused the suspicions of Cloud Silk, who stood beneath the window to eavesdrop—unsuccessfully, as it turned out; but through a tiny hole in the paper covering she saw Five Dragons hand the stranger a paper parcel, and assumed it was money.

Over the summer the stranger haunted the rice emporium regularly. One day, after he had left, Cloud Silk flung open the door and spotted Five Dragons on top of the wardrobe; he had loosened a brick stopper in the rafters and was stuffing a wooden box into the space.

Why put it there? Cloud Silk asked. Aren't you afraid a rat might run off with it?

Why are you always sneaking around, looking into things that don't concern you? I can't even take a leak without feeling your eyes on me. After plugging up the hiding place, he dusted himself off and eased down off the wardrobe onto his bed, and from there to the floor.

You're the sneaky one. I'd like to know what you and that country cousin of yours are up to.

I'll tell you, he said. It won't make any difference. He took a deep breath, looked up at the brick in the rafters, which fit snugly in place and kept the wooden cashbox away from prying eyes, as it had for years. Now that Cloud Silk had discovered its hiding place, maybe it was time to put it somewhere else, somewhere safer. An expression of irritation on his face failed to conceal how invigorated he had become as a result of dealings with his cousin; his passion was renewed. I'm going to buy some land, he said. Three thousand acres.

Buy land? Cloud Silk studied his face. He was serious, she could tell that from his expression and the slight stammer on the word *land*. Have you gone completely insane? Where is this land you're buying?

It's the land my childhood home stands on. A thousand acres of paddy land, another thousand acres of cotton fields, plus the main house, threshing ground, and other buildings. A white-hot glare flowed from his good eye for the second time as he picked up a brush and dusted himself off. Slightly blackened flakes of skin fell through the bristles and floated to the ground. It was a vow I made when I left, he continued. I made it to a little boy and repeated it at my parents' gravesite. Now it's time to fulfill that vow. My cousin gave me a stack of Maple-Poplar Village land deeds. They're all in that wooden box.

You really have lost your mind. I thought you meant you were buying a burial plot. With an agonizing shake of her head, she went on, Where did the money come from?

I saved it up, one coin at a time. All those years of eating, drinking, and whoring around, I never spent my own hard-earned money. He pointed to the ceiling with the brush as a blissful look spread across his face. The first money I ever earned is inside that box, the silver dollar your father gave me for the backbreaking work I did.

You . . . Cloud Silk did not complete her thought. She was struck by the notion that she was looking into the face of a stranger. During nearly a quarter of a century with him she had had that feeling before, but never so powerfully or so urgently as now. She turned her back to him and began to sob. At that moment, she realized how pitifully fragile he was. Owing to a pessimistic view of the world, she believed that all people are condemned to live in isolation, beyond the help of others, that they must hide their cashboxes in the rafters or in a wall somewhere or beneath floorboards, that they spend part of their time walking in the light of day, and part hidden in darkness, where no one can see them. That little wooden box hidden in the rafters, for instance, seemed to contain Five Dragons's soul, leaping in frenzy one moment, sobbing the next.

It was the seventh day of the seventh lunar month: Cloud Silk lit votive candles at noon, as custom required, to pay respects to her ancestors and whatever other ghostly spirits her imagination could conjure. She completed the sacrificial rites alone, since the rest of the family showed total indifference. Then, after extinguishing the candles, she watched a puff of pale blue smoke rise from the altar, holding its shape until it reached the ancestors' portraits, where it fanned out to enshroud the furniture in the room and wrap itself around the family members sitting at the table. Her gaze fell devoutly on her father's portrait; it glowed intermittently. She believed she had seen a Buddhist light pointing the way across the chasm of delusion.

I just saw the light of Buddha, she exclaimed to Five Dragons. That's a good omen. Now maybe peace will return to this house.

Stop dreaming, he said nonchalantly. Peace will never return to this house as long as a single one of us lives. He stepped on a burning sheet of spirit money that had floated from the altar to the floor, then spat on the cinders.

A commotion broke the night calm on Brick Mason Avenue, bringing the residents out of their bamboo cots and rattan chairs to witness the sight of the local dyer's third daughter-in-law chasing Rice Boy. Howling and cursing, she was on the heels of her gimp quarry, who carried a pair of scissors.

Rice Boy ran into the shop, leaving his pursuer standing in the doorway, where she turned and provided spectators with a fitful explanation of what had happened. They didn't know whether to laugh or cry: Rice Boy had crept up while she was asleep and slit the crotch of her shorts with his scissors.

After his wife ran away to become a whore, I guess he went crazy over women, someone said with a grin.

Then why doesn't he cut open his mother's crotch? the young woman complained as she kicked the closed door. You people in there are guttersnipes, you're despicable.

The two families had feuded for years, but this time the dyer was clearly the injured party, and Cloud Silk's anger over the incident sent her to bed for three days; a sufferer of migraines during unhappy times, she was now reduced to smearing cooling salves on her forehead and covering them with peppermint leaves. The flow of tears was endless, owing partly to the prickly salves and partly to grief.

After calling Rice Boy to her bedside, she looked with exasperation at her son, who stood, stone-faced, clutching his old harmonica.

How could you do something like that? When word gets out you'll never find another wife. Recalling the popular saying, If the upper beam is crooked, the lower beam cannot be straight, she sighed and added, You're just like your father. Wild animals have better manners than you two.

I need a woman. I can't sleep without one, Rice Boy replied firmly, his head down as he tapped his teeth rhythmically with the harmonica. He felt no shame over the incident.

How am I supposed to find you a new wife? Sadly she realized that the light of Buddha she had seen during the Festival of Ghosts was a sham, meant to deceive her. That or wishful thinking, since her hopes were always being dashed by reality. Her thoughts turned to Snow Talent, the daughter-in-law who had run away. Blame it all on the slut, damn her, she said. You could cut her to ribbons and I'd still despise her. I spent two hundred silver dollars to bring her across our threshold. But instead of providing the Feng clan with an heir, she poisons our porridge, then runs off.

Snow Talent was stupid, Rice Boy sniggered as he cleaned the holes of his harmonica with a matchstick. If I had poisoned the porridge, no one would have tasted the arsenic, and you'd all be in hell chatting with King Yama by now.

Shut your mouth! Cloud Silk pounded the rush mat beneath her with her fists. This family will kill me yet. She was too ill to worry about the heat; cool air snaking up between her fingers slithered cruelly around and over her frail body. She turned to see her son's retreating back. Who wouldn't like to poison this family? she remarked. I've thought about it for twenty years. I just never found the courage.

As her pregnancy neared its end, Redolence grew more vocal in her complaints of aches, pains, and dwindling energy. Finally she took to bed and spent her time listening to the phonograph, abandoning her household duties altogether. One day she told Kindling Boy that she had predicted the gender of the fetus by tossing a wetted needle into the air: It stuck straight up in a lump of clay. According to her mother, that meant he would have a son. Who can you people count on to continue the family line, if not me? she asked with a palpable sense of pride. Her husband merely smiled, preferring to remain noncommital. Kindling Boy was not interested in such things.

Cricket jars, once all but eliminated, made a reappearance in a corner of the storeroom. One day Kindling Boy lifted one of the lids and flipped in a single green soybean, then watched the savage red-headed cricket chomp down on it. He was awestruck by his cricket king's appetite and vitality. Just then Five Dragons waddled into the storeroom and stood behind his son to quietly observe the feeding. Try rice, he said at length.

They won't eat it, Kindling Boy replied. My crickets only eat soybeans.

There isn't a human alive who doesn't eat rice, and no dumb animals either. Even immortals eat rice, Five Dragons remarked confidently as he scooped up a handful and dumped it into the jar. The cricket ignored it. Five Dragons was disappointed. It's not hungry, he said as he clapped the lid back on the jar. Wait till it's crazed with hunger, then give it some rice, and see whether it eats it or not.

Wary of his father's domineering, unpredictable ways, Kindling Boy picked up the jar with his king of crickets and headed quickly for the door. His father shouted him to a halt. This was not a casual visit.

Your wife's going to have her baby soon, isn't she?

Any day now. She says it's a boy.

Boy or girl, it doesn't matter. It's one more mouth to feed. No joy showed on Five Dragons's face. She can have it at her parents' home. I want you to send her there tomorrow.

Why can't she have it here?

Don't you understand? he said emotionlessly. A woman's not supposed to have a baby at home when a male member of the family is sick. Her bloody emanations could be fatal to me. Noting the puzzled look on his son's face, he added, It's a Maple-Poplar Village belief. I used to think it was a silly superstition, but things are different now, and in my condition, I can't afford to take anything for granted.

Was this some sort of joke? Kindling Boy held his tongue for a moment, trying to work up the nerve to defy his father. Finally he smiled and said, After striving to outdo other men all your life, how could you suddenly be afraid of a pregnant woman? He turned and walked into the yard, cricket jar in hand. Then: What if she refuses? You know how stubborn she can be. What if she demands to have her baby at home?

I'll get someone to carry her out, Five Dragons replied. What could be simpler?

Redolence surprised Kindling Boy by acceding to the request without a murmur. I might as well go home, she said, since your mother wouldn't take care of me, anyway. My mother says the first month is very important, and if I'm not well taken care of, I could get really sick. She then went to her mother-in-law for money. I can't ask my own family to support me, she said. This child belongs to the Feng clan, and it's only right that you pay the bills. Cloud Silk, still confined to her bed, held a peppermint leaf to her aching forehead, barely able to contain her disgust over such a blatant demand. But when she took out her cashbox, Redolence sneered at the money clutched in the outstretched hand. Do you really expect to send me off with a few measly coins? Maybe you don't care about losing face, but I won't have my family laugh at me. With no way out of her predicament, Cloud Silk went into the northern wing, where a brief search turned up the jade bracelet that Cloud Weave had left behind. She rubbed the charred spots from force of habit and said, I don't have any cash lying around, so take this. It will bring at least a hundred at the pawn shop. The gold is fine, the jade is pure. It's a family heirloom that can ward off evil. At length Redolence accepted the paltry sum of cash and the bracelet, deftly sliding the latter onto her wrist, then raising her arm to take an appreciative look. Well, then, she said in an offhanded manner, I'll just wear it and keep evil at bay.

On the road to her home, Kindling Boy noticed the jade bracelet on his wife's wrist, but thought nothing of it, having no eye for jewelry. She was the daughter of the renowned South City coffinmaker, in whose shopfront was displayed an array of cottonwood coffins, and every time Kindling Boy visited his in-laws it felt like a trip through a cemetery. This time, as he and Redolence walked past the local cotton mill, they saw it had been turned into a barracks. Japanese soldiers were holding drills behind coils of barbed wire, their shouts carrying into the distance.

Look at the stumpy legs and stubbly beards on those funny Japanese soldiers, Redolence said from the rickshaw bench. The joy of coming home had turned her gaunt face ruddy and vigorous. She took Kindling Boy's hand. And listen to that silly gibberish they speak.

Funny? You wouldn't think it was so funny with one of their bayonets sticking through you.

Well, I think they're cute. She giggled and looked over at her husband, who didn't feel like arguing. Women come into the world with a weak mind, he was thinking, then keep changing it. Absurd thoughts like hers did not surprise him.

Just past noon on August 13 two youthful and very drunk Japanese soldiers staggered out of the military barracks in South City and forced their way past the sentry, determined to seek out some special entertainment: Out of a liquor-induced fanaticism they had devised a scheme to see who could slaughter the most people.

Their first victims were a melon peddler and his customer just outside the barracks gate. When the peddler saw the Japanese soldiers approach, bayonets drawn, he walked up cradling half a watermelon. Thirsty, officers? He smiled and offered it to them. It's sweet, crunchy, and thin-skinned. If you don't like it, it's free. The soldiers exchanged grins. Their breath stank of alcohol. Sensing danger in their wild cackles, the peddler threw down the watermelon and ran for the safety of his pushcart. But he was a step too slow for the glinting bayonet that buried itself in his naked back. Amid the impaled man's screeches, the soldier withdrew his blood-streaked bayonet and wiggled a single finger in front of his buddy. *ICHI—ICHI—ICHI,* he shouted.

The killing spree followed the meandering alleys of South City in a frenzy of indiscriminate bloodletting that left a chorus of agonizing shrieks and mournful wails up one street and down the other. Finally the Japanese soldiers spotted a terrified, slow-moving pregnant woman in front of the coffinmaker's shop at the exact same moment, and the drive to win the contest propelled them onto the steps of the coffin shop. Two bayonets entered the bulging abdomen simultaneously.

News of the tragic events in South City reached Brick Mason Avenue around nightfall. Rice Boy handed Five Dragons the evening newspaper, on which photos of the murder victims were splashed across the front page. One, a woman, lay in a pool of blood, her belly sliced open to expose a pasty, fully formed fetus, half in and half out of the destroyed womb. Noticing the lines and shadows of several coffins fanned out behind her, he called to Cloud Silk. Come look at this and tell me who the woman is. But his wife, who was in the kitchen making a pot of date-and-lotus-seed soup, turned her nose up at the gory front page. You look at it if you like it so much. Things like that make me sick. Five Dragons kept staring at the dead woman's face. I said take a look, he repeated, more loudly, and tell me if it's Redolence.

Cloud Silk paled the moment she looked at the paper; the first thing she noticed was the bracelet on the dead woman's wrist. Oh no! she gasped, pointing to the grainy outline of the jade bracelet. It's her, it's Redolence! Her blood ran cold. She was carrying the Feng clan's heir. Those monsters.

On the following day, Kindling Boy dragged two black-lacquered cypress coffins home from South City, one large and one small. Redolence's body filled the larger one; her male infant, dead before it even had a taste of life, lay in the smaller one. The proprietress of the coffin shop insisted that Redolence and her offspring be returned to the Feng home for three days. She suspected that the Fengs had planned the whole thing, that on the pretext of sending their daughter home they had led her straight into a trap. Kindling Boy, grief-stricken, did not argue the point. Instead he loaded the coffins onto two lumber wagons and led them through the chaotic streets, past fearful residents, some of whom stood in doorways arguing bitterly over the exact number of victims of the killing spree. Kindling Boy recalled how pleased Redolence had been to reveal that she was going to give him a son, and how he had teased her cruelly—**You wouldn't think it was so funny with one of their bayonets sticking through you.** He shook his head sadly, keenly aware of the prophetic power of the human tongue.

For three blistering days the bodies of Redolence and her son lay in state; the family placed ice around the coffins and Cloud Silk sprayed at least eight bottles of toilet water in the room, but the stench of death was too powerful. Only a few people dropped by to offer condolences; everyone seemed to be in mourning as the presence of death filled the summer days following the South City killings; the wake at the rice emporium caused hardly a ripple.

Kindling Boy, cotton stuffed up his nostrils, maintained

a vigil between the two coffins in accordance with the wishes of his in-laws. During those three days he seemed numb, watching the jade bracelet dig into Redolence's discolored flesh as the arm grew more and more bloated. The dim sound of a moan fell on his ears; wondering if it had come from the corpse, he stood and pulled back the sheet. Her face was turning hideously purple around a gaping mouth in which a blackened pit was lodged between tongue and gums; maybe an apricot pit, possibly plum, he couldn't tell for sure; he knew without a doubt that it was the remains of the last thing Redolence had ever eaten.

You killed my wife. On the day of the funeral Kindling Boy sought out the source of his crippling grief. If you hadn't sent her home to have the baby, he accosted his father, they'd both be alive today.

You're blaming me? Five Dragons gazed calmly at his son from his rocking chair as he rhythmically tapped the armrests. Don't make me laugh. He closed his eyes. The blood of a great many people is on my hands, but not theirs. Rabbits don't eat the grass around their own burrows. In my two years of schooling I learned that much at least.

If we'd kept her here, she'd be alive and I'd have a son to hold, Kindling Boy said, his lids drooping from a lack of sleep. With a yawn he lay on the counter and muttered, My own father killed my wife and son.

Go find those two Japanese soldiers if you want to settle scores. Five Dragons drew his trusty Mauser and laid it in the palm of his hand. You can have this if you'll bring back their heads. Have you got the balls? Well, have you?

The only response was a loud snore—Kindling Boy was fast asleep on the counter. Having buried his wife and son in the Feng burial plot outside the city, he could finally get some rest.

The idea that the city was an immense, ornamental grave-yard occurred often to Five Dragons at night. That's what cities are for: They come into being for the sake of the dead. Throngs of people materialize among crowded, noisy streets, only to disappear, like drops of water evaporating in the sun's rays. Throngs of them are murdered, or carried away by disease, or killed by depression and apoplexy, or impaled on Japanese bayonets, or dispatched by Japanese bullets. For them the city is a gigantic coffin that emits thick black industrial smoke, scented powder, and the hidden odor of women's sex as soon as the lid is raised. An arm, shapeless yet limber and powerful, grows out of the coffin, which contains gold and silver, fancy clothes and delicacies. The arm reaches into the streets and alleys to drag wanderers into the cold depths.

In the quiet of the night Five Dragons dimly perceived that outstretched black hand. Grasping his Mauser, he moved his sweat-soaked rush mat from the northern wing out into the yard, and from there to the storeroom, always keeping one step ahead of the menacing black hand. Settling finally on the storeroom, he rolled up his mat and fell asleep naked on a mound of rice. It was, after all, rice, and rice alone, that had a calming, cooling effect on him; all his life it had comforted him. Now it was late at night, and the watchman's bamboo clappers sounded rhythmically up and down Brick Mason Avenue. In the distance a train rumbled down the tracks with a lulling cadence; from the other direction came a faint whistle, as a ship eased away from its mooring. Time passes, but the world hasn't changed. Meanwhile I get older and weaker, caught up in a tug of war with the black hand of death. A succession of morbid images appeared before Five Dragons's eyes—all those corpses, different in manner of pose, yet united in final destination. At that moment he came face-to-face with his one and only, his real fear: death.

Death. Five Dragons sat up, suddenly wide awake with the crystallization of this notion. Scooping up handfuls of rice, he poured it over his head. The soft flowing sound was soothing; the rice cooled him as it brushed his skin; it was burying him, covering his scars and every inch of rotting, suppurating flesh. It eased his tension and turned his thoughts to happier episodes from his childhood in Maple-Poplar Village: the mischievous taunting of newlyweds outside bridal chambers; the baffling outbursts of children's laughter as they watched hogs being slaughtered on the threshing floor; his sole youthful sexual experience, when, at the age of eighteen, he and his sister-in-law had played in tall grass. His emotions built: If not for that devastating flood, he was thinking, Maple-Poplar Village would be a safer place for me. The difference between town and country is the frequency of death. Back during those peaceful, promising times, he recalled, on average only a single old villager died each year; but in the city, where chaos reigns and human perversities run rampant, someone new passes through the netherworld gates nearly every day, plummeting straight to the depths of the Nine Springs.

Five Dragons envisioned his reception when he returned home a conquering hero. Now he owned three thousand acres of land in Maple-Poplar Village, which was being tilled by local farmers. His cousin would lead a delegation to welcome him at the village entrance, where ninety strings of firecrackers hanging from trees would be exploded, and ninety tables would be set up around the newly rebuilt ancestral hall for a welcoming banquet that would include ninety vats of homemade rice wine. Five Dragons would not drink, of course, since that was the one stricture to which he had adhered all his life, in his quest to remain clearheaded at all times. What will I do while my fellow villagers are stuffing themselves and getting drunk? Maybe, he thought, I'll take a walk around that dark, rich earth I've missed for so long, or survey the paddy fields on the left bank of the river and the poppy fields on the right. His cousin had said that in the spring the farmers had planted only those two crops on his land, as instructed; he knew all about current trends in agricultural production.

Five Dragons positioned himself in the path of a cool breeze sweeping in through the transom, carrying odors from the chemical plant and the fragrance of roadside acacias. He stuck his head out to look at night-darkened Brick Mason Avenue. Autumn was well under way, so there were no people sleeping outside to cool off; cobblestones glimmered like fresh snow under the streetlamps. Fall weather was becoming more and more pronounced, and as Five Dragons reflected on time's ruthless passage and the progressive deterioration of his health, his mood soured; he roared at the deserted street: FUCK ALL YOUR WOMEN!

Fuck all your women. The curse exhausted every last ounce of energy, allowing him finally to slump weakly against the splintery transom sill, as the hand of death gently stroked his hair. He curled into a ball. Don't touch me, he sobbed in response to the illusory sensation, don't you touch me. What do you think you're doing?

Perfect silence covered Brick Mason Avenue as midnight came and went. A solitary figure standing beneath the awning of the grocery store glanced at the rice emporium from time to time. Five Dragons spotted the stranger, but his weak eyes and the enveloping darkness kept him from seeing who it was and what he was doing there.

14

CLOUD SILK ENGAGED A SORCERER FROM SOUTH CITY TO rid the shop of a ghost. A string of calamities had convinced her that an evil spirit dwelt there, one that had to be exorcised.

One drizzly morning the mystic appeared at the door, an ancient Taoist cape draped over his shoulders. Brandishing a sword, he performed a spirit dance around the shop, under the watchful eyes of Cloud Silk and Five Dragons. Her heart was filled with reverence and awe; he sat in a rocking chair sipping tea, seemingly indifferent to the exorcist's antics. Until the man spread a sheet of yellow paper on the floor in preparation for nabbing the ghost, that is. Five Dragons's loud cackles broke the spell. What are you laughing at? Cloud Silk scolded. You'll scare the ghost off. I'm laughing at you, he replied. At how seriously you're taking this nonsense. After all my years around quacks and charlatans, do you really think I can't spot a phony?

The sorcerer's sword was slicing toward the yellow paper. His ruddy face glowed and his expression was sublimely enigmatic as he pressed the blade against the yellow paper to reveal ghostly blood. See there! he shouted to Cloud Silk, then stopped in disbelief: There was no blood, not a drop, nothing but a solitary gash from his sword.

It can't bleed without magic powder, Five Dragons commented. He leaned back and roared a second time, his face suffused with the gleeful look of a man who has pulled off a successful prank. I switched the paper, he continued. I know the tricks of the exorcist trade.

Who said you could switch my paper? the embarrassed sorcerer said defensively, sheathing his sword. The ghost will annihilate your entire family as nonbelievers.

Does the name Five Dragons mean nothing to you? Cheat the gullible all you want, but what makes you think you can get away with your tricks in *my* home? Five Dragons shut his eyes, his laughter having taken him to the brink of sheer exhaustion. Let me lie here awhile. The truth is, only I know where the ghost is.

Cloud Silk saw the sorcerer out the door and paid him for his efforts. I think I already caught my ghost, he said. There's one living in the midst of your family, but his head is fastened securely to his neck. The mystic's expression was a mixture of cunning and mystery, and as Cloud Silk gazed at his lips, moist and red like a woman's, her curiosity got the best of her. This ghost, where is it? The sorcerer pointed to the yard with his sword. Lying there in the rocking chair, he said softly.

Cloud Silk stood on the steps and watched the sorcerer walk off. There was, she believed, truth in what he said.

Summer had ended with a dramatic change in the lives of the rice-emporium brothers: Both had regained their bachelorhood. No one in the neighborhood doubted that it was retribution for all the evil deeds of the interloper, Five Dragons.

During the warm weather, the neighbors had gotten used to hearing the strains of a harmonica—melancholic, tinny, off-key—but they hoped that as the chilled air of autumn settled in, their ears would be spared. Their hopes were dashed when they spotted Rice Boy hobbling after the daughter of the bamboo-goods shop owner as he blew on his harmonica, his musicianship a perfect accompaniment to his ineptitude as a runner. The shrieking girl was scared witless; observers noted the baffling fury in Rice Boy's gloomy eyes.

At first everyone assumed that Rice Boy was sex-crazed, but the grade-school teacher on East Street disagreed. Having once updated the Feng clan genealogy, he had a deeper understanding of the family. Rice Boy has a weak psychological makeup, he pronounced to local gossips, and in a family like that, he's sure to suffer a nervous breakdown sooner or later. Would you be capable of suffocating your own sister at the age of ten? That boy was never given any breathing room. He's unbalanced. One more disaster in his life will send him over the edge.

Feeling that Rice Boy may well have needed the consoling presence of a woman, Cloud Silk asked around, hoping to find him a suitable wife. At one place she was advised to buy a girl, one of those with straw tags pinned to their hair, from the trader in human cargo who operated out of a wooden ark moored alongside the wharf. She grimaced. No son of the Feng clan will sink so low as to buy a wife from one of those people, she said. I wouldn't be caught dead doing that, even if Rice Boy asked me to. Fortunately, her other son was less trouble. Following the death of his wife and child, Kindling Boy returned easily to his dissolute life-style. With the early-autumn arrival of the gambling season, he spent more time in gambling houses at Three Corners than he did at home, and his frequent absences from home kept the pressure off his mother.

One day he showed up to borrow money for lottery tickets, and brought astonishing news with him. He had seen Jade Embrace at Three Corners with some Japanese soldiers who were raiding a gambling establishment.

That's impossible. She couldn't believe her ears. He's in Shanghai getting rich. It doesn't make sense for him to come here to work for the Japanese.

Why would I lie to you? He's wearing Japanese boots and carrying a Japanese pistol. I think he's their interpreter.

Why didn't you bring him home? Disbelief still showed in Cloud Silk's eyes. Her son responded by holding out his hand for lottery money. She pushed it aside. I don't have it, she said. Go ask your father if you have the nerve. She was trying to picture Jade Embrace's pale, lovely face, which he had inherited from Cloud Weave. But pleasant thoughts were short-lived: After all I did for the ungrateful bastard, he doesn't even have the decency to come see me. You'd think he'd at least come pay his respects.

I called out to him, but he pretended he didn't know me. If he'll ignore his own cousin, what's to keep him from doing the same to his aunt? Kindling Boy held his hand out again. Why all the concern, anyway? he asked with a laugh. You don't need him to take care of you in your old age or see you to your final resting spot. We'll be at your bedside when you're too old to get around, so why not show a little gratitude beforehand?

I don't need you, I don't need anybody. I'm spending my last days in the Purple Bamboo nunnery. Regarding her son with anger, she grabbed a broom propped against the wall and smacked his hand with it. I don't have any money, I said. Go get it from your father.

Not likely. I won't see any of his money till he's dead and buried. With a curl of his lip, Kindling Boy withdrew his hand, resigned to failure. But don't think you've had the last word, he said as he headed to his room. I'll just sell some of my furnishings. She stood in the yard holding the broom, assuming he was making idle threats. But he soon emerged with a redwood chair over his head. She tried to stop him. How dare you! Unmoved, he easily shoved her out of the way; in that regard, at least, he resembled the youthful Five Dragons. I'll start with this, he said casually, then come back for the bed. With my wife and child gone, I don't need this stuff. In desperation, Cloud Silk thought of Five Dragons. Only he could control his son. She turned and called to him.

A moment later, Five Dragons appeared at the window, vinegar dripping from his naked body. By squinting, he was able to make out his wife and son in the yard. He appeared to be scratching himself down below with one hand and tugging on his shoulder with the other; loose folds of flesh quivered.

Sell it, go ahead, sell it. Except for the rice, I don't give a shit about anything in this house. Sell it all, I don't care.

Astonished, Cloud Silk let go of the chair and plopped down on the ground, where she sat in stunned silence. Soon she was sobbing and cursing her husband and sons, cut from the same cloth. What have I done to deserve this? She began banging her forehead on a rock. If heaven won't allow me a decent life, she mumbled, why can't I at least die in peace? Why doesn't one of those Japanese bullets have my name on it?

Dying's easy, Five Dragons remarked from the window. It's living that's hard. He was still scratching himself. What are you crying about? There isn't a blemish anywhere on your fair skin. I'm the one who's suffering, with scars and open sores all over, not to mention the pus and blood and crawling vermin. My cock aches and itches so bad I wouldn't be surprised if it dropped off.

With his parents' attention diverted elsewhere, Kindling Boy slipped out the gate with his redwood armchair and sold it to the secondhand dealer for less money than it would take to buy a sheet of tickets for the fall lottery. He stepped outside, utterly dejected; all he could afford, he reckoned, was a small bet on a horserace.

The next day Jade Embrace led a squad of Japanese MPs down Brick Mason Avenue, from east to west. Rice Boy ran home to tell his mother, who rushed outside just as Jade Embrace was passing. She called to him. He turned with a smile and looked straight at her without missing a step; she thought she heard him say Auntie, but couldn't be sure. Then, when he reached the grocery store, he turned and waved. I'll come see you. The self-congratulatory sound of his voice carried far down the street.

What's their hurry? Cloud Silk asked Rice Boy.

It's killing time, he replied. What do you think?

Maybe we should see what he knows about Snow Talent, she said as she watched the khaki-clad figures disappear from view beyond the intersection. He's a bad person, she went on. If he sold her into prostitution, I'll slap the son of a bitch across his face.

Rice Boy sneered and bent over to pick up an apple core, which he flung at the intersection. It barely got airborne before tumbling to the ground, far short of its destination. Fuck your mother, Rice Boy cursed, with an angry stomp of his foot. And fuck your grandmother, too.

Cloud Silk turned and went inside. Five Dragons sneaked up behind her, a strange look on his face. Two of the clerks stood nearby; having heard of Jade Embrace's return, they could not escape the feeling that there would be trouble.

So Abao's son is back, Five Dragons remarked, looking glum. It is him, isn't it?

It's him, all right. My sister's son. She needed to set the record straight.

It's Abao's son. Five Dragons edged along the wall toward the main part of the house, listing slightly to the right. This is how they walk, father and son, he said. Their right shoulders slump, did you know that? Swordsmen and murderers used to walk that way. You don't want to mess with their kind.

You messed with them. Any regrets?

No. I never regret things I've done. Five Dragons leaned against the wall to catch his breath. His smile seemed forced. I dreamt about Abao's son last night, he went on. My dreams always come true, as you know, since you've seen him with your own eyes. It's payback time. He's come to settle accounts.

Dogs up and down Brick Mason Avenue unleashed a frenzy of barking in the direction of the rice emporium, waking neighbors, who rushed to their windows in time to see some black-clad men slip out of the rice emporium and into the darkness, making hardly a sound. It was Japanese MPs, followed by the interpreter, Jade Embrace, who was dragging someone along like a sack of rice. People froze with fear when they saw it was Five Dragons.

A sack of rice perfectly describes the disease-ridden Five Dragons. Denied the time to put on shoes and socks, he scraped the cobblestones with his bare feet; some of the neighbors heard tortured moans, others concentrated on his eyes, the good one staring into the sky, the powerful light of former days extinguished.

Once again the affairs of the rice emporium were a topic of discussion in North City. Teahouse customers said the Japanese MPs had arrested Five Dragons for storing up explosives, that they had found eight carbines and two pistols hidden in mounds of rice. No one mentioned the role Jade Embrace may have played in the incident. The troubles of the rice emporium—complex, ever changing, and deep-rooted—easily transcended the boundaries of the people's imagination and understanding. For all anyone knew, only the members of the family themselves could fathom the real reason for this particular calamity.

On the following day, the shop opened for business an hour later than usual, but it did open, and customers timidly tried to pry information out of the clerks, who evaded the issue. Cloud Silk sat behind the counter as if in a trance, eyes red and swollen from crying, or from a lack of sleep, or both. When the muted sounds of gossip reached her ears, she looked up and glared at the people filling the shop. Are you here to buy rice or wag your tongues? Her anger growing, she jumped up and flung her abacus into the crowd, and in a voice that had grown hoarse overnight, she rasped, Wagging tongues, wagging tongues. Wait till your turn comes, then we'll see how much you like wagging those damned tongues.

Five Dragons had no idea how far Jade Embrace dragged him, but he was aware of the ropes binding his wrists and of his instinctive struggle to break free of his captor's grasp; lacking the strength for either, he was forced to suffer the humiliation through to the end. He felt like an ox being led to slaughter: Back in Maple-Poplar Village, draft animals too sick to pull a plow were trussed up like this before being sent to the butcher's.

They dragged him into the Japanese MP headquarters, located on the ground floor of a sundries shop, where he was picked up head and feet by Jade Embrace and one of the MPs and tossed into a basement room; he landed weakly, like a bundle of straw, very much the way he'd landed after jumping off the coal car years earlier. A gas lamp hanging from the ceiling made it possible to survey his surroundings: damp walls virtually covered with dark bloodstains, some in the form of streaks, others like flowers in bloom. His hand brushed against a cloth shoe, from which emerged a series of squeaks; wide-eyed he watched as a rat emerged and skittered out of sight through the barred door. Maybe, he thought, a few kernels of rice were hidden in the shoe, but once his hand was inside, he felt something wet and sticky: a small puddle of fresh blood.

Around midnight the interrogation began; since he didn't understand a word his Japanese interrogator said, he focused his attention on Jade Embrace's moist red lips. Now that summer was gone, the lines of youth had vanished without a trace, and in the glare of the gas lamp, Jade Embrace's face had a macabre quality. He doesn't look like Abao now, Five Dragons thought to himself. Nor like Sixth Master or Cloud Weave. If anything, he's a younger version of me.

You were turned in for storing up weapons at home, a crime punishable by death, Jade Embrace asked. Are you ready to confess?

Who turned me in? Five Dragons asked as he shut his eyes. I'd like to know who it was.

We can't tell you that. But you'd be surprised if you knew, Jade Embrace replied with a sly grin. He walked up and grabbed Five Dragons by the hair to get a better look at his waxen, scabrous face. Who were you planning to use those weapons on? Me? The Japanese Imperial Forces?

No. I was taking them back to Maple-Poplar Village. I'm tired of this life, but I need protection against my enemies.

The world is filled with your enemies. You've got the blood of dozens of people on your hands. If I hadn't come for you, somebody else would have. I can't believe you don't understand that people who kill wind up being killed themselves.

That's not it. What ruined me was this venereal disease. I never thought I'd be done in by a scummy whore. With a look of abject sadness he shook his head in agony. Are you my enemy? he asked Jade Embrace. Are you avenging your parents?

I'm doing this for myself. I've hated you from the first time I saw you, as a little boy, and I've never stopped. I can't explain it, except to say that hate is something you're born with.

You're so much like me—like I used to be, anyway. Despite the pain, Five Dragons raised his bound arms and gently stroked Jade Embrace's white-gloved hand. Could you let go of my hair? Five Dragons asked. Weak as I am, I can't take much more.

Don't you think I know that? I want you to suffer precisely *because* you can't take it. Jade Embrace was enjoying himself. His cheeks were deeply dimpled. He released his grip and pulled up his glove. Do you know how many instruments of torture we have here? We can use the water torture, the fumigation torture, the tiger bench, the scalding swing, and more. They say pain has never bothered you, but I can heat a skewer and run it through all five fingers of each hand, like shish kebab you buy on the street.

Five Dragons was tortured from midnight till dawn. They kept moving him from one ingenious machine to the next, until every sore and scab on his body had split open, and a mixture of blood and pus dripped to the floor as if from a leaky spigot, to merge with the blood of former victims. Jade Embrace never heard the hoped-for moans, which either bore out his victim's legendary disdain of pain or was a sign that he no longer had the strength even for that. In the predawn hours, with his head drooping and his eyes shut, Five Dragons seemed to be fast asleep, without a care in the world. Jade Embrace, who was by then panting from exhaustion, freed his victim's limbs from the tiger bench and stuck his finger under his nose to see if he was still breathing. Strong and even as ever. The man's pain threshold was astonishing; that he could live through a night of unimaginable torture seemed to bear out the belief that he was indestructible.

Jade Embrace emptied a bucket of water into Five Dragons's face, then stood back to watch him open his eyes; a peculiar look of compassion appeared.

Finished? Five Dragons asked. Can you take me home now?

We'll wait till it's light out. Jade Embrace's gloved hand was inspecting Five Dragons's face, searching out a spot free of sores and scabs. The search ended at the eyes. One was dull and lifeless, covered by a cloudy membrane; in the other he saw his own reflection. He touched the sight-less eye. Who blinded you?

Your maternal grandfather. He was one of my enemies.

He probably didn't have time to finish the job, Jade Embrace remarked as he picked the metal skewer up off the floor. I'll do it for him. Without another word he jabbed it into Five Dragons's left eye—once, twice, three times—until he heard the sound he had been waiting for: not a moan this time, but a drawn-out, ear-shattering scream.

That morning two manure gatherers nearly tripped over Five Dragons in the outhouse behind the sundries shop; they both knew him, but at first could not link the bat-tered man lying in a pool of shit, pus, and dried blood with Five Dragons, who had terrorized the northern part of town for all those years. Too great a change in too short a time—a single summer. When they delivered him to the Brick Mason Avenue rice emporium on their dung cart, they asked Cloud Silk what it was all about. Holding her nose, she just stared blankly down at Five Dragons as he lay on a bamboo cot. I don't know, she said at last. I have no idea why this happened.

Unable to stand the stench rising from Five Dragons's body, Cloud Silk went to get some clean clothes. But he drifted back into consciousness and grabbed her hand. Don't worry about that, he said as befouled blood oozed from his eye again, gliding down his cheek like red paint. Tell me, was it you who told about the guns I hid in the rice?

No, it wasn't me. She pulled back her hand. I'll go get a doctor. You're a mess.

How would I know? I can't see. His voice was weak

and raspy, but the look on his face showed he was still thinking clearly. No need to pretend any longer, he said with a wry smile. I'm dying, and you can stop being afraid of me.

I never was afraid of you. You've got no one but yourself to blame for what's happened to you. Her attention was caught by some flies that swarmed over from the wall to buzz around Five Dragons. A few landed on his leg, attracted by the festering sores. The sight made her sick to her stomach, so she shooed them away with her fan; but they regrouped and were back in no time. She stood stiffly to the side and watched the loathsome insects dine on exposed thigh, liberated from his ripped, blood-soaked white satin trousers; one of his pendulous testicles was visible, along with a considerable section of his diseased, festering groin. The sight reminded her of the passionless yet incessant sexual activity of their early years together. She nearly vomited. How had they made it this far with their lives entwined? And what did it all mean?

Cloud Silk went inside to wake Rice Boy and Kindling Boy after Five Dragons lost consciousness again. Your damned cousin tortured your father nearly to death. I want you to carry him over to the bathtub. We have to make him presentable for when he meets the King of Hell.

So the brothers carried Five Dragons to the bathtub, which was still filled with his rice-vinegar bath. Rice Boy peeled off his father's undershirt while Kindling Boy cut off the bloody shorts with a pair of scissors and tossed them aside. Then Rice Boy bent over and splashed rice vinegar over his father's body. The old bastard probably won't last more than a few days, he said. With loathing in his eyes, his brother stared at the rotting skin. How can he stink so much? he remarked, seeing it all as somehow comical. He smells worse than shit.

Cloud Silk carried a kettle of scalding water over from the kitchen and poured it slowly over Five Dragons's body. Hot things have never bothered him, she said as she touched the kettle. This is the only thing that will wash away the stench. Shocked awake by the scalding water, Five Dragons instinctively wrapped his arms around his head. Cloud Silk saw fear on his face, a look of helpless isolation.

Who's whipping me?

Nobody, it's hot water. I'm giving you a bath.

I can't see. Did you boil the water? It's like a lash. A gasp escaped from Five Dragons's mouth. I don't need a bath, he said. I'm not dying. It'll take more than this to kill me.

What do you want, then? Tell me.

I want to go home. Five Dragons strained to open his eyes wide, as if to look at the faces around him; but of course he saw nothing. I can't put it off any longer, he said. I have to return to Maple-Poplar Village now.

Don't be foolish. It's too far. What if you die on the road?

So what? You never worried about what happened to me before, and this is no time to start. Five Dragons groaned. Go find a railway worker called Old Sun and tell him to reserve a boxcar for me. I came by train, and I'll return the same way.

You're being ridiculous. I can understand why you want to return to where you were born, but you don't need an entire boxcar to do that. Do you know how much it will cost?

I said I want an entire boxcar. **I'm taking a boxcarful**

of our finest white rice with me, he said forcefully. Dimly he could hear his sons giggle. He knew it sounded illogical, but it was the key element in his plan to return home. He needed a carload of snow-white, fragrant rice, since that was the only thing that stood between him and calamities, natural and man-made.

The rice-emporium brothers argued all afternoon over who would accompany their father home, a task neither wanted. Cloud Silk found Kindling Boy's attitude particularly annoying. You'd actually let your brother make the trip with his crippled leg? His neck went taut. Crippled leg? He can outrun me if he's chasing a woman. Did I get more than him when we split up the property? No! A fight seemed inevitable, when Cloud Silk, who was growing increasingly anxious, decided to flip a coin to see who went and who stayed. Rice Boy was heads, Kindling Boy tails. The coin hit the ground and rolled up to Kindling Boy's foot. Tails.

He glanced at his father, who lay unconscious on the cot. My bad luck, he grumbled. But I won't rest until I find his money. Do you know where he keeps it?

He spent it all on land in Maple-Poplar Village. He hasn't got any left.

Land's the same as money. He has to have deeds to prove ownership, so where does he keep them?

In a little wooden box, Cloud Silk said through clenched teeth. I saw him hide it in the rafters in the northern wing.

Kindling Boy searched for the box all afternoon. He stood on a ladder and knocked out every ceiling brick with a hammer, but apart from a few well-fed rats and some clouds of dust, he found nothing. The box, where is it? he roared at his mother after jumping down off the ladder. Maybe you took it.

You know he's never trusted me. How could I get my hands on anything of his? You might as well stop looking, she said. You could tear the house apart, and still you wouldn't find anything. He's a master at hiding stuff. If you want to get your hands on that box, you'll have to ask him for it.

Kindling Boy's mood turned from anger to resignation as he moved the ladder out into the yard. The sad thing was, he understood his father perfectly, and knew he'd have to be on his deathbed before he'd reveal the location of the box, if then. Raising the ladder over his head, he flung it to the ground to vent his anger, then watched his father's eyelids flutter; suffering and confusion showed on his face in response to the clatter of the bamboo ladder on the hard ground.

What was that? Five Dragons demanded. I can't see what's making that noise.

A ladder. Feeling a perverse urge to torment his father, Kindling Boy dragged the ladder along the ground, banging its legs noisily. I'm fixing it. Plug your ears if it bothers you.

I thought it was the rumble of tracks. I thought we were on the train already.

The first rain of autumn fell that night, raising a wet tattoo on Brick Mason Avenue's cobblestones; water coursed down the rain gutters and soaked the ancient bamboo cot in the yard. It was Five Dragons's favorite piece of furniture, and under the onslaught of the heavy rain, every strip of bamboo shone, wet and glistening.

After packing what Five Dragons and Kindling Boy would need on the trip, Cloud Silk opened the window to watch the rain fall, leisurely and languid, with no sign of stopping anytime soon. She reached out to it. It'll keep up like this all night, she said, cupping raindrops in her hand. Suddenly she was reminded of something her mother, Madam Zhu, had said long ago: Whenever an evil creature is born, the heavens weep, and when that creature dies, the sky clears.

TRACKS OF THE SOUTHERN RAILWAY STRETCHED AS FAR as the eye could see, sandwiched between luxuriant growths of bushes that rustled wetly. The sodden sky began to clear over the riverbank as the black boxcars rumbled by; rays of sunlight poking through mist and rain illuminated the surface of the river and turned the wheels and cars a dull gold.

The sun should be up by the time we reach Xuzhou, the engineer shouted to the motorman.

Hard to say, the motorman replied as he climbed out of the grimy cab and looked skyward. Let it rain. In times like these, when you can't say in the morning if you'll still be alive that night, a little rain can't hurt. And if it doesn't bother people, it sure as hell can't hurt the freight.

The sky was not visible from inside the boxcar; at first, trickles of rain seeped in through the cracks, but eventually even they stopped. The train rumbled across the bridge heading north. Kindling Boy tried to force the ventilation window, but it was sealed half open with three rivets, leaving just enough room for his arm, and making it impossible to see any more of the bleak scenery than an occasional bare branch whizzing by.

The car was filled with new rice, on top of which

the two men—father and son—perched. Five Dragons lay quietly in the sliver of daylight passing through the ventilation window. Kindling Boy watched his father's wasted frame rock from side to side with the train, his face floating like a sheet of paper in the darkness, arms and legs spread out over the rice like twigs.

We're supposed to be heading north. Why does it feel like we're heading south? Five Dragons asked anxiously.

We're heading north, all right, Kindling Boy said, absently combing his fingers through the rice and glancing contemptuously at his father. Even on your deathbed you won't trust anyone.

North. Five Dragons nodded and shut his eyes. Heading north, he repeated, north to Maple-Poplar Village. The conquering hero returns. As a boy I saw people return triumphantly from the city, and at most they brought back a wagonful of rice. But I'm returning with a boxcar full of it, more than anyone could eat in a lifetime.

Kindling Boy, bored by the seemingly endless trip, wished he'd brought some crickets along. Several had survived the cold and wetness of early autumn, and all he had to do was prod them with a twig to get them fighting.

What have I got left? Five Dragons asked. Only this rice. His hand inched across the mound until he touched Kindling Boy's sleeve. Here, feel me, then tell me what I've got left. I'm missing toes, I'm blind in both eyes, and my skin feels like it's being scraped with a hasp. So tell me, what have I got left?

You're still breathing. Kindling Boy pushed his father's hand away, repulsed by the thought of physical contact.

That's right, I'm still breathing, Five Dragons echoed him softly with a self-mocking smile. He reached up to grab something out of the air, and brought it down to his chest; then his hand slipped weakly down to his disease-ravaged genitals, where it rested for a moment before moving up again, past his withered, flabby chest and on up to the two rows of hard, sleek teeth made of pure gold. Lovingly he brushed his finger across them and sighed heavily. And my gold teeth, I still have them. As a boy I saw people with one or two gold teeth, but I've got a whole mouthful of them. See my gold teeth, Kindling Boy? Gold never goes bad. Even if I've got nothing else, I've always got my gold teeth.

Kindling Boy's attention was caught by the narrow glints of light emerging from between his father's wasted lips; he knew what those glints represented. Leaning closer, he listened to the labored, chilled breaths from his father's nostrils; detecting the heavy stench of death, he was reminded of the wooden box his mother had told them about. He grew worried. Where's the box? Hurry up, tell me where you hid it. Seized by a sudden rage, he began shaking his father, obsessed with the need to learn where the box was hidden before he stopped breathing. Five Dragons's body reacted to the violent shaking by curling up like a leaf swirling in the wind. RICE—His head moved toward the mound of rice as he uttered one last word.

You hid it in the rice? his son shouted anxiously. But the shout fell on deaf ears. Kindling Boy was digging frantically through mounds of rice in search of the wooden box when he heard the barely audible death rattle behind him; his hands didn't skip a beat. Finally, deep down in one of the mounds, he found what he was looking for: a heavy wooden box. He carried it over to the ventilation window and opened it. He was stunned. No land deeds, no money, nothing but rice, a boxful of rice that gave off a mysterious pale blue glare in the light filtering through the tiny window.

With a frenzied roar, he fell upon his father's corpse. You're a rotten cheat, even in death! he bellowed, scooping up handfuls of rice and flinging it into his father's dead face, quickly covering up the features and filling the space around them. Then a glint of yellow light where Five Dragons's mouth had been caught his eye. Glimmers of light fought through the whiteness covering the withered lips and danced in the darkness of the cramped space. Gold teeth. The seductive glimmers coming from the gold teeth drew him toward them.

Driven by greed, Kindling Boy pried open his father's icy lips and stuck his fingers inside to remove the teeth. First he yanked out the uppers, then concentrated on the lowers, his task made easier by the gap above. He dumped the rice out of the wooden box and replaced it with the gold teeth, which rattled around, producing a crisp, wonderful sound.

Five Dragons never heard the gold teeth leave his body. The last sound to fill his ears was the rhythmic clatter of iron wheels on steel tracks, and he knew he was on a train taking him away from disaster. The sound of rain in the wildwoods had died out; maybe the sun had vanquished the first autumn rain. In the vast yet tranquil realm of his imagination, he tried to picture the scene surrounding his birth, but nothing came. He knew only that he had been an orphan ever since he could remember, and that he had fled Maple-Poplar Village during a catastrophic flood. The last image he ever saw was of himself floating on the surface of a boundless expanse of water, moving farther and farther away, like an uprooted rice plant, or a solitary puff of raw cotton.